No Good Deed

David R Bishop & J Scott Cordero

Published by My Little Island in the Ether, LLC, 2023.

© 2023 by David R Bishop and J Scott Cordero
ISBN: 979-8-9899068-0-2

All rights reserved. No part of this publication may be reproduced in any form or by any means, including scanning, photocopying, or otherwise without written permission of the copyright holder.

My Little Island in the Ether, LLC
PO Box 419
Lewistown, MT 59457

David & Scott thank Gloria Bishop, Janet Cordero, Kimberlee Decker, Dana Kinsey, and Danyeil Luna for their feedback and support.

David dedicates this novel to Gloria & Kimberlee. He would also like to thank Scott for letting him sweat the details.

Scott dedicates this novel to his bride. *Thank you for your steadfast love and support, for giving me the time to pursue my dream, and for believing in me before I did.*

Prologue

Emily signaled then turned right as she caressed her belly and smiled.

Three more weeks.

As she pulled up to the house, Emily took a deep breath, psyching herself up for the next task.

This was truly the only part of pregnancy she didn't like, getting in and out of the car. She'd learned to cope with that claustrophobic feeling of the steering wheel being closer than it should be while the pedals felt farther than they should but getting her and her belly in or out only seemed to become more difficult with each passing day.

She shouldered her purse, put her right hand on the steering wheel, her left on the door frame, and started the pull, push, scoot combination she'd come up with to manipulate her body and extricate herself. She always thought of Houdini and his straitjacket and chains, the time ticking away to apparent doom.

Well, this may not be as theatrical, but it sure feels just as dramatic.

When she finally had herself out, she looked over the top of the car and trained her realtor's eye on the front of the house. A large oak tree standing on the front right corner of the brick ranch house shaded a full third of the closely manicured lawn, including the flowerbed exploding with pink, red, yellow, and orange.

She pulled a digital camera from her purse, powered it up, and snapped a couple of shots, checking them as she walked to the front door to retrieve the key from the lockbox.

Opening the front door she stepped into the foyer.

Emily's lips parted into a satisfied smile. Fresh paint. New Berber carpeting. She walked through the house; counting three bedrooms and two baths as she wandered her way around.

Emily moved into the kitchen. It was, as expected, immaculate. The appliances were all brand new and high-end.

And the stove?

A smile curved her lips.

Gas.

She turned the stove to 350 degrees and heard a *whoosh*.

Her smile broadened.

But the *whoosh* didn't stop and a second later, Emily instinctively turned away from the oven, closed her eyes, and wrapped her arms around her belly as the room was enveloped in flame.

PART 1
Chapter 1

Jennifer Robinson knocked on her brother and sister-in-law's front door. Ex-sister-in-law, she corrected herself. Well, Ex didn't quite fit either. She was deceased, not divorced. Jennifer tugged uncomfortably at her jacket.

How was she supposed to refer to Emily? What was the proper etiquette? Why hadn't she stopped by a bookstore or library in the last six months to find that out? Surely, Dear Abby or Ann Landers or Miss Manners would have known the proper term to use when your brother's pregnant wife suddenly becomes the burnt marshmallow portion of a S'more.

There she went again. Jennifer tugged again at her jacket. Whenever she got nervous or distressed her humor went beyond dark, right to Dante's ninth ring. It had been that way all her life and it was the one thing her husband, Bill, had politely said of her that was less than beautiful.

Yeah, well, he thinks he looks like Tom Cruise naked.

Jennifer pinched herself. She had to focus. This wasn't about her husband's misplaced vanity or even what to call Emily. But she always referred to Emily in the present tense and only informed a speaker she was dead if they asked.

Dead.

That was the word she used. Not "passed away" or "passed on" or "passed over." Emily hadn't passed anything. She'd been killed, practically incinerated. "Passed away" was too soft a phrase.

Jennifer hated soft phrases. Once when she and Bill were at a dinner party, she'd spent a short time speaking to a Navy pilot. He'd referred to his bombing of buildings and installations during the Gulf War as "servicing the target." Jennifer couldn't help herself.

"Servicing the target?" She'd almost sprayed the man with the white wine in her mouth. "Sounds like something a hooker does."

She'd not won points with the pilot, her husband, nor the host and hostess with that remark. But she just thought he should call it what it was.

His job was to deliver death and destruction in a tiny package, so if he wanted to sugar-coat it, he should say he was a delivery driver for Uncle Sam's Parcel Service.

Now Jennifer stood at the front door of Eric's, *and Emily's*, house. She was tired of doing this, driving from her home in Chicago Heights through Chicago up to Cary once a month. Today, it was through snow and ice, cursing as she ended up behind a snowplow, jumping the berm of snow piled in front of Eric's driveway, and then sliding and trudging through the un-shoveled driveway and walkway. Just to check on a brother who'd spent the time since her last visit ignoring his phone, his mail, his job, and his life.

Every month. Show up. Clean the house. Sort his mail. Pay his bills Check his voicemails. Feed him. Browbeat him. Cajole him. Threaten. Guilt. Anything to light a fire under him, hoping that would help him keep moving forward. It didn't. But she kept trying.

Was it too early to call it just *his* house, she wondered to herself. No. Probably not. After all, Jennifer wasn't looking for him to run out and replace Emily. She just wanted her brother to engage in life again.

Every month she would open the door to his house and find a month's worth of mail lying on the foyer floor. Dishes were scattered throughout the house, crusted with the remains of food. She brought groceries with her every time, homemade and store-bought casseroles and other foods Eric could simply heat in the microwave. She would find the Stouffer's lasagna sitting on the dining room table for what looked like weeks with only a small scoop missing. Her Tupperware containers, crusty with the remains of the homemade items, would be scattered throughout the living room, dining room, and kitchen.

The only thing that appeared in any order was any correspondence addressed solely to Emily. That she would find unopened, bundled with a rubber band, and lying on the table by the front door, waiting for Emily to peruse when she arrived home.

Today, she had no groceries with her. She had no cleaning supplies. It was time for some tough love. She liked that phrase. What she was doing today was for Eric's good. She loved him too much to let him continue down the path he was treading. He'd turned into some type of zombie leach. She liked that analogy too. He wasn't a flesh-eating animated corpse, but some

Chapter 2

Jennifer put her hand on the doorknob, twisted, and pushed. The do swung freely until it connected with the pile of mail that lay exactly where it'd fallen through the mail slot. She shook her head and stepped through the doorway into the foyer, not bothering to watch where she stepped. Envelopes crinkled and quickly dampened from the ice clinging to the soles of her snow boots. The house stank of booze and neglect.

"Eric," Jennifer called out.

Nothing. Not a sound. No TV or stereo or even a microwave. If she didn't know better, she might think Eric was out.

She continued into the house and surveyed the lasagna box sitting on the living room sofa, with only a couple of bites missing. Last month's Tupperware containers of dried food were piled haphazardly on the coffee table next to the—

Jennifer stopped as if she'd bumped into a wall. Her jaw dropped. Eric had taken more than ten steps back this last month.

There on the coffee table were not one or even two empty bottles of liquor, but three. She read the labels. Jack Daniel's. Patron. Skyy. She moved completely into the living room and discovered the doors to the seldom-used liquor cabinet standing wide open. Eric and Emily weren't drinkers and when they did it was wine. Eric, she knew, enjoyed a beer or two during a Sunday football game, but the hard liquor was for entertaining. They could buy a forty-dollar bottle of Patron for margaritas and that could last them a year or more.

She walked to the liquor cabinet and found it devoid of alcohol. The mixes were still there as well as a book on how to make certain drinks, but all the alcohol was gone. Turning to shout his name, she screamed in surprise.

Sitting in the recliner, a picture in one hand and a half-empty bottle of Seagram's Seven whiskey balanced precariously on his thigh, Eric couldn't have been farther from Jennifer if he'd been at some bar on the other side of the world. His glazed eyes, red from tears or alcohol, she couldn't say, stared at something beyond the walls of the room.

"You couldn't have said something?" Her voice deepened into a bad imitation of Eric's. "Hey, Sis, good to see you. How ya been?"

Eric didn't react. His boyish face, puffy with liquor, was covered by a scruffy beard which did help hide his gaunt, waxy complexion but along with the bags under his eyes and untrimmed hair gave him the appearance of a homeless addict. His blue sweatshirt and jeans had the look of many days of wearing but no laundering and stank of dried food and spilled liquor, sweat, tears, and dirt.

Jennifer walked over and stood in front of him. "Hellooo," She sang as she waved her hand in front of his face.

Still no response.

Pity party, table of one.

Jennifer shook her head in reproach as much to herself as to Eric. This was supposed to be a day of tough love she reminded herself, not passive/aggressive love. She turned from him and without thinking grabbed the empty liquor bottles off of the coffee table.

"Jody and Julie say 'Hello.'" She moved to the kitchen where she stared horrified. If she hadn't known better, she'd have thought someone had broken in and gone rifling through the drawers and cabinets looking for the secret hidey-hole of the family jewels. Every cupboard was open; its contents spilling out like the entrails of some butchered animal. Drawers were completely out, lying upside down on the floor.

Eric was looking for something, but if it was the tools needed to make a tuna fish sandwich or what the kitchen might look like if some thief was looking for the family jewels, well, only Eric could tell her if he'd found what he'd been looking for.

Her next thought was out of her mouth before she could stop it. "Eric, you. *Freaking. Self-absorbed. SLOB.*" She screamed as she spun around towards the living room. "Why can't you get off your—" She shut her mouth with a snap. She was here for tough love, she reminded herself, not middle-school name-calling. She took a deep breath and counted to ten while she pummeled the air.

She let out her breath in a long slow release and then moved to the cupboard below the kitchen sink, careful where she walked this time. Broken glass gleamed on the floor like the snow and ice on the walkway outside. She retrieved a garbage bag and decided to pick up the rest of the house first. Dropping the bottles into the bag, she made her way back to the living room.

Eric hadn't moved. Still didn't acknowledge his sister's presence.

Jennifer sighed, trying to be as loud as she could as she began straightening up the living room. She pulled the cushions from the sofa and slapped them like a doctor slapping a baby's bottom to make it breathe. She nearly choked on the dust. She slammed the liquor cabinet doors shut and piled the flatware with a crash. Once or twice she winced; sure she'd broken a plate. It was a little passive/aggressive, she knew, but she reasoned it was okay if Eric responded. He didn't.

Dropping the pile of collected dishes on the dining room table, Jennifer marched back to Eric. *"Did you hear me?"* She nudged his foot with hers."

Still nothing.

Sighing in disgust, her eyes fell upon his and Emily's office. She could see the business answering machine's red light blinking it had multiple messages. This room was off-limits to everyone but Eric and Emily, Eric had always been adamant on that point. The rest of their home was an open house for play, but the office was for work.

This'll get you off your backside.

"You know what," she said over her shoulder as she stamped into the office, "I'm going to check your messages." She pushed the play button.

The machine beeped and then announced in its mechanical male voice there were six new messages.

"Hi." The voice seemed a little uncertain. "This is Paul Stephens. I was calling about the house on Gunther and was wondering if it was still available. Please call me at..."

Jennifer scooped up a pen and scribbled the number down Paul Stephens rattled off. "When's the last time you checked your messages?" The machine answered the question for Eric.

Monday, November Thirteenth.

"Eric. This message is over a month old."

The second message started.

"This message is for Mr. Messer." This voice was accusing. "This is Tony from Critter Getters Pest Control. We've not received the last two quarterly payments."

Jennifer winced. Every month she'd collected the mail at the front door, sorted through it, and paid the bills with Eric's checkbook she'd found on the table next to the rubber-banded correspondence for Emily. But she hadn't known about this bill. The voice continued.

"If we do not receive payment by Thursday, the thirtieth of November, I'm afraid we'll have to suspend your service and pursue this matter in small claims court or through a collection agency. Please call me..."

Again Jennifer scratched down the name and phone number on the pad as the machine let her know when this message had been received.

Wednesday, November 15th.

"Hi. This is Paul Stephens, again. I called a week or two ago about the house on Gunther. I noticed the *For Sale* sign is still in the front yard. I'd really like to set up a time to see it. Please call me..."

"Eric, this guy's called twice about a listing." She listened to the man repeat his number and then end the call wishing Eric a Happy Thanksgiving.

Wednesday, November 22nd.

"Mr. Messer. This is Cammie Reynolds from Prudential. I've got a gentleman here who's interested in the Gunther listing. Says he's tried contacting you, but with no response. Since you're still the agent of listing, I thought it a courtesy to call you..."

Jennifer stopped listening to the messages and stormed into the living room. "Eric, you gotta snap out of this." She pleaded.

Still nothing.

She stared at her brother in exasperated silence. What was going to get through to him? What was going to wake him up? And then she blurted out the one thing she'd kept buried all these months as she watched him slide deeper and deeper into this funk and depression.

"Emily's dead. You're not."

Eric's head snapped back, his entire body jerked, as if Jennifer had jumped on him and slapped him. But the statement did get Eric's attention.

His eyes narrowed and his face tightened as he looked up at Jennifer. He stared at her hard and cold.

Jennifer felt herself want to take a step back from his glare, but she willed herself to stand her ground. She'd finally got him to acknowledge her. It was time to say what she'd come here to say. She cleared her throat.

"I can understand what you're going through—"

Eric's eyes narrowed even further to cold, black dangerous slits and he cut across her like a straight razor. "You can't *possibly* imagine what *I'm* going through." His voice sounded rough like it hadn't been used in a long time. "Until Bill, Jody, and Julie are killed..." his voice faltered as his eyes glossed over with fresh tears. He wiped them away furiously. "Until you have closed casket funerals for Bill and the kids because their bodies were virtually *cremated*, you have absolutely *no* idea. If you had to sit there, *day after day and night after night,* trying not to, but still imagining how much pain they'd been in, how they'd screamed and called your name. Maybe then *you* could tell me *you* understand."

Jennifer placed her hands, now clenched into fists, on her hips. At the moment, that seemed the safest place. She could feel it deep inside herself, a seething anger making its way from the pit of her soul up to her mouth wanting to spew hot words at him, making its way to her hands wanting to slap him.

He was right of course. She didn't know what he was going through, and she couldn't and didn't want to understand or even imagine his pain. But he'd tapped into her greatest fear, every mother's greatest fear, losing a child. And that fear had seared her emotionally as surely as if he'd stuck her with a hot poker. Bill was devastating, but the girls...

"How dare you," Jennifer spat pure venom. "How *dare* you say something like that to me after all I've done for you." She turned away from him before she really did jump on him and start pummeling. "You're not the only one hurting here. We all loved her. We all miss her. We all miss you. I didn't lose just a sister that day. I lost a brother."

Jennifer's vision blurred as the hot sting of tears veiled her eyes, but she willed them away. She would not cry. Not today. She had more to say, and she never would if she started crying. She stared hard at the liquor cabinet for a long moment.

"We were supposed to make Christmas cookies today, the girls and me. For Santa. But Jody said I just *had* to check on Uncle Eric. *Had* to make sure he was okay. Santa's cookies could wait. Uncle Eric couldn't.

"You remember Jody, don't you? Your favorite niece. Probably your favorite person in the world after Emily. You've never said it, and Julie's never felt like a second-rate niece, but you've always lit up in a way different with Jody. The girls don't see it. But I do. So does Bill. You've never forgotten either girl's birthday. Until you forgot Jody's last weekend. She was devastated. She was afraid something had happened to you like Aunt Emily. It was very difficult to convince her otherwise since you don't answer the phone or return calls. But we managed it."

Jennifer turned away. She could feel the moisture gathering in her eyes again and knew she would be unable to stop it this time. She bolted to the front door, swung it open, and then stopped. She called over her shoulder. "Jody—.... the girls would...the girls and I—all of us...would love to see you next week. For Christmas." She closed the door and fled down the walkway to the driveway and her car.

Chapter 3

An hour later, Eric still sat in the recliner, holding the whiskey bottle in one hand and the photo in his other. It was a picture of Emily. She had just placed their first *Sold!* Placard on the *For Sale* sign above their picture. She had laughed as she'd done this, and Eric had snapped the photo without her knowledge. It was a great shot. Emily was so naturally photogenic and this one had captured more than her smile and the sparkle in her eye, but her enthusiasm for life as well.

That picture was at once a blessing and a curse for Eric. The image was so wonderfully powerful, able to move Eric beyond the captured still life into the moving moment where he lived and relived and relived. He could feel the heat of that day on his skin, the crisp bite of Fall air mixing with Emily's perfume in his nostrils, and hear Emily's peel of laughter ringing in his ears.

It kept him from falling apart; at least Eric saw it that way. Otherwise, everywhere he went, everywhere he looked, reality threatened to squash him. He'd stopped sleeping in their bedroom. Emily had forbidden a television in the room, stating bedrooms existed for two purposes only, sleeping and sex. And that's exactly what they did. They slept together and they made love together in that room.

Every time he went into the bedroom, every time he thought about the bedroom, images of Emily scooting into him while drowsily telling him she was cold, of him kissing her ear to wake her up to eat the breakfast he'd prepared for her, of lovemaking, crashed into his mind's eye like an eighteen-wheeler crashing into a plate glass window.

Not even the alcohol could blur those images. But he still tried.

He'd taken to sleeping on the sofa, the one piece of furniture farthest away from their bedroom. If they'd had a bench in the foyer, he would've slept there.

The office was the same. One day, when a blizzard struck, they'd decided since they weren't going to be out selling houses that day, they'd dress in the silliest clothes they could find and try to make each other laugh as they returned calls. Emily was quite good at that game, using various parts of her body to make obscene gestures. Try as he might, he just couldn't get the same laughter or jaw-dropping silence out of her. They had their first real fight as a couple in the office. They'd gone to bed angry that night, Emily sleeping in their room and he in the guest room.

The guest room. He couldn't stay in that room either. For one thing, it was too close to their bedroom, and, of course, there were memories in that room as well.

It was the same for the kitchen, the dining room, and the laundry room. Any room in the house where his mind's eye could pull up a memory of Emily. Eric could only find solace in the small space between the sofa and the recliner. He ate because his sister brought him food, but he wasn't hungry. A bite or two in and he would feel his stomach begin to churn.

So he grasped the photograph and its ability to transport him from his hellish present to a more beautiful past. And he grasped it the way a victim experiencing the panicky sensation of drowning will claw at anything to save himself.

Eric had spent the day moving between replaying that memory of Emily and imagining her pain and her screams. He hadn't been lying to Jennifer about that. It was the one consuming nightmare he lived and relived day and night. And the thought of the baby, what it (he could no longer refer to it as he, as his son) felt, what its screams must've sounded like, what its pain must've felt like, was beyond nightmare. This was a torment no human was supposed to know, a torment beyond a man's physical, mental, or emotional endurance. It paralyzed him.

The nightmare of her screams always overcame the good memories, but he forced himself to think about that first sale, the day she told him she was pregnant, the day she finally told him she was going to have his son, even the memory of their first fight, which had become one of those clichés "we laugh about it now, but at the time..." for the both of them. Her remembered laughter and her imagined screams were a constant battle raging in his psyche.

The memory trying to advance at the moment was his last conversation with Emily. It had been over the phone, not in person. The last time he said,

'I love you,' to her had been into the receiver, not her ear. It'd been a good phone call; he was thankful for that.

"Shouldn't be too long. I'm just gonna take a quick look at a house and then I'll be on my way home."

But she hadn't made it home. He couldn't remember the rest of the conversation, couldn't remember her saying, "I love you," or, "Goodbye," but his mind could imagine the sound of her screams, as she burned to death.

That's what he'd been doing when Jennifer had come into the house. He was locked in that struggle, the nightmare of 'what is' winning over 'what was'. He hadn't heard her, couldn't hear her over Emily's and the baby's screams in his head. There'd been no intent for meanness. Well, maybe there had been a little, and now he felt ashamed as he looked at the picture of Emily and realized how disappointed she would be in him for hurting his sister like that. Hurting his niece.

He wanted to say nieces, but Jennifer was right. Jody was his favorite. He was glad to hear Julie didn't seem to notice, but...Jody was his favorite. Probably because Jody was such a tomboy. She was into dolls and liked pink like her sister, Julie, but she also loved watching football, playing baseball, and shooting hoops with her dad and Uncle Eric.

No. Those weren't why Jody was his favorite. Jody was his favorite because Jody was the reason Eric was going to be a dad. Or would have been. Despite the searing stab of pain in his heart, a smile spread across Eric's face as he remembered the day he and Emily decided to have a baby.

They'd spent a long weekend with Bill, Jennifer, and the kids at a cabin Bill's family owned at Lake Lou Yaeger. The cabin was fantastic. The lake was amazing. The weather was spectacular. It'd been a day of pancakes on the terrace with a view of the lake, Jody insisting on climbing up into Eric's lap and sharing his breakfast. Telling him he needed more sauce on his pancakes. Teaching the children to ski, feeling the exhilaration as Jody got up on her feet and stayed there. Surf and turf on the grill with all the adults having just a little too much to drink.

As they sat around the table on the terrace, after this final meal together, Bill set up his phone to take a photo. It was perfect. Bill had said something humorous. All the adults were laughing as they looked at the camera. Julie and Jody were smiling, faces smeared with hot fudge sundae. The sky behind them was a soft pink.

Eric and Emily had placed their copy of the photograph on the wall in their home office where it could also be seen from the living room. If Eric stretched a little to his left and craned his neck up, he could see it. He did so now. His mind drifted back to that day, or more specifically, that night.

He and Emily had just finished making love, and as they lay entangled in each other they both blurted out at the same time, "I want a Jody of my own."

Well, Eric didn't have a Jody of his own. He didn't have Emily either. But he still had his niece, Jody. Only...Uncle Eric had missed Jody's birthday. Missed it completely. It had never even crossed his mind. She'd been devastated. Bill and Jennifer had had to console her.

A stuttering sigh escaped Eric. He'd hurt his sister and his nieces. Probably Bill as well.

"I'm sorry, Emily." He said it out loud. He always spoke out loud to Emily, as if she were in the room. As if she had just finished reprimanding him for being such a jerk to Jennifer. Emily's voice filled his head. She was telling him he needed to apologize to Jennifer as well.

"I will, Emily. I'll go over there for Christmas, and I'll say I'm sorry and I love you, okay?" He could see Emily smile, like the one in the picture, and tell him 'Thank you.' He could feel her hand on his cheek, her lips on his, and the weight of her in his lap.

Closing his eyes, he smiled, breathed in her perfume, or was that ash? The smell of hair burning. And now she was screaming and calling his name.

His eyes opened with a start as his breath caught in his throat, his Adam's apple seemed to swell to the size of a pineapple.

"What am I gonna do, Emily? Tell me, what am I supposed to do?" The sobbing started again. It racked his body like Laurence Taylor and Brian Bosworth hitting a quarterback from the left and the right simultaneously over and over again. "What am I supposed to do?" He repeated. "I can't do this anymore. I don't—...I don't want to do this anymore. I don't...want to be without you."

That was it, Eric realized. He didn't want to be without Emily. Here, this world, this life, was without Emily. She was gone, and she couldn't come back. Wherever she was right now, that's where he wanted to be.

"What do I do?"

Eric looked at the photo and his eyes settled on the word *Sold!* That was it. Emily was talking to him, guiding him. She was answering his question. Emily couldn't come back to him. But he could go to her.

But before he went, he needed to make certain financial arrangements and create one last event of good memories.

"How?"

A plan began to formulate in his brain. A simple yet elegant plan. The pieces fell effortlessly into place in only a matter of minutes.

"Thank you," Eric said as he kissed the picture. He ran through the steps. First, he needed to sell a house. He needed to sell a house quickly. Which meant he needed a motivated buyer. He had a house to sell, and he had a motivated buyer.

What was that guy's name?

Eric jumped up, spilling the remains of the whiskey bottle over himself and the recliner, and headed for the office. The message indicator light was no longer blinking; all the messages had been played. But Jennifer had written the numbers down, she'd told him. Right beside the answering machine laid the pad and pen with Jennifer's scribbles. The name was at the top of the page. Paul Stephens.

Eric took a deep breath and dialed Paul Stephens' number.

A male voice answered on the third ring. "Hello."

"Hi. This is Eric Messer. May I speak with—?"

"Mr. Messer." The man interrupted, sounding genuinely pleased. "Thanks for returning my call."

"I wanted to apologize for taking so long to get back to you."

"No problem, no problem at all."

"Are you still interested in the—"

"Absolutely." Paul Stephens interrupted again sounding very excited.

"Great. When would you like to see it?"

"How about this afternoon? Two o'clock?"

Eric glanced at his watch.

12:30.

"Sure. That sounds good. I'll see you then."

"Wonderful. I look forward to finally meeting you."

"Me too, Mr. Stephens."

Eric placed the receiver back in its cradle and started for the stairs. He was only now aware that his jeans were damp with whiskey.

"Sorry about that, Honey." He said to the picture still clutched in his hand. He was feeling better, not quite himself, he never thought he'd feel like that again, but better until he started up the stairs.

As soon as he placed his foot on the first step, it seemed to stick, like the runner had jelly on it. By the time he reached the third step, he felt those lead-lined clothes again. He trudged up the stairs slowly. As he reached the second floor, he felt winded, like he'd been sprinting up and down the stairs. He stood there for a full five minutes before attempting to move to the bedroom, staring at the closed door across the hall, the baby's room.

When he finally did move, it was like wearing lead-lined clothes and wading through molasses. But he pushed through, forcing himself to shower and shave and finally finding himself standing in front of a closet full of suits, shirts, and ties. He reached out to grab a plain white dress shirt but stopped.

Her favorite color on me was blue.

He smiled as he pulled a blue dress shirt from its hanger and put it on.

And she loved that tie.

He moved to the tie rack and began thumbing through the ties.

It's midnight blue.

The smile slipped from his face. He began pulling ties off and tossing them over his shoulder.

It's midnight blue.

He yanked a blue tie from the rack and studied it carefully before tossing it to the floor. He started ripping ties from the rack and tossing them down.

Midnight blue with charcoal and silver in a swirling pattern.

The rack hung denuded of its wardrobe of ties. Panic seized Eric. Sweat beaded on his forehead and dampened his armpits. His heart grew cold. He felt his knees burn when they hit the carpet.

And there it was, lying across his dress shoes like an anesthetized snake. He yanked it to himself as if he were a twelve-year-old little leaguer receiving his state championship trophy. He wrapped it around his neck, tied the knot, and stood up to look at it in the mirror. He smiled at the reflection as he gently smoothed down the tie, then stopped as a thought grabbed hold.

I just freaked out over a tie.

Eric wandered over and slumped wearily onto the bed. He looked at the picture of Emily placing the *Sold!* placard. He picked it up.

"Help me, Emily. Please help me."

He leaned forward with his elbows on his knees, buried his head in his hands, and started to cry.

Chapter 4

Eric cursed under his breath as he glanced at the digital clock above the radio.

2:38

He dialed the number on his cell phone he had for Paul again and again he got a recorded message saying that number was not in service. He ended the call and tossed the phone onto the passenger seat, pressing the accelerator a little farther down. He'd pushed the Ford Expedition a little faster than he liked on the icy roads, and he still felt he was crawling.

"*Perfect*," Eric said sarcastically as he saw a Mercedes-Benz S65, metallic black, sitting in the driveway of the house. "Nice car," he said, smirking at the admiration he heard in his voice.

He pulled to a stop at the curb in front of the house, put the SUV in park, and turned the engine off. As he opened the door, the wind bit through his navy blue slacks, giving him the sensation his pants were suddenly starched. He looked up. The forecast had been for snow in the late afternoon and evening, and by the looks of it, the weatherman was going to be a hit with the kids. There'd be more snow on the ground by Christmas Day. The sky was thick with it.

Hugging his overcoat to himself, he marched up to the Benz, not catching the purr of the engine until he was right up to it. Eric could, however, hear quite clearly emanating from the Benz's stereo system some old crooner singing lazily about Rudy the Red-Nosed Reindeer. The engine cut as the driver's side door opened. Paul Stephens stepped out of the vehicle.

He wore black slip-on loafers, cuffed black wool slacks, and a black three-quarter length classic leather coat buttoned up to a scarf wrapped neatly around his neck. A thick stock of short wavy dark hair, vibrant green eyes, and even features completed his appearance.

"Mr. Messer." Paul tugged off a black leather glove and extended his hand towards Eric. "Great to finally meet you."

Eric scrambled to get his glove off and accepted Paul's hand. "Great to meet you. I'm sorry I made you wait."

Paul slipped his hand back into his glove. "No problem. It happens. Especially in weather like this."

Eric put his glove back on. "I tried calling your number but kept getting an out-of-service message."

Paul waved the comment off. "My cell phone died, and I couldn't find the charger, so I just left it at home." He hugged himself for warmth.

Eric gestured towards the house. "Shall we take a look?"

"Yes, please." Paul turned and started making his way towards the house.

Eric turned too and saw the picture of him and Emily emblazoning the *For Sale* sign. It was his favorite picture of the two of them together. It had been taken for the signs they would be plunging into front yards together. It'd been the photographer's first shot and she'd remarked that was it, though she took a dozen more. Eric and Emily knew she'd been right as soon as they saw the proofs.

Eric could feel his clothes taking on the lead-lining. Molasses bubbled up from the ground, rooting him to the spot.

"You coming?"

Eric shot Paul a confused glance.

Paul gestured at the front door.

Eric could feel the molasses ebb away as he looked at Paul. The lead lining also lifted from his body as he managed a weak smile and said, "Sorry." He trudged up to the front door. "Shall we see the house?"

Eric retrieved the house key from the electronic lockbox, unlocked the door, pushed it open, and offered the threshold to Paul.

Paul crossed into the house and Eric followed. He was starting into his spiel when he noticed Paul wasn't listening, but already giving himself an unguided tour. Eric hurried to catch up. Paul moved from room to room, giving each room a cursory glance at best. When Paul went upstairs to the second floor, Eric decided not to follow but to wait at the fireplace in the living room.

He didn't have to wait long. Paul couldn't have been upstairs more than a minute before his feet could be heard descending the staircase. He breezed into the living room and leaned against the mantle.

"Do you have any questions I can answer?" Eric felt a little deflated and there wasn't much conviction in his question.

"No," Paul said. He clapped his gloved hands together and grinned, revealing a fortune in capped teeth. "I'll take it."

Reaching into his outside jacket pocket, he pulled out an envelope and handed it to Eric. "I'm going out of town for the holidays, but if you could go ahead and start the ball rolling on this, I'd appreciate it."

Eric took the envelope. "And what if they don't accept your offer." Eric knew they would. Of course, they would. He hadn't shown the house in he couldn't remember how long, even before Emily's death. Hadn't had a bite, even a nibble, in months.

Paul nodded at the envelope.

Eric opened it. Inside was a check with Paul Stephens' signature and the Payable To field left blank. The amount written in was a full ten grand over the asking price.

This guy knew he was going to buy this house before he even got here.

Paul pointed to the Payable To field. "I didn't know who to make it out to. Figured you could handle that for me."

Something about this whole thing was leaving Eric feeling unsettled. He should be happy, ecstatic even, but this wasn't just out of the ordinary. It was irregular. People didn't hand you six-figure blank checks and tell you to handle it. People didn't spend that kind of money on a house they'd spent less time in than the nastiest public john And, nothing against the house or the neighborhood, but if you had that kind of money, why would you be interested in this house?

Paul pulled the glove from his right hand again and extended it towards Eric. "Thank you for your time."

Eric took the hand again. "Thank you." Eric motioned for the front door, and the two men went outside.

"I'll call you when everything's ready," Eric said as he locked the house up and put the key back in the electronic lockbox.

"Actually, I'll be out of the country, so I'll just call you when I get back." Paul pulled out his keys and pushed a button on the key fob. The Mercedes beeped, the lights flickered, and Eric could hear the purr of the engine.

Paul opened the car door. "I guess now you can put one of those SOLD signs up in the front, Huh?" He pointed to the sign of Eric and Emily.

"Well, usually I wait –."

"Wait for what?" Paul interrupted as he fell into the car and closed the door. He lowered the power window.

Eric marveled at the near-quiet hum of the motor. Nothing on this car, outside of the stereo system, was loud. This car was the epitome of "walking softly but carrying a big stick."

"I'm paying cash," Paul explained as patiently as explaining how money works to a six-year-old. "This'll be a cinch." Paul dropped the engine into reverse and began backing out of the driveway. He beeped a goodbye and sped away.

Eric waved and then shook his head after the Benz dropped out of sight. *This guy has never spent a single day in the real world.*

He pocketed the envelope and pulled out his cell phone. Slipping off a glove, he dialed the number to his attorney.

"Law offices of Burgess, Myers, and Kemp," the receptionist announced in a soft but crisp voice that always made Eric think he'd caught her reapplying lipstick. "How may I direct your call?"

"Joseph Kemp, please," Eric answered.

The receptionist asked him to hold and then his ear was filled with Johnny Mathis passing around the coffee and pumpkin pie.

Eric loved this version of Sleigh Ride and he started to hum along when—

"Joseph Kemp's office. This is Sofia. How may I help you?"

"Hey, Sofia. This is Eric Messer."

"Hi, Mr. Messer."

Eric could hear the smile in her voice.

"I was just about to call you. Mr. Kemp just dropped off the changes to the will you requested. Before I typed it up, I wanted to make sure we had them all. Do you have a moment?"

Eric said he did, and Sofia reviewed all the changes. "That's all of them," Eric said.

"Great," Sofia exclaimed. "I'll get it typed up and ready for signature immediately."

"Thank you," Eric said. "And the trust papers?"

"That will take a little longer to draw up," Sofia responded. "But Mr. Kemp is aware you want to sign them before you leave for your sister's. Don't worry, Mr. Messer. "They'll be ready."

Eric thanked Sofia and disconnected the call after wishing her a Merry Christmas. He pulled out his keys as he walked around to the back of the Expedition. He unlocked and lifted the back gate of the vehicle and reached into a small cardboard box. Taking out a *Sold* placard, he made his way towards the picture of him and Emily.

But as he drew closer to the sign, the harder it was to put one foot in front of the other. The lead lining in his clothes was returning. The molasses was no longer bubbling up from the ground but raining over him, draping him like the third blanket a mother puts on a child to help break a fever.

The *Sold* placard felt heavy, like a tombstone. Exhaustion was setting in, he wanted to drop to the ground, curl into a fetal position, and rest, sleep for a long time. Maybe forever. The placard, a fitting marker. But he knew that wouldn't be possible. He could hear it again, faint like the edge of a dream.

He slipped the sign into the T-groove with the last of his strength. Snow and a little sleet began to fall as the wind howled, announcing the storm would be more ice than snow. But Eric couldn't hear it. All he heard were their screams, Emily's, and the baby's, growing louder in his head like a distant train coming closer.

Chapter 5

Eric made his way into Chicago Heights and to his sister's neighborhood. He couldn't help but smile as he imagined his sister's face when she opened the front door to find him standing there. She had sincerely meant her offer for him to come for Christmas, and she would have prepared space and food for him, but she would have also sincerely believed there was no way he would come.

He glanced at the seat beside him, checking for the twentieth time since he'd left his house that the neatly wrapped Christmas presents were still there. This morning he'd made his way into a Toys-R-Us store thinking he'd be in and out in less than thirty minutes. He couldn't have been more wrong. A throng of adults stood at the locked doors like teenagers waiting to get into a rock concert. When the manager began unlocking the doors and the throng surged forward, Eric remembered The Who concert when eleven people were trampled to death. Rock stars and Elmo had a lot more in common at Christmas than people thought.

Once inside, Eric realized he had no idea what to get his nieces. He'd wandered lost and confused like a child might in an antique store. Or maybe it was more like the running of the bulls in Pamplona. He'd never been more jostled in his life. Not even a rock concert, and he was sure one woman had purposefully rib-checked him when she thought he was going for the last Millennium Falcon on the shelf.

Finally, a young lady stocking shelves took pity on him. She helped him pick out the perfect gift for any girl of six and eight - Barbie. And now lying beside him, looking like gift-wrapped mausoleums, were two identical Barbie's.

His brother-in-law was easier. He gave him the same gift every year-Captain Morgan's spiced rum. And for Jennifer...Eric usually begged Emily to get something for Jennifer and Emily always found the perfect gift. Emily and Jennifer had a lot of the same tastes, so all Emily had to do was buy something she'd love to have herself, which also had the added benefit of giving Eric an idea of what to get Emily for her birthday. This year, Eric had decided to give her a bottle of wine he thought would go rather nicely with the Christmas turkey.

Eric pulled into the driveway and cut the engine. He looked over the house and front yard. Multi-colored lights stretched across the trim of the roof, around the trim of the windows and front door, and spiraled up the trunk of the Maple tree, and over the front hedge.

Scooping up the gifts as he got out of the Expedition, Eric headed to the front door. The breeze, thank God it's only a breeze he thought, cut through his jeans, cuffed his ears, and clipped his nose. The sky showed blue-gray, which was just as well, Eric thought. He hated those days when the sky was an eye-squinting, dazzling blue with the sun shining bright and not one ounce of warmth in the day.

What was it Jody had told him last year? His niece had been a precocious five at the time when she announced to him that the sun tended to be hot, but not in winter because of the snow. She'd rolled her eyes and asked, "Don't you get the weather channel, Uncle Eric?" Her tone suggested she thought he was a step below her hamster on the intelligence ladder. Now she was a precocious six-year-old. What new knowledge would she bestow upon him now, he wondered.

Eric hitched a smile onto his face. It didn't quite make it to his eyes.

Fake it till you make it.

He knocked on the front door, nearly dropping the bottle of wine. He caught it as the door opened. He almost dropped the wine again as his legs were gathered in a strong embrace. A muffled "Uncle Eric" came from his thighs. He looked down to see the top of Jody's head, her auburn hair still damaged by bed head, her body still wrapped in footed pajamas. The sound of Jimmy Stewart screaming, "Merry Christmas movie house," came through the open door.

"Jody," Jennifer reprimanded. "Wait 'til I get there to open the door."

"Merry Christmas, Sis," Eric shouted to his sister as she came to the front door.

Jennifer couldn't have looked more stunned. "Eric?" She grabbed his neck in a bear hug. He thought she'd given him whiplash. "You came." She kissed his cheek and then let him go. "Let me help you." She grabbed the wine and the rum from him and then knelt to talk to Jody.

"Jody, Sweetheart, what have Daddy and I told you about opening the front door?"

Jody's face reddened as she stared down hard at the feet of her pajamas. "I'm sorry, Mommy, I forgot."

"Remember what we said about strangers?"

Jody's head shot up. "Uncle Eric's not a stranger." Her tone suggested to Eric she thought the hamster, Mommy, and Uncle Eric should all be riding the short bus.

"She's got a point, you know." Eric wasn't sure if he meant the point about being a stranger or riding the short bus.

Jennifer shot him a 'you're not helping' look. "Shut up, Uncle Eric." She looked back at Jody as if to start back into the browbeating but stopped. Jody had already moved on.

"Presents," she was screaming as she pointed to the two packages still in Eric's arms. She danced about his legs.

"Sweetheart," Jennifer said as she shifted the rum and wine to one arm, scooped the two packages out of Eric's hands, and handed them to Jody. "Why don't you put these presents from Uncle Eric under the tree, okay?"

Jody's eyes bulged as she snatched the two brightly wrapped packages from her mother and sped off toward the living room, announcing to her sister that they had more presents.

Jennifer eyed her brother coyly. "Barbie's?"

Eric felt the heat of embarrassment brush his cheek. "Yeah. Do they like Barbie?"

"Like her?" Jennifer rolled her eyes. "They've each got a harem. Makes me feel bad for Ken."

Eric stared nonplussed.

"Too bad he's a eunuch."

Eric burst out laughing. It was so spontaneous, so foreign, he hadn't so much as snickered in the past six months, that he jumped at the sound of it. It was a deep, loud belly laugh. His head felt light from the sound of it, the rush of endorphins in the brain intoxicating him.

Jennifer brightened. "Now there's the old Eric." She drew him into an embrace with her free hand. "I've missed you, Bro."

The comment steadied him, the lightheadedness drifting away, and he changed the subject back to Barbie. "I got them both the same one."

Relief enveloped Jennifer's body like a sixty-pound rucksack had just been taken off her back. A smile spread across her face. "That's perfect." She said. "They won't have anything to fight over. Well, except 'til Jody cuts off the hair on hers."

"Cuts off the hair?" He could feel a laugh bubbling up inside him. "Why on earth does she do that?"

"She's just really into that close-cropped, G.I. Jane look." Jennifer moved towards the living room and beckoned him to follow. "Julie's got a harem and Jody's got a platoon."

As she reached the Christmas tree, she held up the presents for her and Bill. The bottles of alcohol weren't in gift boxes, just the paper drawn up around them and tied off with a ribbon. "Now I wonder what these could be." She gave a light shake to the bottle in her right hand.

Eric pointed to the bottle in her left hand. "That one should go well with dinner tomorrow."

She looked a little disappointed. "Well, I won't be opening this one tonight."

She set them under the tree. "One guess as to which one Bill will be opening." She stood back up. "Opening *your* present on Christmas Eve has become his little tradition."

"Lunch is ready," Bill announced as he walked into the living room carrying a tray of tuna fish sandwiches. "Hey, Eric." He set the tray down on the coffee table and offered a warm hand to Eric which he accepted. Bill pulled Eric into a hug. "Merry Christmas, Man. Thanks for coming."

Eric could feel the genuineness in his embrace. "Thanks. Merry Christmas."

Bill released him and then eyed his present under the tree. "Oh, it will be." He smiled and winked.

Jennifer came over to Bill and playfully elbowed him in the ribs. "Shameless." She saw the girls, who'd grabbed sandwiches and replanted themselves in front of the television, eating. "Stop."

"Aw, Mom," came the exasperated chorus from the girls.

"Don't 'Aw, Mom' me. You don't have plates and we haven't said grace yet."

"Grace," the girls screamed in stereo and began giggling.

"That's enough." Jennifer sounded stern, but Eric could see the corner of her mouth crook suppressing the smile.

"I've got it." Bill took off for the kitchen and returned with paper plates and cups of milk for the girls. "Eric? Beer?"

"Sure," Eric said as he picked up a sandwich and placed it on a paper plate.

Bill nodded and then looked at Jennifer.

"Diet Pepsi," she replied.

"No, Honey," Bill said. "I thought you could make yourself useful and get us a couple of beers."

"Oh, did you?" She moved to Bill, an impish sort of smile spreading across her face, and whispered into his ear. "I thought I made myself useful last night."

Usually, when he heard them talk like this, he'd remark that it was gross, that he didn't want to know his sister was having sex, or that the two of them should get a room. On that last one, his sister would always look him square in the eye and tell him they already had. This time, however, Eric felt a pang, not of pain but of envy and a light dusting of jealousy.

Jennifer couldn't see the look on Eric's face, but Bill could. He shifted away from Jennifer as if he'd been jabbed in the ribs.

"Jenny," he whispered as his eyes shot quickly from her to Eric and back.

Jennifer cringed, closing her eyes, and exhaling a remonstrating breath.

Perhaps the girls sensed the awkward silence between the adults in the room, Jennifer later pondered, but it was at this moment they bounced over to Eric and taking the plate from his hands and grabbing a hand each, tugged him towards their place on the floor in front of the television.

"Come on, Uncle Eric," they beseeched, "watch the Grinch with us."

Eric let himself be dragged and pushed to the floor beside them. He did enjoy his two nieces and, it seemed to him, that they were crazy about him.

"I love that cartoon." He told them. "Back when your mom and I were kids—," he stopped as his nieces started laughing.

"The *real* Grinch, Uncle Eric." Jody had that short bus tone again.

Eric looked bemusedly at Jennifer who answered, "Jim Carey."

"Ah," Eric said, turning back to his nieces. "Have you guys ever seen the cartoon?"

"We're too old for cartoons," Julie said in a sober tone as Jody nodded in serious agreement.

Eric turned back to Jennifer, but it was Bill who responded this time. "Welcome to our world."

The rest of the day passed with more Christmas movies interrupted by board games (Jody stomped everyone at Candy Land and Julie only stopped gloating after winning at Simon when her mother reminded her Santa Claus didn't leave presents for sore winners) and dinner (homemade Chili).

Eric ate two bowls of chili before realizing he'd just eaten more food in one day than he had in the past week.

At seven-thirty, Bill came into the living room carrying a Tom Collins glass filled with ice cubes in one hand and a can of Coke in the other and announced it was time to open one present each.

The girls opened their present from some relative on Bill's side. It was *Chutes and Ladders* and the girls begged Eric and their parents to play. Bill and Jennifer declined as the film *A Christmas Story* started on TNT. Eric ended up playing two very cutthroat games with the girls. Jody won both games. He never knew someone that young and cute could be that vicious.

Jody asked for another game, but it was time for bed. Santa Claus didn't visit naughty girls who beat on their uncles and didn't go to bed on time. With the girls in bed, Eric helped himself to some of his present to Bill and watched the rest of the movie with Jennifer in silence. Bill sat on the floor cursing as he assembled the indoor playhouse they'd gotten for the girls.

As the credits rolled, Eric said goodnight and headed off to the guest room to bed. It had been a good day. The best he'd had in six months. He hadn't thought it possible. He'd thought that once Emily died, the intangibles like joy and laughter ceased to be.

But today, he'd laughed and eaten and had enjoyed his nieces and his sister and brother-in-law. It hadn't taken long for the smile to be genuine. He chuckled as he thought of Jody jumping up, leaning into Julie, and shouting, "In yo' face," as she won her second game of Chutes and Ladders.

The chuckle died away as Eric's mind pointed out something he hadn't noticed. There had been no screaming the entire day. There had been no image of fire playing in his mind's eye. When Eric thought about it now, he hadn't thought of Emily or the baby all day. He felt a pang of betrayal at this. A betrayal of his plan. A betrayal to his wife.

"I'm sorry, Emily," Eric said softly. "Merry Christmas."

He rolled onto his side and closed his eyes. There'd been no screaming today. Only laughter.

Eric drifted off, a smile curving his lips. It had been a very good day.

Chapter 6

Christmas Day passed much in the same way as the day before. The morning had been filled with squeals of delight as the girls moved from present to present. They'd loved their Barbie dolls very much, and true to form when the girls appeared at the table for Christmas dinner, Jody's Barbie was sporting a fresh buzz cut. Jody was singing and dancing her Barbie across the table.

"I guess this one's Sinead O'Connor." Jennifer rolled her eyes.

Eric nearly spewed dressing across the table. Julie, however, upon seeing her uncle, did spew turkey across the table laughing at him, which earned her a weighty reprimand from her mother. Jody was ordered to put down Barbie O'Connor and the rest of dinner had gone on spew free. Jennifer had even admitted that the wine had gone spectacularly with dinner.

The rest of the day and evening passed playing charades as well as *Trouble* and other board games.

"Okay, you two," Jennifer had said as she grabbed the board game, "time to go to bed."

"Awww Mom," the girls moaned in miserable unison.

"Don't 'Awww Mom' me." Jennifer packed up the board game.

"We'll go on one condition," Julie said.

Jennifer turned to face her oldest daughter. Eyebrows raised. "Just the one?"

Julie quailed at her mother's look, but Jody hastily spoke up in her place. "Uncle Eric tucks us in."

"This isn't a democracy," Bill started to say, but Eric interrupted him.

"Those seem like fair terms to me," Eric offered.

Eric looked up to meet his sister's eyebrow-raised glare. "If it's okay with the President. Or are you a martinet? Or is it...Queen?"

The girls had no idea what their uncle was talking about, but they could tell by the tone of his voice, the mocking look on his face, and their mother's inability to keep the smile from curling the corner of her lip that Uncle Eric had just won. They giggled and shouted, "Hooray."

Jennifer turned back to Julie and Jody. "Then I suggest you girls kiss me and your father and get your little rears up the stairs toot sweet."

Jody guffawed.

"What?" Jennifer exclaimed a little irritated.

"You told us to fart up the stairs." Jody laughed.

Julie rolled her eyes soberly and then grabbed her sister by the arm. "Honestly, you are such a child," she said as she guided her from the room.

But Eric, Jennifer, and Bill heard them break into laughter as they ran up the stairs.

"And I'd better hear you brushing your teeth," Jennifer called after them.

"You can hear them brushing their teeth from here?" Eric asked his sister, a mild skepticism flavoring his tone.

Jennifer only nodded. "It's a gift."

Bill caught Eric's attention and mouthed *Tell me about it* to which Jennifer replied, "I heard that, Bill."

Bill and Eric burst out laughing.

Eric finished his laughter with a yawn. "I think I'll tuck them in and then tuck myself in." He got up and started walking to the stairs, where he stopped, one foot on the first step. "By the way, Sis, who says 'toot sweet' anymore?" He ran up the stairs, hearing a pillow hit the staircase below him.

He tucked the girls in, read them a story, and then retired to the guestroom. He pulled off his jeans and shirt, chuckling all the while about the girls, Barbie O'Connor, toot sweet, Bill opening his present with a glass of ice and can of coke in hand. Eric climbed into bed and rolled over to turn off the bedside light.

On the bedside table, Jennifer had set a copy of the picture taken at Lake Lou Yaeger. It hadn't been there Christmas Eve. Jennifer must've done it sometime during the day. Eric focused on the image of Emily laughing at whatever Bill had said, her face frozen in that smile Eric loved.

The picture wiped the smile off Eric's face as cleanly as a teacher wiping chalk from a blackboard with an eraser. The picture blurred as Eric realized he hadn't thought of Emily once that day. He'd had fun. Enjoyed himself like he'd had when she'd been alive. And that was wrong, somehow. He didn't have the right to have fun. He didn't have the right to enjoy himself, especially like he had when they'd been together. That was a special kind of happiness, a special kind of joy he no longer had a right to experience.

Eric turned off the light and cried for a long time. And when he wiped the last tear from his cheek, he remembered the plan. Like Emily, it hadn't entered his mind all day. But he was thinking about it now. He reviewed the plan and checked off the points he'd completed. Only one more thing left to do. Well, two more. And then…he drifted off to sleep thinking of his reunion with Emily.

The next morning he avoided his sister and the kids by pretending to sleep in. Bill had already left for work by seven-thirty. Eventually, he'd gotten up, showered, dressed, packed, and headed to the kitchen.

The girls were too busy with Christmas toys to notice Uncle Eric just yet, but Jennifer sensed a problem as soon as his foot hit the tiled floor.

She cocked her head. "You okay?"

"Yeah." He shrugged her off as he retrieved a cup and filled it with coffee. He added milk and sugar. "Just a little hung over from the frivolity that is Christmas."

Jennifer went back to rinsing the breakfast dishes. "You going back today?"

Eric noted a slight wariness in her voice, like she didn't want him to go, but didn't feel she had the right.

"Yes." Then he added. "I need to think about getting back to work, putting my life back together."

That last statement had done the trick. Jennifer brightened and made him a big breakfast to send him on his way. He'd eaten, but the food didn't sit well on his belly.

Jennifer had watched him as she cleaned the kitchen and had tried engaging him in small talk, but Eric didn't bite.

When his car was packed and he'd said goodbye to the girls, he and Jennifer had stood at the front door a long time in awkward silence. He'd had a good time and part of him didn't want to leave. But what could he do? He couldn't just move in with them and expect the girls to mute the screaming with their laughter. And even if he could, the girls would go back to school the following week.

He had a plan. He had to stick to the plan.

"You can stay as long as you like. You don't have to go, you know. Not yet." But there was a resignation in her voice. She knew he would leave.

"Thanks for everything, Sis." He'd opened his arms for a hug.

She'd come at him, slipped her arms around him, and pulled him hard to her. She'd held him hard for a long time. He could still feel the strength of her embrace as he pulled into the parking lot of the dingy pawn shop.

Eric cut the engine and sat steeling himself for the cold that was December weather in inner-city Chicago. The snow here had lost its White Christmas luster, taking on the lesser virtues of its surrounding environment. Hope had long since left this neighborhood and bleakness hung on it heavier and colder than any Northwestern blizzard. The pawn shop had lost the 'N' and the 'S' years ago so the sign read *Paw Hop*. In a different frame of mind, this might have made Eric laugh with the mental image of a dog dressed in socks hopping up and down.

But Eric's mind was focused on the next step in the plan. Buy a gun. When he'd first formulated the plan, he thought this might be the hardest part. After using the gun, of course. Remembering the photograph on the bedside table, however, Eric realized these last two steps were the easiest. Eric had no intention of enduring another holiday, birthday, or any other day for that matter, without Emily.

Eric opened the Expedition's door and stepped into the frigid wind. Despite the cold, Eric walked slowly towards the store entrance like a kid walking up to the principal's door. He just couldn't shake the image of his sister when she finally let him go, looked hard into his eyes, and asked again, "Are you okay?"

The chime echoed above his head as he opened and stepped through the glass door smeared with neglect. A phantom graveled voice yelled out, "Be with you in a minute" as he let the door close behind him. He looked around. If a yard sale and a flea market had decided to hook up and procreate, this might be what the result of their union would look like.

Making his way to the glass cases, he looked through the dustiness, still thinking about her face. Maybe it was more than just wanting him to stay, worrying that he wasn't okay, he began to wonder. Maybe she knew what he was planning to do. Maybe she knew she'd never see him again. Eric felt a shiver run through him at this thought. He'd never want to hurt his sister.

"What can I do you for?"

Eric looked up to see a man straight out of a Charles Dickens novel. He was as dingy and dusty as his store. Eric suppressed an urge to call the man Old Joe, the name of the rickety old pawnbroker in *A Christmas Carol*. Instead, Eric dropped his eye on the case that held the quarry he'd come for. Jabbing the glass, Eric said, "I'll take that one."

The old man grinned; his teeth just as dingy as the rest of him. He pulled a key ring from his pocket and finding the proper key, unlocked the case. "A classic," he said as he pulled out what Eric had been pointing at, a Nickel-plated, snub nose .38 special with a pearl handle grip. The sight of the pistol, shining from reflected light, felt completely wrong cradled in the thick, dirty hand of the pawn shop dealer, and Eric remembered a verse from the Bible about a pearl in the snout of a pig.

The old man made a quick jerk with his hand, popping the cylinder out. He eyed the chambers, ensuring they were each clear, then checked the inside of the barrel, before jerking the pistol again. The cylinder made a sharp click as it fell into place.

Eric now wanted to say, "Thanks Pecos Bill" as the old man shifted the weapon one-handed so that when he extended the pistol across the counter, he was offering the grip to Eric.

Eric took the .38, surprised by the weight. Eric hadn't held many weapons before, okay only a loaded water pistol when he was eight years old, but he was sure this one would do.

Eric grunted something that sounded like agreement and set the pistol down on the glass counter.

"You wanna box o' rounds?"

"Yeah."

"What type?"

"Type?"

The man behind the counter seemed unfazed by Eric's lack of knowledge. He turned to a shelf behind him. "Just depends on what you want to use it for. If you want some cheap rounds to take to the range," he grabbed a box off the shelf and placed them on the counter, "these'll work." He turned back to the shelf. "Now if you're looking for home protection, I'd recommend a hollow point. A lot of people prefer the Federal."

He grabbed another box off the shelf. "Now these babies," he turned to Eric, "are the Gold Dot hollow point. Made by Speer." He set the box down, opened it, and slid out a black plastic tray filled with rows of bullets. It made Eric think about what an egg carton might look like if Rambo were the Easter Bunny.

He pulled a bullet out and held it up to Eric. "Someone tries to break into your house," his face twitched into a malevolent smile, "and this little beauty'll take his head clean off."

Eric had no idea who Federal or Speer was, but he did understand the last statement the man said.

Take his head clean off.

If Eric was going to eat a bullet, he wanted to make sure he only had to eat one. He didn't want to wake up to find all he'd done was blow off his face, or worse, end up a vegetable strapped to a bed with enough tubes coming out of him to look like a Borg from *Star Trek*.

"I'll take it." Eric took the bullet from the man's hand and rolled it between his fingers, feeling the cold smoothness of it. It was small, not more than an inch and a half in length. Something so small could do that much damage. Eric wondered what that said about humanity and its value of life. Not much, he figured.

"Okay." The old man fished through a stack of papers. "Just need you to fill out a background check. You know the government. Won't tell you the truth about Area Fifty-One, but by God, they think they got the right to know what brand toilet paper you wipe with." He rolled his eyes. "Walmart can sell you a shotgun to shoot your wife with the same day but buy a handgun for the range or home protection and you gotta wait three days."

"Three days?" Eric stopped filling out the paperwork. "I have to wait three days?"

The old man could sense he had an audience and started heating up. "Yup. Call it a cooling-off period. Cooling-off period." He repeated, incredulity flying out of his mouth like spittle. He drew a breath to start full into his prepared rant when Eric interrupted him.

"I can't wait three days."

He knew how it sounded, but he didn't care. He had the nerve to kill himself today. Had the desire to die today. He didn't trust himself to swallow a bottle of pills, slice his wrists with a razor, or even run his SUV into a cement pylon at a hundred miles an hour. Those methods took too much time, and he could see them coming. But he wouldn't see the bullet. Just a quick spasm of his finger and lights out.

I don't know if I'll be able to go through with it in three days.

But the old man did care how it sounded. His gray brows lowered in suspicion as his body went taut. "I don't care for visits from the Feds."

Eric raised his hands. "I didn't mean it like that." His mind groped for some good explanation. "It's a birthday present for my brother-in-law."

This guy's never gonna believe this.

"His birthday's tomorrow. I didn't know what to get him and he just happened to mention yesterday that he'd always wanted a .38."

Eric didn't know what he was marveling at more, how brilliantly he'd just lied or how lamely. He knew the man wouldn't buy it.

But the old man appeared more than willing to buy what Eric was selling. "Well, that's different." He winked. "But you still got to wait the three days. You'll just have to give it to him late."

"He's waited this long," Eric nodded in agreement, "what's another couple of days?"

Eric finished the background check information and paid for the pistol and ammunition with his credit card. He thanked the old man as he pocketed his receipt and turned to leave.

"Oh," the old man said.

Eric turned back to him.

"Hope your brother-in-law has a very happy birthday." He winked and smiled another malevolent, dingy smile.

Eric nodded and left.

The wind had picked up, but Eric didn't notice. He didn't feel the drop in temperature that had taken place during the time he'd been in the store. It still wasn't as cold as the ice forming inside him.

Eric opened the Expedition's door and climbed in. He shut the door and stared at nothing for a long time before opening his phone. His wallpaper was a headshot taken of Emily at the same time they had the couple's picture taken for their business. He rubbed a finger over the screen's surface. "I'm sorry."

Chapter 7

Eric wandered his way through downtown Chicago and back onto the interstate. He'd expected to have a gun sitting on the seat beside him and its absence had him feeling as lost and as purposeless as he had been in the last six months.

It was ironic, he'd thought to himself more than once, that the only reason he'd found for living was so he could kill himself. Now without the instrument to kill himself, he had no reason to live.

The interstate had the regular flow of business traffic, and the additional holiday traffic was surprisingly light. He used to like the interstate because it gave him time to think. Now he tried hard to keep his mind idling, a task made easier by concentrating on the drive. Traffic moved at a brisk clip and soon he was at the sign welcoming travelers to Cary.

He'd passed that sign more times than he could remember. It had become nothing more than a marker for distance and time traveled, an announcement he was almost home, the trip nearly complete, and a gauge against where he'd been. No matter how large or exciting the places had been, they were all found wanting in comparison to home.

And Cary was home, had been his home all his life. He'd been born there and until this very moment, until seeing the sign today, Eric would have sworn he'd be buried there. His parents were buried there, as were his grandparents. Except for the four years at Northwestern University, Eric had lived nowhere else. Emily had been born there as well. And like him, had only left to attend Northwestern.

Now the sign was a tombstone, a reminder that all he had left were memories. He hated that sign. Felt the urge to plow the sign down and leave it just broken splinters under his Expedition. He had no desire to go home. Didn't think he could stand the idea of being in that house alone. There were too many memories, and the irony was, Eric mused humorlessly, the good memories more than outweighed the bad ones. Good memories hurt more to remember.

So instead of making the left into his neighborhood, Eric went straight, looking for someplace to escape the household filled with remembrances. But the street was jammed with stores and restaurants and memories. He took a right and then another right and then a left. Everywhere he turned, restaurants, the movie house, the high school, neighborhoods they'd sold houses in, he could see more memories. Eric felt a wave of claustrophobic panic pass over him. There was no place he could go, no place he could escape a memory. He was trapped. He thought about turning around and leaving Cary, just driving until he couldn't stand the interior of his vehicle, then maybe renting a room in some hotel in some town he'd never heard of. Maybe then he could rest.

Eric had just turned his SUV around when he noticed a sign for a bar. It wasn't much, just an end unit of a newly built and, not surprisingly, bland mini-mall. The lighted sign read 'Molly O'Malley's Irish Tavern.' It had green clovers for the apostrophes and a rose in a beer mug completed the motif. Eric chuckled. Nothing about the mini-mall, with its off-white stucco and institutionalized architecture, or the end unit, with one big square window in the front by the glass door entrance, faintly resembled an Irish tavern, not even the sign. Eric decided to stop anyway. Hanging below the sign was a white streamer with red letters announcing, *'Grand Opening.'*

This area had just been a couple of empty commercial lots, not used since before Eric and Emily were born. Eric had never given it any thought other than if he wanted to get into commercial development, which he didn't, it was probably the best place to start. He had never discussed this with Emily, though, and she had never mentioned the property to him.

This was someplace new, someplace without any memories. It was safe, and it would probably be open late. They might even let him stay there all night if he passed out, though he doubted it.

He pulled into a parking spot, cut the engine, and hopped out. He moved at a brisk pace, not from the chill, but from the draw, the pull, to this new-found oasis. He had to chuckle again. He felt almost giddy.

He opened the door and stepped inside. A quick scan of the place told him that the words 'Irish' and 'Tavern' on the sign with the clovers provided the only Irish ambiance. The faint smell of a Chicago-style pizza with everything wafted in the air. Dull black and white linoleum tile covered the floor. Faux wood paneling, not dark but blonde, ended halfway up the wall where stark white paint took over.

Old black and white pictures of Chicago and Mobsters hung on the wall. Several square brown Formica tables littered the center of the room and a couple of booths sat against the front window. In the front corner opposite the door was a small platform and a music stand. Taped to the stand was a handwritten note announcing karaoke every Friday, Saturday, and Sunday. Currently, a jukebox was blasting Bob Seger's "Hollywood Nights." As far as Eric knew, Bob Seger wasn't Irish.

Eric made his way to the bar which took up a full two-thirds of the back wall. He'd never been to Ireland, but he'd read enough books, seen enough television and movies, and been in a couple of Irish pubs in Chicago to know that even somebody who claimed to be Irish on their great-great-great grandmother's side would have been embarrassed to admit that in here.

Eric sat on a stool at the bar as a burly man with shaggy hair and beard and a worn flannel shirt finished filling mugs with draught beer and growled what he could get him. Looking at the beer taps and dismissing them outright, Eric's eyes flit over the shelves of liquor on the glass wall behind the bar. He didn't care for beer unless he was watching a football game with his buddies. He preferred a glass of wine for a nightcap with Emily, and margaritas were his favorite at a party.

He had the feeling asking the bartender (and he was using the term loosely) for the house white might earn him more than the dirty look he was receiving right now. Eric stifled a shudder. What would this place consider a house white? Eric also had the suspicion this guy's idea of a margarita was a shot of Tequila with a suck of lime and a lick of salt.

Truth was, Eric had to admit to himself, that he was a social drinker, or had been before Emily died. After…? Well, he also had to admit to himself, that he preferred to drink alone, not knowing or caring what he drank so long as it kept him numb.

Eric had the distinct impression the bartender now glowering down at him, looking more like a bear or a silverback gorilla with his fists resting on the already scratched bar, was trying to intimidate him and the even more distinct impression it was working. His eyes darted over the man's shoulder and spotted a bottle. He pointed at the bottle and squeaked, "Can you give me, oh, I forget the name for it, but could you give me a glass," Eric held up his hands as if holding a glass, "and put some, ah, Jack Daniels," he mimed pouring liquid into the glass, "and some soda in it?"

The bartender just stood there glaring for a moment before saying, "A Jack and Coke" in a tone that sounded like he too agreed with Eric's niece about the hamster and the short bus.

Eric winced.

Jack and Coke. I'm such an idiot.

The man turned and snatched a glass from below the counter. "Freaking charades."

"He's just jealous." A voice behind Eric spoke, causing him to jump.

Eric looked into the mirror over the bar. Behind him over his right shoulder, stood Paul Stephens. He smiled and waved into the mirror when he saw Eric looking at him.

The bartender set the glass down in front of Eric. "Here's your glass of Jack Daniels with some soda in it."

"I believe that's called a Jack and Coke actually," Paul offered.

The bartender shot Paul a look of disdain.

Paul appeared not to notice. "Do you have anything over eighteen years in a malt?" He leaned in, making eye contact with the bartender.

The bartender's eyes dropped as if he was suddenly very interested in something on the floor, but he quickly recovered. He looked back up, though not at Paul, responding with bland indifference. "I got Johnny Walker Red Label and twelve-year-old Glenlivet. Whaddaya want?" His constantly shifting gaze belied his nonchalant attitude.

Paul made an unimpressed face. "Just give me a Sam Adams."

The bartender traipsed off to get Paul's beer.

Paul turned to Eric, pointing to the stool beside him. "May I?"

"Oh, yeah, sure." Eric took a sip of his drink as the bartender sat a glass of beer in front of Paul and sauntered away to help other customers.

Paul sat down on the stool. "Did you have a nice Christmas?" He picked up his glass and drank.

"Very nice, thank you. You?" Eric was only being polite. He didn't care how Paul's Christmas had been, but now that he asked, he was quite interested. He'd been a little more than surprised to see Paul in Cary, but he couldn't put his finger on why. Now he remembered. Paul had said he'd be out of the country on business.

Paul seemed to have read his mind. "Business went very well, tied up in a day. So I came on back." He took another swallow. "Thought I'd drive out to Cary from the office to see just how long the commute would be. Speaking of which, have you had a chance to check on the sale yet?"

Eric sipped his drink and grimaced. It was mostly ice with a whole lot of bourbon and faintly flavored carbonated water. "Not today, but everything should be ready to go. The sellers accepted your offer—"

"Great." He gave Eric a huge smile. "I'll tell the movers they can deliver the furniture the day after tomorrow."

"It doesn't really work like that."

"Why not?" Paul took another swallow of his beer and said in the tone of a child explaining to an adult why he had the right to hit Jimmy, "It's my house now."

"Technically it's not your house yet."

Paul waved him off, looking annoyed as he finished off his beer and called out to the bartender for another round. He sat in silence for a long moment before speaking. "Look…I've been living out of a suitcase and a hotel room for too long. Now this is a done deal. I'm not backing out and the seller's not backing out. But if it'll make you feel better, call the seller, and see if it's okay with them. If they squabble, up the price by…three thousand. Call it a rental fee if you have to, but I need to be in that house the day after tomorrow."

The bartender dropped off another Sam Adams and a Jack and Coke. Eric felt pressured to finish his first drink. He did so in two lip-puckering, eye-squinting gulps. Paul picked up his glass and took a long swallow.

"Now enough about that business." Paul's tone indicated the subject was indeed closed and he at once seemed to relax. "Tell me about the town of Cary."

"Like what?" Eric stifled the irritated expression that had started creeping across his face at the word 'Cary' with a long pull from his drink, which, like the first one, was a lot of whiskey with a little carbonated water. He wanted to sit in silence and drink. He wanted to be numb. He didn't want to think, to remember, and he sure didn't want to give a talking tour of the town. He came in here to get away from town. Couldn't this guy see that? Eric started to feel annoyed. This guy has the money to live anywhere, so why does he buy a house in Cary when he works in Chicago? A town he knows nothing about. Who does that? What single rich guy wants to live in the Burbs when he can afford to live in the city?

Feeling emboldened by the alcohol, Eric opened his mouth to share these thoughts with Paul when Paul announced, "I'm starving. I could go for some wings. What about you?"

Eric's stomach growled its desire for wings, and he realized he hadn't eaten anything since the morning. He nodded. "Sure."

Paul nodded, then turned and shouted at the bartender, "We'd like a couple dozen wings, a couple orders of fries, and some," he turned back to Eric, "You like blue cheese?"

Eric nodded.

Paul turned back to the bartender. "Blue cheese dressing."

The bartender, feeling emboldened by the space between him and Paul, shouted back harshly, "We ain't got no blue cheese dressing."

Paul waited until the man looked at him. "Sure you do."

Eric couldn't see the look on Paul's face, but he could see the bartender's reaction to it. The man's face paled. His eyes widened as his mouth fell open. He closed it with a sharp snap of teeth Eric could hear. The man suddenly looked exhausted. He nodded wearily. "I'll get on it," he said as he shuffled to the kitchen.

Deciding he would not like to see whatever look had been on Paul's face directed at him, Eric cleared his throat and began telling Paul about the town. He thought he was a pretty good guide telling Paul not only local history and politics but civic information and traffic patterns of the surrounding communities as well. Paul was a great tourist, listening actively and asking questions.

The wings and fries came and with them another round. Eric's stomach rumbled again as the mouthwatering steam rose from the wings, invading his nostrils. He and Paul devoured the food as their conversation moved to other inane subjects like Midwest and New York weather.

Eric was feeling pretty good, not great, not even close to how he felt at his sister's, but he couldn't hear his wife screaming and he didn't feel much of anything. Yet, he still wasn't ready to face the house alone.

Finally, Paul yawned. "I'm sorry, but as my nanny used to say, 'My belly's full and my diaper's dry. Time for a nap.'"

Eric looked at his watch.

10:15 already?

"Do you recommend any place around here? I don't think I should make the trip back to Chicago." Paul pointed to his beer.

"Well as far as hotels—"

Paul groaned. "I can't stand another night in a hotel. I need something a little more like home. What about a B and B?"

Eric was just about to recommend a place when he had an idea. "Well, if you really want something more like a home, I've got a guestroom."

Paul shot him a puzzled look.

"If you don't mind. And it'd save you a buck." Eric thought he'd laugh at that last comment. Paul wasn't living on a budget, maybe a monthly trust fund allowance, but certainly not a budget. "At any rate, you wouldn't have to find the place and then check in."

"I am pretty tired," Paul said wearily. He finished off his beer. "If it's not too much trouble."

"No trouble at all," Eric reassured him. "It's actually a win-win situation."

"How so?" Paul motioned for the check as he pulled his wallet out of his pocket.

Eric felt heat on the back of his neck. He hadn't meant to say that. He was just thinking that Paul crashing in his guestroom kept Paul out of a hotel and kept him from being alone in the house. But he didn't want to tell Paul that. He finished off his drink with a grimace.

"Well, I can't really vouch for the bed's comfort, but in the morning I can take you to breakfast and then sign the papers. We'll be done before ten."

Paul laughed. "Sounds like my last night with my ex-wife."

Chapter 8

Eric awoke with a crick in his neck and the morning sunlight stabbing through his closed eyelids straight into his brain. He'd been dreaming. He and Emily were sitting in a restaurant discussing baby names. Eric was making her laugh thinking up silly and archaic names, something couples have done for centuries, just one of those ordinary things made extraordinary when happening to you. Emily was laughing. It was so good to hear her laugh and Eric could remember thinking as she roared at the names Parsifal Euripides for a boy and Persephone Andromeda for a girl that all he had to do was keep thinking up names and this dream, and her laughter, would never have to end.

But the dream had ended, and Emily's laughter had evaporated like a drop of water on the pavement in the summer sun. And now the sun was pouring through the windows and his neck protested the night's reposing and his brain the evening's imbibing. Shielding his eyes with one hand, he rubbed his neck with the other and waited for the living room to come into focus.

He'd fallen asleep in the recliner, a habit he'd taken to the day Emily died. He spent as little time as possible in their bedroom. When he showered, he used the guest bathroom downstairs and only went into their upstairs bedroom long enough to grab a change of clothes.

Sunday morning, when he'd packed for his visit to Jennifer's, had been the longest he'd been in the room in six months, and he'd felt like a stranger perusing someone else's personal space. Well, not so much a stranger. More like an amnesia victim moving through a room hoping to stir up memories and recover the life he'd lost. The room seemed familiar, but he wasn't sure if that was because he remembered or because people told him it was supposed to be.

Otherwise, his roaming about the house consisted of moving from the recliner to the downstairs bathroom to the kitchen and back. His sister's monthly visits of cleaning and tidying up had enabled him this luxury. But now she was done coming around. She'd told him so on Saturday, and one thing he knew about his sister, she said what she meant and meant what she said.

Jennifer was the only person who had been in the house since Emily had—

Eric sat bolt upright, which caused his hungover brain to jostle inside his skull. He'd suddenly remembered he had another person in the house right now. Paul Stephens was upstairs in the guestroom, probably, Eric thought as he massaged his temple, sleeping off a terrific hangover.

"I guess I should go check on him," Eric mumbled to himself as he pulled himself reluctantly out of the recliner and shuffled to the staircase.

The phone on the end table began to ring, sounding like some shrill school fire alarm to Eric's head. He scrambled for the cordless receiver.

"Hello?" He didn't recognize his own voice. It seemed to have dropped a few husky octaves.

"Hey. It's Paul." Not only did he sound like he'd been up for hours, Eric realized, he sounded well rested. "How ya doing this morning?"

"Fine," Eric said, wincing at Paul's cheerfulness.

Paul chuckled. "You sound like Barry White with the flu."

"You know any good remedies?" Eric rubbed his temple.

"Take two raw eggs, a teaspoon of Tabasco sauce, and a scoop of coffee grounds, put 'em in a glass of Pepsi, and drink."

Eric groaned. "That sounds disgusting. Does it really work?"

"No, but you're so nauseated you forget you've got a hangover." Paul chuckled again. "Drink water. Lots of it. Best thing for you really."

"Thanks." Eric started moving towards the kitchen. "So you're not calling me from my guestroom."

"No rest for the workaholic. But I was thinking you could meet me in the city for lunch to sign the papers if it wouldn't be too much trouble."

Eric grabbed a glass, filled it from the tap, and took a long swallow. It tasted great. "Sure, I guess I could do that." At least he would be out of the house.

"Great." Paul sounded relieved. "Do you know the Dearborn Street Oyster Bar? In the South Loop?"

For a guy who's just moved here, Eric thought, he's picked up a lay of the land fast. Eric screwed up his eyes in thought. "I've never heard of the place."

"If you're heading south on Dearborn, it's on the left after you cross over Van Buren. If you hit Congress Parkway, you've gone too far."

"I think I can find the place." Eric pulled a torn envelope out of the trash and found a pen. He wrote down the information.

"Great. One o'clock?"

Eric looked at the clock on the stove. A quarter till ten. "One's great"

"Thanks. I need to go, but I'll see you later, then."

The phone clicked before Eric could say goodbye. He set the receiver down on the counter, downed his glass of water, and poured another from the tap. It tasted just as good as the first. He finished the second glass, picked up the receiver, and dialed his broker's office. After confirming all the paperwork was ready to go, Eric poured a third glass of water and drank it on his way to the guest bathroom.

He showered and shaved, then ran to the master bedroom in a towel. Taking a deep breath and closing his eyes, he put his hand on the doorknob and visualized it first. Boxers and socks in the dresser. Jeans and a sweatshirt in the closet. Sneakers...

His eyes popped open. Where were his sneakers? Were they in the luggage? In the car? *When did I wear them last?* He felt his chest tighten with panic. *Where* were his *sneakers?*

Eric forced himself to inhale deeply, hold his breath to the count of ten, and then exhale. They were probably on the living room floor where he kicked them off before crashing in the recliner.

Allowing his body to shrug with relief, he made himself take a few deep, slow breaths. When he felt calmer, he inhaled one deep, steeling breath and then opened the door. He entered the room and scrambled to the dresser like a scared kid running through a darkened cellar. He ripped open a drawer and grabbed blindly, pulling out two pairs of boxers. He threw one pair down and then yanked open another drawer and withdrew a pair of socks.

Now he crossed to the closet, wondering if he would make it out of this room alive. His heart was thudding, his breath quickening.

Thank God the closet door is open.

Eric kept his eyes focused on a pair of jeans and his favorite Northwestern sweatshirt and tore them off the hangers. He could hear the *Snap* as the plastic hangers broke, but he didn't care. Better them than him he thought as he raced for the door. He was out of the room in less than twenty seconds. He dressed in the guestroom, in the luxuriating calm only a child knows after running through a darkened cellar and living to tell the tale.

The one thing Eric told himself, admonished really, was not to be late for lunch. He'd been late returning Paul's call, late meeting Paul to show him the house, and had slept late that morning. He repeated in his head *Don't be late, don't be late* like a mantra as he picked up the contract from the broker, removed the lockbox and keys from the property, and called the sellers (who'd been very put out by Eric's desire to take possession of the house early until he promised to drop off the one-month rent check of three thousand dollars the next day) and hit the road for the South Loop.

Besides the unprofessionalism of tardiness, Eric found he didn't want to disappoint Paul. He found himself liking Paul. The man was pushy and financially out of touch with reality, but he did seem to be genuine. Not to mention Paul got him out of the house and distracted enough to not hear his wife screaming. And he had nothing better to do for another day. He couldn't pick up the handgun till tomorrow.

But despite his best efforts, he found himself at five minutes till One stuck in downtown traffic, the cabbie behind him honking and gesturing rudely for Eric to move.

"Move where?" Eric yelled into the rearview mirror. He watched the light change from red to green to yellow and back to red and wondered why he hadn't just taken the train. The cabbie honked again, and Eric suppressed the urge to get out of his SUV, pull the cabbie through the window, and beat him. The only thing stopping him was the realization that as soon as he was out of his vehicle the cabbie would be out of his. Eric's delusions of Bruce Lee grandeur were tempered by the knowledge he'd never been in a fight, not since grade school anyway.

At one-thirty, Eric finally pulled into the paid parking area near the restaurant. A red Volvo was pulling out of a spot which Eric tore into, brakes squealing, cut the engine, and sped walked to the restaurant. He checked his watch as he opened the door.

One thirty-five.

Eric didn't have a chance to grimace. As soon as he entered the restaurant, Paul's arm was up waving him over. Eric waved acknowledgment and headed to the table.

Paul had a bottle of Samuel Adams and a plate of oysters on the table in front of him. His suit jacket was hanging off the back of the chair to his right. His shirt sleeves were rolled up and his collar and tie were loosened.

"Sorry, I'm late." Eric began as he sat down across from Paul.

"Don't worry about it," Paul said as he smiled. "I figured by the freight train coming outta the recliner this morning you'd probably be late." He gestured to the plate of oysters. "Want one?"

"No, not really." It was out of his mouth before he realized. Usually, if a client offered him something, he didn't turn it down, no matter how much he might loathe that thing, not wanting to offend. He never knew what little offense might lose you a sale. But for some reason, he had the feeling it would be okay with Paul.

Paul laughed. "Cool. More for me." He slipped a raw oyster into his mouth and swallowed.

Eric couldn't help but think of a show he'd seen on the Discovery channel about sea-faring birds. It had featured a pelican scooping a fish into its gullet and swallowing it. He could have sworn that Paul wore the same satisfied look as the pelican.

"Whatcha drinking?" Paul took a swig from his bottle.

Eric looked at the bottle in Paul's hand. "Beer, I guess."

Paul nodded. "I was going to have the Jambalaya. I've been told it's pretty good."

"I'll try it too then."

Paul motioned for the waitress to come over. The young lady shot each of them a broad smile. "Two bowls of Jambalaya and a Sam Adams for my friend."

The woman wrote down the order, smiled at each man, and left, promising to be back momentarily with Eric's beer.

"Now that that's done," Paul said as he scooped up another raw oyster, "let's get the other piece of business out of the way." He popped the oyster into his mouth and closed his eyes, chewing this one.

Eric reached over, pulled the paperwork and a pen out of his jacket pocket, and handed them across the table to Paul.

Pushing the plate of oysters away from him, Paul took the pen and the paperwork and placed them on the table in front of himself.

The waitress dropped off Eric's beer without Paul noticing. He appeared to be reading each line before initialing or signing.

Eric sat in silence waiting, sipping his beer. This could take a while, he thought to himself.

But Paul seemed to be a speed reader. Within a couple of minutes, he had initialed and signed all the correct sections and handed them along with the pen back to Eric.

Eric accepted the papers and pen and handed over the keys to the house which Paul accepted and pocketed in his suit's breast pocket.

"Now we can relax and enjoy the food and the company." Paul picked up another oyster and deposited it into his mouth. He swallowed. "Which reminds me. Last night while we watched Sports Center on ESPN, you mentioned you were a big Bulls fan. Still true?"

We watched Sports Center?

"Ah, yeah. Why?"

"Cuz I happen to have two tickets to tonight's game." Paul pulled the tickets from his shirt pocket and held them up to Eric's face with all the triumph of a newly engaged woman showing the rock off to her girlfriends. "Client gave them to me this morning."

Eric looked at the tickets. He was excited, of course. He'd been to Bulls games before, but what captured his attention was the seating listed on the tickets.

"These are courtside." Eric wanted to reach out and touch them like they were a million dollars in dollar bills but suppressed the urge.

"Yup." Paul slipped them back into his shirt pocket.

"Exactly what do you do for a living?" Eric couldn't believe he'd let that slip out of his mouth, but Paul didn't seem to mind.

"Imports and exports. Do you want to go?"

"I do, but—"

"But what?" Paul interrupted. "You love the Bulls and I've got tickets. Besides, I owe you for coming into the city for thirty seconds."

"But the game's not till this evening." Eric wasn't sure why he was objecting. It wouldn't be a bad way to spend his last night on this earth, he told himself, but it still felt wrong. Maybe because he knew he would be killing himself the next day.

Paul geared up to start pushing. He sat on the edge of his seat, pulling the tickets from his pocket and holding them in Eric's face again. "Courtside. You have to go." He kept the tickets in Eric's face. "Here's the plan. We eat lunch. I call the office and say I'm taking the rest of the day off. You show me around Chicago. I mean, you got to know some of the hot spots. Maybe even some of the touristy places. Then we'll swing by my hotel. I'll change into more suitable attire for the game. We go to dinner then to the game." He pushed the tickets right under Eric's nose. "We'll sit so close to the action you won't *believe* how fast the game actually moves."

Eric stared at the tickets.

Courtside.

"Come on," Paul goaded.

Eric bit his lip. This was a once-in-a-lifetime offer. He'd be an idiot to pass it up.

"You're quite the motivational speaker," Eric said.

Paul smiled. "I'm the Tony Robbins of this table." He waggled the tickets.

Eric nodded over the tickets to Paul. "Okay."

Chapter 9

As it turned out, Eric was much better at talking tours of Cary than walking tours of Chicago, and absolutely horrible at driving tours, which Paul pointed out as they sat in yet another downtown traffic jam.

"At least we'd be moving," Paul said as he wistfully watched a family of tourists walking along the sidewalk, the father checking a map as his wife and children pointed and snapped photos with their smartphones.

Until this moment, Eric never realized just what a homebody he'd always been. He'd been to Chicago, of course, more times than he could remember, but he'd very rarely driven. If he did, it was an evening on the weekend when traffic seemed to move. Or maybe he didn't care because he was stuck in traffic with Emily heading to some event he didn't want to attend or stuck in traffic with Emily heading to some event he knew she didn't want to attend. They would be talking and making promises to each other about what they would do for the faithful spouse to attend.

One time, after Eric had finished describing to her just how he would show his appreciation once he got her back home and into the bedroom, Emily, without missing a beat, sighed and said, "I'd settle for you taking out the trash without being nagged." Eric had burst out laughing, which had caused Emily to burst out laughing. That night, before fulfilling his promise in the bedroom, he'd fulfilled her wish in the kitchen.

"Ground control to Eric," Paul said. "Come in Eric."

"Huh?" Eric looked at Paul who was pointing out the windshield. The traffic was moving but they were not, which now Eric could hear was causing a lot of angry honking behind him.

Angry honking, he thought, and that made him think of another time stuck in Chicago traffic when Emily had observed, "How can a honk be angry? It's the same honk no matter what. Now a goose could have an angry honk, but a car?" At that moment a little compact car's horn blew, sounding just like an angry goose.

Eric chuckled.

"Dude," Paul said forcefully but not impatiently.

Eric came back to reality, stepped on the gas, and thought, this is why I don't come to Chicago. Like Cary, all of Eric's best memories were of Emily and him. Of course, he had memories of going to a Cubs game with his dad (a hope he'd had of creating memories with a son of his own one day) and school trips, but there was something different when you were with the woman you loved.

So the truth was, he had to admit to himself, was his heart wasn't in it. It was a truth Paul had recognized as well.

"Let's just call it," Paul said with a resigned chuckle. "We'll go to my hotel so I can change and head out."

"Where are you staying?" Eric asked, hoping Paul hadn't heard the relief in his voice.

"The Drake," Paul answered. "Do you know where that is?"

Eric felt ice kiss his heart. The Drake. Emily had always wanted them to spend an anniversary weekend there. They'd watched some Julia Roberts flick, Eric could never remember the title, some romantic comedy, where Julia Roberts's character stays at the Drake while she plots to sabotage a friend's wedding. Emily had gone on and on how they should stay at the Drake, maybe even in the same room Julia Roberts did.

"We can buy the movie to find out which room." She had squeezed his hand, the way she always did when she was excited and had what she thought was a brilliant idea.

Eric had laughed at Emily and her girlish excitement. The memory, now, reminded him of his nieces when they'd opened their Barbie dolls on Christmas Morning just two days ago. He'd never taken her up on the idea and Emily had let it drop only bringing it up on the rare occasion the film came on television. Now, as he drove towards the Drake, regret lashed at his heart like a downed electrical line in a lightning storm. What he wouldn't give to have memories of them at the Drake, eating, laughing, making love instead of no memory at all.

Paul was saying something, but Eric wasn't paying attention. He was suddenly regretting taking Paul up on his offer of a driving tour and dinner and tickets to the Bulls game. He wanted to be on his couch with a bottle in his hand, his head numb, and his feelings tucked nicely away in an alcoholic stupor.

He didn't remember driving to the Drake, handing his keys off to a valet, or following Eric up to his room, which was not the room Julia Roberts had stayed in.

"The *Presidential* Suite." Eric had blurted out incredulously in response to Paul telling him the room in which he was occupying.

"What gives?"

Eric had been waiting for ten minutes to put that question to Paul Stephens. This guy was living in the Presidential Suite of the Drake Hotel. Not splurging for the weekend or renting a standard room on some sort of business fair.

Living. In the Presidential Suite.

Eric had taken the personal tour, comparing it with the house Paul Stephens had just purchased. The house was nice but there was no comparison. He thought about the people who'd sold the house and wondered how they'd feel knowing the guy who bought it must've decided to find out what living in the projects was like.

"What do you mean?" Paul moved to the bar and pulled out a tumbler and an ice bucket.

Eric stared in disbelief at Paul from the tan suede couch he was sitting on. "Whaddaya mean what do I mean?" Eric waved his arms in an expansive gesture, taking in the room. "This."

Paul dropped ice cubes into the tumbler. "This...what?"

"This place." Eric looked around the room. "When you bought the house, were you just bored and decided to go slumming?"

Paul laughed. "That's funny." He opened a bottle on the bar in front of him and poured the golden liquid into the tumbler. It looked like watered-down apple juice. "Do you want one?"

"What is it?" Eric asked, eying the bottle.

"Scotch," Paul replied as he pulled out another tumbler, set it on the bar, and began filling it with ice.

"Sure." Eric shifted his eye from the bottle. He had started stronger than he'd intended. He'd wanted it to sound conversational, but ten minutes thinking about this suite, which must've been costing him more than an arm and leg, more like an arm, leg, and kidney, and the house had worked Eric towards accusation.

"I'm sorry, it's none of my business," Eric said, hoping Paul had been as obtuse as he'd appeared when he first walked into the room.

Paul poured Scotch into the second tumbler, then picked up both tumblers and walked to the sofa where Eric was sitting. He handed the second tumbler to Eric and took a sip of his own.

"Oh, I don't mind." Paul sat down in a suede chair across from the sofa and threw his legs onto the matching ottoman. He was dressed the same way he was when Eric met him; black loafers, Vibram stamped on the bottom, black socks and slacks, and a black turtleneck sweater.

Eric stared at the word Vibram. Even this guy's shoes cost more than one of Eric's suits and accessories. Eric had the feeling again he was dealing with someone who had no grip on the reality that most people were born with a handle on. Nothing about this guy was middle-class or even upper-class. Only the filthy rich could comprehend Paul's lack of understanding.

Filthy is an adjective most people assign to people that rich to indicate that the amount of wealth was a sin. It cut you off from mankind. You forgot you lived, bled, stank, died like everyone else. Those economically beneath you were biologically beneath you as well, an inferior species.

But that didn't fit Paul. Paul, after all, was hanging out with solidly middle-class Eric and had been slurping down oysters at lunch. Of course, Eric couldn't help but feel a little too casual in his jeans and sweatshirt when he thought about the price of Paul's attire.

He looked up at Paul who was looking patiently back at him. He wasn't giving Eric the same scrutinizing gaze and at once Eric felt a little ashamed. He cleared his throat and took a sip of the scotch. It burned his mouth and throat, and he couldn't help the grunt of dismay or his eyes watering. He set the glass down on the coffee table, wondering how anyone could enjoy it. He understood now when Emily told him, without ever tasting it, that beer tasted like horse pee. He would gladly drink horse pee, with or without ice, than that again.

"I guess I'm trying to figure out why a guy who can afford a place like this would be interested in...not that there's anything wrong with the house I sold you, but...you've been here like a month. What possible interest could you have in a house like the one you bought? I mean...you could be renting a mansion or an apartment in the city."

Paul sipped his scotch weighing his words like the heavy glass in his hands. "I hate hotels. I hate the way they look, the way they smell. And you can never forget you're in a hotel." His nose wrinkled with some foul odor only he could smell. "You park in a lot, go to a front desk, get a mag card, not even a key anymore, pass by a hall of doors to get to your door, and go into the same master bedroom everyone around you is in." He stood up and walked over to the marble fireplace glowing brightly from the perfect fire.

Eric looked at the fire. You only got fires like that in places like this.

Paul continued as he placed a hand on the mantle and stared into the fire. "You unpack, trying to fit your clothes in a couple of drawers, but there's no way to hide the luggage. You sleep on the same sheets everyone around you is sleeping on, making love on. And even if you can disconnect from all that, you can still hear everyone around you shower, watch TV, make love."

Paul turned towards Eric, leaning on the mantle. "So I pay a little extra..." He grinned sheepishly. "Okay, a *lot* extra, and by the grace of God it only seems like a little extra, so my bedroom doesn't look like everybody else's bedroom. And I don't hear everybody else's shower, or television, or lovemaking. Here," he gestured around the room, "at least I don't feel like I'm in a hotel. It may not be home, but at least I can pretend it isn't a hotel." He took another sip of his drink. "I'm only here, anywhere for that matter, for six months to a year. I used to rent a mansion or an apartment downtown when I was staying in a new city, but have you priced a furnished mansion? Not only the price but then I have to endure someone's misguided tastes in décor. And few people rent unfurnished mansions. What would be the point? Besides, I hate throwing money away and that's all renting is."

He moved back to the mini bar. "No, it's cheaper to buy a little place, decorate it the way I want, and then sell it when I leave, or turn it into a rental property."

Eric thought about it. It made sense. Everyone he'd ever helped purchase their first house had confessed their primary reason for buying was, "I'm just so tired of renting." And he was never thrilled when he had to stay in a hotel for more than a couple of nights, even on vacation. How many times had he been awakened in the early morning wishing he could've rented the rooms on either side of him? So why should he hold it against Paul that he could afford to do just that? If he'd had the money, he would've probably upgraded his hotel room to something nicer, something a little more private; and when he and Emily were amorous, something a lot more private.

Paul refreshed his glass and asked if Eric wanted something else. "Scotch isn't for everybody, an acquired taste for most."

Eric looked at his glass on the coffee table, paling with the melting ice. "Oh. That's okay. I'm fine."

Paul nodded and looked at his watch. "There's a nice little theme joint in the lobby." Paul moved back to his chair in front of Eric. "Do you like seafood?"

"Sure," Eric said as he reached instinctively for the glass on the coffee table before catching himself.

Paul laughed. He took a sip of his drink. "We've got reservations at six." He set his drink down on the coffee table. "Let's go."

Paul led the way out of the Presidential Suite and down the hall to the elevator. He asked Eric how often he went to Bulls games and confessed he didn't get the chance to go to many sporting events himself. Usually, he worked long hours, but it was the holidays and he'd decided to give himself a treat and not work more than nine or ten hours a day through New Years.

Again the ride in the elevator was smooth. Eric decided that like cars, you got what you paid for with elevators. This elevator had to be the Cadillac or Mercedes of vertical transportation. Paul talked about some of the games he'd gotten to see over the years including a couple of Super Bowl games in box seats.

As they entered the restaurant, Paul took Eric over to the bar. "Come on," Paul said with a childlike enthusiasm. "You've *got* to see this."

Paul marched up to the bar and began scrutinizing it the way a rancher might a prized heifer he was considering purchasing, or maybe a kid trying to find his favorite candy bar.

"Ah ha," Paul exclaimed in triumph. He pointed at the bar as he faced Eric.

Eric looked unimpressed at the bar. Its surface looked battered, a stark contrast to its surroundings. But Paul was practically dancing with delight at what he pointed at. Eric scrutinized the two letters carved into the bar top.

"M, M." He looked at Paul. "So what?"

"So what?" Paul looked wounded. "M, M. Marilyn Monroe, that's what."

"Marilyn Monroe?" Eric looked back at the bar with renewed interest. "How do you know?"

"Bartender told me. The bar's covered with the initials of famous people all carved by the celebrities themselves."

Eric looked. Paul was right. The bar top was covered with initials carved into the rough wood. The wood was not covered in shellac or varnish, but left untreated, waiting for the initials of new famous people.

> "Can I get you gentlemen anything?" The bartender stood ready for their order. Eric decided on a Samuel Adams while Paul wanted a white wine.

The Maitre'd informed them their table was ready and after confirming their drinks would be sent to their table, they followed him.

The waitress, another of Paul's devotees, placed a tall, frosty pilsner glass in front of Eric and a glass of Vin Santo in front of Paul. Eric ordered the clam chowder followed by chili and sea bass. Paul decided on a dozen raw oysters and the Surf & Turf.

Eric passed the time waiting for the food answering all of Paul's questions about his life, growing up in Cary, his time at Northwestern. When the main course arrived, Eric found he'd barely touched his clam chowder.

The sea bass with chili was delicious and Eric ate with a voracious appetite. He would've loved dessert, but Paul informed him they'd need to run, or they'd miss their ride. Paul paid the check with a couple of one-hundred-dollar bills left on the table and got up.

Eric dragged his feet, but followed Paul out of the restaurant, down the steps to the revolving door, and out into the crisp Chicago evening. As if by the magic that was Paul, a cab pulled up just as Paul gave the doorman a warm greeting, his breath fogging before him. Paul moved to the back door, opened it, and slid into the backseat.

What? No limo?

Eric moved to the cab and got in, closing the door as the driver moved the cab into traffic. The cab swerved in and out of traffic, skirting vehicles and pedestrians with no more space than a razor has on the skin. He was quiet, working with a concentration Eric had rarely seen in the most focused of people, able to see room for his cab even before it was there.

Paul sat back and relaxed, reliving some of the dinner conversation and making leisurely observations on the downtown scenery. Eric marveled at Paul's apparent lack of interest in the driving conditions. His right arm was already fatigued by the constant clutching at the imaginary hand brake on the passenger-side door. Passengers in other vehicles might have thought Eric was having either some form of seizure or suffering the attack of an unknown, unseen assailant as he thrashed and flinched from all the near misses.

Eric thought he might jump from the cab and kiss the sidewalk as the cabbie pulled up to United Center, but he didn't.

Paul thanked the cabbie as he handed him a fifty-dollar bill and said, "There's another hundred for you if you're here when the game's over." Paul was pointing through the floorboard of the backseat to the piece of asphalt the vehicle was parked on.

The cabbie's eyes had bulged at the fifty-dollar bill, the fare hadn't been twenty dollars, but they popped right out of his skull at the offer of a C-note. The cabbie's eyes rolled over an imaginary abacus as he calculated what other fares he could handle if they weren't across town and still be back in time by the game's end. It didn't take him a minute to agree to the terms.

Paul nodded, shook the cabbie's hand, and motioned for Eric to get out of the cab. As soon as Eric and Paul were out of the cab, the driver gunned the engine and sped off, letting the force of his acceleration close the rear door. Paul pulled out the tickets, handed one to Eric, and after pocketing his own, set off for the entrance. "I'd be a Miami Heat fan for life if they brought some of that tropical warmth with 'em."

Before Eric knew it, he was sitting in his courtside seat, as the lights went out, plunging the arena into total darkness. Immediately the void was filled with the dazzling twinkle of thousands of cameras taking pictures, of what Eric wasn't sure. Soon a spotlight hit the players as each one was announced. Paul excused himself for the bathroom as guys much taller than Eric had imagined trotted to the bench across from him.

Eric found a new respect for these warriors of the hardwood floor as the game began. He could hear bodies collide, hit the floor, grunt. He could feel the sweat as it showered from the men as they fought over the ball. At least once, he feared he was about to be run over as players scrambled for a loose ball. And that was in just the first five minutes.

Paul walked over during a break in the action, handing Eric a plastic cup emblazoned with the Bulls logo on the side and filled with beer.

"Thanks," Eric took the cup, "I was beginning to wonder if you'd fallen in."

Paul sat down. "Really?"

Eric's head shot back to the game as the dull roar of the crowd exploded. He said sideways. "Actually, I hadn't given you a second thought."

Paul smiled and sipped his beer. "I didn't think so. The only line longer than the beer line was the line for the john. I was beginning to think I'd gotten into the line for the ladies' room."

Eric and Paul didn't speak much during the rest of the game except to agree on bad calls by the referees and high-five each other after three-pointers. As the final buzzer sounded, Eric finished the last of the beer in his hand. It felt good on his throat, now burning from the effort of screaming. He looked across the court to the players (television just didn't do justice to the size and athleticism of these guys) exiting to their respective locker rooms and smiled, glad he'd come. He'd had fun, and though the realization had produced a pang of betrayal in his stomach, the pain had been dull this time, the sense of betrayal less. He wasn't ready to give up his plan with the .38 just yet, but...he was really glad he'd come.

Chapter 10

Paul and Eric found the cab idling right where it was supposed to be. The cabbie, his scarf curled loosely around his neck, leaned against it, enjoying a smoke. The night air had a bite, but the man seemed protected from it by the glow of the cigarette. At the site of his two fares, the cabbie dropped the butt and crushed it under his shoe.

As they approached the cab, Eric noticed a crowd gathering around an ambulance parked at one of the main entrances.

The cabbie, following Eric's gaze, puffed out, "Cops said some guy had a heart attack and died during the game. Didn't you know about it?"

"No," Eric said as paramedics wheeled a shrouded body from the entrance to the rear of the ambulance.

"Guess the guy couldn't take the heat." He hacked more than laughed at his own double entendre.

Eric, however, didn't find it very amusing.

Paul opened the back passenger door and held it for Eric. He coughed as he entered the smoky warmth of the cab. Paul followed and closed the door. The cabbie slid in behind the wheel, dropped the car into Drive, and started moving before asking over his shoulder where to take the two men.

"Back to the Drake," Paul responded as he settled back for the ride.

"Good game?" The cabbie pulled out of the United Center parking lot.

Eric wanted to tell the man it'd been a fantastic game, but all he could manage was a hoarse croak. Something about being courtside had unleashed in him a wild frenzy. Baskets weren't just baskets, but the sun setting in a pot of gold. He screamed like a girl caught in a room full of creepy crawlies.

"Hey," Paul replied, settling even further back into the seat like a man pleasantly buzzed, "it was, "Da Bulls.""

"Da Bulls." The cabbie echoed.

The rest of the ride went by in silence. Eric had no voice to scream as the cabbie navigated through the evening's traffic like a man on the run. The hand brake on the driver's side backseat door still wasn't working, nor was the foot brake.

Eric looked over at Paul who seemed to be melding with the seat; that buzzed grin lying like a sunning lizard across his face. Eric didn't remember Paul drinking any more than he had. He was sure he'd drunk more than Paul, and he wasn't feeling the least bit tipsy. A thought crossed his mind. Could Paul be a user? Maybe not cocaine, the only time they weren't together had been when Paul had gone to the restroom, and he hadn't acted like this until they got into the cab. Crystal Meth maybe? Ecstasy?

Eric wasn't really sure what people acted like on any of these drugs. His expertise on the subject came from films and television, not personal experience. He'd never done anything harder than Ibuprofen for a headache or backache. He could easily put on the screen in his head the scene from "Pulp Fiction" when John Travolta shot up heroin and the next scene showing him driving with that sleepy smile on his face.

"We're here." The cabbie grunted as he pulled the cab to the curb in front of The Drake Hotel, rubbing the front tire and hubcap on the concrete.

Paul shot up as if startled out of a very restful night's sleep. "Okay," Paul said as he pulled his wallet from his inside coat pocket, "that's a hundred for being there." He pulled a crisp bill from his wallet and laid it in the cabbie's ungloved hand like he wanted to feel the weight of the bill on his bare flesh. "And for the fare back." Paul laid a fifty-dollar bill on top of the one-hundred-dollar bill. The cabbie stared hungrily at the bills in his hand.

"Thank *you*, Sir." The cabbie shut his fist tight around the bills and shoved his hand into his jacket pocket. "If there's anything you need Mr. Stephens, you just let me know." The cabbie looked into Paul's eyes and added with emphasis, "Anything."

Eric couldn't help wondering if anything included drugs, or maybe girls, probably both, and most likely a whole lot more, though he was a little confused at how quickly Paul had recovered once the cab was back at the hotel.

"Thanks," Paul said. "I will." He opened the door and slid out of the backseat.

The cabbie smiled and wished them a happy new year.

"Happy New Year," Paul and Eric echoed.

Eric followed Paul and was turning to close the door behind him, but the cab was already shrieking away from the curb into traffic, the door swinging shut by the force of acceleration again.

"Thank God." Paul shrugged with relief as he looked up towards what was perhaps a starry night once you got past the altitude of the city lights. "I don't know about you, but that guy scared me to death."

Eric laughed. "I meant to tell him his passenger brakes weren't working."

Paul looked at him, his eyes wide with understanding. "I know. The whole ride home, I just lay back in the seat with my eyes closed thinking, 'Go to a happy place. Go to a happy place.'"

They both laughed.

"I wish I'd thought of that," Eric admitted. "So why did you ask him to hang out and wait for us?"

"Known entity," Paul responded. "With the luck I've had in Chicago traffic today," he nodded at Eric and then in the direction the cab had sped off, "I figured I didn't want to take my chances with any other drivers."

Eric nodded, then took a breath and admitted something else. "I was starting to wonder if you might be on drugs the way you were just sitting there with that grin on your face." He swallowed. "Maybe this isn't a good time...and maybe I've just seen too many reruns of "CSI" and "Miami Vice," but what exactly do you import and export?"

Paul turned the collar of his coat up and dug his gloved hands into his pockets. Eric had the suspicion that more than the cold of the night air was responsible for the color growing on Paul's face. Paul shifted his weight and looked away from Eric.

"Could you get Mr. Messer's car?" Paul asked as he caught sight of the valet walking towards them.

"Right away, Mr. Stephens." The valet turned and broke into a run.

"Won't they need," Eric's voice trailed off as he fished through his pockets for his claim ticket, but realized he'd never been given one.

"Don't worry about it," Paul said as he glanced sidelong at Eric. He took in a deep breath, held it for a moment, and then let it out. "I do very well in my business, but," he hesitated for a moment before continuing, "but that isn't my only source of income." Paul looked around to make sure they were alone.

Eric felt his heart begin to pound against his sternum. He thought if he looked down, he would see his shirt moving from the impact. Paul, this enigmatic man, was about to reveal...what? Something dark and sinister? Did he really want to know? Would it be one of those 'I've told you now I have to kill you' things people joke about? Only Paul's not joking? Paul was looking conflicted. Could that be it?

And was that a problem? He was picking up a gun tomorrow to kill himself after all. He'd had a great evening, hadn't heard Emily scream once, and never did when he was with Paul. But what about later? No, 'I've told you now I have to kill you' wasn't a problem, not even the point. The point, Emily would have told him, was that was a *really* inappropriate thing to ask.

Eric threw up his hands. "That wasn't fair of me to ask. It's none of my business. Forget I brought it up." He hoped that would be enough to assuage the tension, but Paul was shaking his head.

"No, it's okay." Paul looked Eric in the eye. "It's just not something I like to talk about. I mean, nobody I work with has a clue." He took another breath. "I've got a trust fund, a very sizable trust fund." Paul slumped with shame.

That's it?

Eric was a little disappointed. He thought it would be something a little more...dramatic. Definitely more interesting. Paul wasn't dramatic, but he was interesting. He looked at the man who now stood before him looking as if he'd just confessed to embezzling or killing someone. His heart went out to Paul.

"So what? Who cares?" Eric shrugged.

Paul looked at him, indignation blazing in his eyes. "I do."

"Why?"

"Because I don't want to be written off like those trust fund kids you see on Twenty-Twenty or Sixty Minutes. You've seen them, Mommy and Daddy have millions upon millions. So the kids never have to grow up, never have to work or make their own way." He shook his head in disgust. "The friends I had growing up were proud of the silver spoon. Flaunted it in everyone's faces, especially each other's. Still do. Country clubs during the day, dance clubs at night. Drugs. Women. And men.

Eric wanted to say the parents were partly to blame in those cases, but Paul wasn't finished.

"It's a crazy lifestyle that eats you from the inside out. Totally out of touch with reality. No real idea of what love and friendship are. They don't trust anyone. They're sociopaths." Paul laughed sardonically. "Ironic, isn't it? Everyone admires them. Wants to be them because of the money, but their lives are empty. They're cadavers and they don't know it. They're the real zombies. Living dead."

Eric just stared at Paul. He didn't have a clue what to say.

Paul turned his head as the valet brought Eric's Expedition up to the curb in front of the two men.

Paul smiled at Eric. "I'll stop preaching or venting or whatever I was doing."

The valet jumped out of the idling SUV and trotted past the two men. "All yours, Mr. Messer."

Paul extended his hand. "Anyway, I'll get off my soapbox and let you go home."

Eric took his hand. "Thanks for the evening. I had a really great time." He released his hand, walked over to the Expedition, and turned back towards Paul. "And don't worry, you're anything but a cadaver."

Paul smiled and waved.

Eric waved, climbed into the Expedition, and set off for home, the smell of beer and nachos filling the interior. He sniffed his clothes. He was wearing both. That happens when a basketball and a couple of guys over six foot four come straight at you at full steam. He laughed (he could laugh now) at the memory. There were other memories to laugh at too.

He'd acted like a six-year-old pointing out Santa Claus to his mother when he spotted the actor Bill Murray at the game. But sitting beside John Cusak for almost the entire game without realizing it had made Paul guffaw and spill his beer all over himself. Eric had thought the man to his left was familiar, maybe he'd shown him a house a few years back, but he really couldn't place him. Not until a woman in her mid-thirties walked up during a time-out and asked for his autograph.

Oh well.

Eric found himself pulling into the driveway. He hadn't remembered the drive home he was so lost in the night. He cut the engine and the lights and looked at the house. It was dark, just like it should be this time of night. He and Emily should be lying asleep in their bed, maybe spooning, maybe not, but in the same bed. This was why he slept downstairs, why he wanted a gun, why he wanted to end his life.

No more Emily.

He took a deep breath and held it as he opened the door. He exhaled as he closed the door and stood motionless beside the Expedition, but he didn't inhale. The air was biting cold, and his nose and ears burned, but still, he didn't move, still didn't inhale. His lungs burned and the familiar grayness closed in on his peripheral vision. With it, like some ethereal mist, came the screams, soft, just on the edge of his conscious, but moving towards him, growing in volume.

Eric hadn't heard Emily scream when that house had become a fireball, but he could imagine them with clarity, with the accuracy of a soldier who even decades after combat can recall the report of his weapon, of other weapons, the scream of mortar. Emily's scream had been caught forever on her charred face, mixed with the unmistakable, unthinkable, unholy stench of cooked human flesh. That odor had permeated his clothes and hair. Penetrated his skin and blackened his bones. The faintest whisper of it stayed forever trapped in his brain and invaded his olfactory passages at will.

Maybe if he hadn't been called down to the morgue that night, hadn't insisted on identifying the body even though the Medical Examiner explained he could do that with dental records, maybe he would simply have mourned his wife's passing and moved on with his life. But he had gone to the morgue and smelled his wife's body for the last time, had gazed upon her face, the mouth twisted, lips burned away revealing blackened teeth so that she looked like some sooty and demented jack-o-lantern.

He'd dropped to his knees beside the gurney on which she lay and had vomited uncontrollably. After each regurgitation, he'd sucked in that smell, that new scent of his wife, no longer White Shoulders perfume, and vomited again.

Now he stood in his driveway, the smell of death ruminating in his nostrils without him taking a breath, the screams growing in his ears. Eric willed himself towards the front door as tears began to slide down his cheeks. He reached the door, inhaled the crisp night air, unlocked the door, and went inside the house, closing, but not locking, the door behind him.

Chapter 11

Old Joe was sitting behind the register reading a copy of *Soldier of Fortune* magazine when Eric walked through the front door of the pawn shop.

"Ah, yes," the man looked up with a dingy smile, his voice sounding like a permanent smoker's hack, "the birthday boy." He winked at Eric who managed a weak grin.

The man dredged a keyring out of his pocket, selected a key, and unlocked the glass case holding the snub-nosed .38, a "Sold" tag tied to the trigger guard. He pulled the pistol out and set it on the glass counter in front of Eric.

Eric picked the weapon up, feeling the roughness of the grip in his palm. He wrapped his index finger around the trigger and pulled. The trigger didn't move. Just as well, he thought, as he saw the safety. He would have hated to blow out the glass in the case. It didn't speak well of the place, Eric realized, that he wasn't sure it wasn't loaded and ready to go. The old man hadn't checked it like he had a couple of days before.

Old Joe had grabbed a brown paper bag and was placing the box of ammunition in the bottom of it. "I don't have the box it would've come in." He pointed to gun pouches hanging on the wall. "But I've got some gun pouches you can take a look at. Got 'em in vinyl and leather."

Eric shook his head. He knew it would rouse the old man's suspicions again, but he didn't care. The gun would go from the bag to his hand to his mouth, and besides, he'd already purchased the gun and no longer needed the pretense.

"Suit yourself." The guy behind the counter didn't seem to think he needed the pretense anymore either. He reached for the gun. "I can't let you walk outta here with it in your paw, though."

Eric handed the pistol over to the man who stuck it in the bag with the ammunition, crinkled up the opening like it was a lunch bag, and handed it to Eric.

Eric took the bag from him. "Thanks." He turned to leave.

"Thank you." The old man said. "And Happy New Year."

Happy New Year. The phrase sounded strange in Eric's ears. This would be the first new year without Emily. What could possibly be happy about that? What about the death of your wife could give you cause to celebrate?

And yet, Eric realized, it was just one of many superficial greetings people gave each other like, "How's it going?" People don't really care; don't really want you to answer with the truth. When the cashier asks, he or she's asking out of habit, or more accurately because store policy says good customer service starts with, "How's it going?" and ends with "Have a nice day." People ask about the kids, the spouse, health, and vacations only because it's polite, always fearing you might be the person to mistake politeness for genuineness. So Old Joe didn't mean Happy New Year when he wished it, it's just the one that fitted the time of year.

"Happy New Year," Eric replied. He turned and walked out of the store to his car. He climbed into his SUV and sat looking at the bag. Now that he had it, he wasn't sure what to do. He'd thought he would just go home and kill himself but found he didn't want to go back home. To the house where she died maybe? No. He hadn't found the intestinal fortitude to go there in the past six months, not even a drive-by. He was kidding himself if he thought he could go there today. So where to go? Maybe just right here in the parking lot? That didn't seem fair to the guy in the pawn shop. But why should he care about the guy in the pawn shop?

Eric decided he could at least load the .38 while he pondered the best place to eat a bullet. He opened the bag, pulled out the pistol, and laid it on the passenger seat. Pulling the box of ammunition out, he set it beside the .38 and dropped the paper bag onto the passenger floorboard.

As he picked the .38 back up, he realized he didn't know how to open the cylinder. He hadn't watched the guy closely enough and hadn't asked him how to do it, not wanting to come off like an idiot. He remembered the guy had flipped it open with a flick of his wrist. Eric flicked, but nothing happened. He pushed on the cylinder, but it didn't budge. He was feeling like an idiot now. He thought about going back into the pawn shop and asking Old Joe, but the testosterone in his bloodstream wouldn't allow it.

He ran his fingers over the surface of the pistol looking for a button or latch or something that would release the cylinder. Above the grip on the left side of the firearm was a small oval-shaped button with grooves cut into it. He pushed on it, but nothing happened. He thumbed it forward and the cylinder slipped out.

Way to go, Rambo.

Eric placed the pistol in his lap and reached for the box. He thumbed the tab open and pulled the plastic tray out just enough to see the first row of bullets. After selecting a bullet, Eric picked the pistol up with his left hand and the bullet with his right. He tried inserting the bullet into the cylinder but found his hands were trembling.

He listened to his heartbeat and felt it fluttering in his chest. If he was this nervous, maybe he didn't want to die. Maybe this wasn't the answer. But he knew it was, knew it was nothing but his self-preservation gene kicking in. He did want to die. Did want to leave this world, and rejoin Emily in the next.

Death was not the worst thing that could happen to a man, Eric had come to realize. There were lots of experiences in life where death was a welcomed relief. Suffering from a debilitating terminal disease.

He closed his eyes and forced himself to take slow, deliberate breaths. The fluttering ceased. With his eyes still closed, he moved the bullet to the cylinder.

His cell phone shrilled, startling him. He dropped the bullet as he jerked his head back into the headrest, causing a light sensation of whiplash. He leaned forward quickly to find the bullet as if it was the lit butt of a cigarette, smacking his head against the steering column. The horn peeled.

Eric rubbed his neck and head as he dropped the .38 on the passenger seat, snatched up his cell phone, and hit the green button.

"Yeah?" He shouted as he felt his forehead for swelling. He was irritated now, but he wasn't sure who he was more irritated with; whoever was calling, interrupting his preparations for death, or himself, so conditioned like Pavlov's dog to salivate and answer the phone whenever and wherever it rang.

"Tell me you like hockey." It was Paul.

"Huh?"

"Hockey. You love it, right?"

"Yeah, sure." He looked down for the bullet and spotted it on the floorboard resting against his right foot.

"I just got a couple of tickets to tomorrow night's Black Hawk's game." He practically shouted as he added, " On the glass."

"Oh." Eric reached down, careful not to hit the steering wheel this time, and picked up the bullet.

"Tell me you're in."

Eric looked at the bullet between his thumb and forefinger. "Well, I don't know."

"Don't know? They're *on the glass*, Man." There was the slightest hint of a plea in Paul's voice.

Eric tried to think of some excuse. "I've got this thing I've got—"

Paul cut in. "Beg off. Tell 'em you're sick, tell 'em something's come up, a family emergency, whatever. Just get out of it and tell me you're in." Now there was out-and-out groveling in Paul's voice. He sounded desperate like his life depended on it.

Life depended on it; Eric mused. He was sitting in his car with a bullet in his hand and a gun on the passenger seat talking to a guy whose biggest worry was finding someone to go to a hockey game with him.

On the glass.

What a life, what a very charmed life Mr. Paul Stephens had. Eric felt a sharp pang of resentment for which he at once felt ashamed. Paul may lead a charmed life, but he'd illustrated many times, he liked sharing that charm with others. From the tips he'd left waitresses to the cabbie the night before, Paul had no problems sharing the wealth.

And really. What was another day? Besides, what better way to go out than a night courtside followed by a night on the glass? He'd only ever been to one Black Hawks game and then he was so far up he needed binoculars to see the players, never mind the puck. Not only that, but Paul had also told him over lunch yesterday he didn't know anyone in Chicago and preferred not to socialize too much with his colleagues.

"I'm in."

"Fantastic." Paul's voice was a mixture of excitement and relief. "Tell you what. I took today and tomorrow off because the decorator and the movers are supposed to be here at the house today. Why don't you come over tomorrow for lunch and see the place? Then I'll drive us into the city for the game."

"Sounds great." It really did sound great. Eric found himself looking forward to it. "Anything you want me to bring?"

"No, I got it covered. Well, I better let you go. See you between twelve and one tomorrow, Buddy. Thanks."

"See you tomorrow." Eric hit the End Call button and set his cell phone in the cup holder. He rolled the bullet between his thumb and forefinger and shook his head, marveling at his indecisiveness, how easily he'd talked himself out of killing himself. He was just about to eat a bullet one minute, and then looking forward to a hockey game the next.

What's another day?

Eric looked over at the .38 resting on the seat beside him and then back to the bullet. He thought about all those television shows and films where a character shrugs and says something like, "The guy's been rotting in jail for twelve years for a crime he didn't commit. What's one more day?" It was never the guy in jail saying that. That guy was never flippant, never resigned to the idea of even another minute of incarceration once there was evidence that cleared him after twelve years. He was ready to get out now, right at that moment.

So maybe I don't want to die.

That thought stopped him from rolling the bullet. Maybe he didn't want to die. But how could he live? Without her?

"I miss you so much, Emily." Eric closed his eyes and saw her. She wasn't screaming. She was whole again. Those lips he loved to kiss, loved to feel on his skin, were still there, now curled into that knowing smile of hers, when she got past the machismo of the man to what was getting to him.

"I love you, Emily."

Her eyes sparkled with the recognition of his love.

"Tell me what to do."

She put a finger to her mouth to quiet him then mouthed, "Wait."

Eric opened his eyes, feeling the wetness of tears on his cheeks. He wiped his eyes and placed the bullet back in the box. He closed the box and the cylinder on the .38.

Emily hadn't said not to kill himself, hadn't told him it was wrong to think like that. She didn't have to. She knew he knew. And yet, he was still confused, conflicted. But he decided to listen to his wife. He would wait.

Eric reached over and retrieved the paper bag from the passenger-side floorboard, dropped the box and pistol into it, and rolled the bag up. Opening the glove box, he laid the bag inside and closed it.

Wait.

Chapter 12

Eric drove up to Paul's new house and parked on the street. In the driveway was Paul's Mercedes. Parked behind it was a 1957 Cadillac Eldorado Biarritz convertible with a pink champagne paint job and a white rag top.

Eric got out of his SUV and walked over to the Caddy. The car was in pristine condition. The wide whitewalls on the tires gleamed. The chrome blazed in the crisp afternoon sun. Eric looked through the windows. The interior, two-tone white with red, couldn't have been cleaner since the first day the car sat in a showroom fifty years before. He took a step back to admire the profile. There was absolutely nothing cooler on a car, Eric thought than fins. That was back when Detroit was serious about building cars.

Eric whistled, walking around the car. Outside of the pink champagne paint job, which had to be new, that just wasn't a color they used back in the Fifties, the car had to be original.

As he finished walking around the vehicle, the front door opened. Eric heard her before he saw her.

"Oh, Darling," her voice boomed from inside the house, "I think you'll be more than pleased with my selections." She pronounced the word 'darling' as if she were high-class English or at least Manhattan Chic. There was also a hint of flirtatiousness in her voice. "I know exactly how to bring out the man inside the man."

She stepped out onto the loggia and growled a laugh. Eric thought that must be the same sound a tiger makes when she first catches the scent of her next meal.

Paul, if that's your girlfriend, Eric thought, my opinion of you has just dropped past the toilet and straight into the septic tank.

The woman was wearing black ankle-high lace-up boots with a potentially fatal high heel, hot pink tights, a black skirt suit, the skirt so tight she had to roll her hips and scissor her legs to walk, and a black hat with a brim so wide, Eric wasn't sure how she made it out the door. The right gust of wind and she'd be airborne.

Paul followed, wearing a sober expression. "I'm sure," seemed to be the extent of conversation he could muster.

"Love, love, kisses, kisses." She made smooching noises towards each of Paul's cheeks before turning away from him, though her hand did linger on his shoulder.

Eric had been sure that women like this one were simply characters in film and television; that no one like her could exist in the real world. But here she was, in the flesh.

She slipped on a pair of winged sunglasses as she rolled and scissored her way to the driver's side door, waving a four-fingered 'goodbye' in Eric's face. She poured herself into the Caddy. Eric was sure she would close the door on the brim of her chapeau, but she didn't.

She fired up the car and blew a few more kisses Paul's way who returned her kisses with a weak wave and a look of nausea as she pulled out of the drive.

Eric watched the car until it drove out of sight, then walked up to the front door where Paul still stood, looking intently for any sign the woman was coming back.

"Who was that?" Eric threw a thumb over his shoulder in the direction the Caddy had gone.

"More like, what was that?" Paul took a breath and exhaled. "You don't want to know." He turned towards Eric. "She's an interior decorator. One of the best in Chicago. Picked out all the furnishings for the house. She was here for *six* hours yesterday."

"Six hours?"

"She moved the ottoman *eight* times. And then she shows up this morning with a Ming vase full of flowers saying, 'This just absolutely has to go in the foyer, Darling.'" Paul's impression of the woman was dead on and Eric couldn't help but laugh.

"It isn't funny, Eric. And then she re-arranged and re-fluffed every single pillow in the house twice and still found time to move the ottoman again."

"Wow. That must've driven you nuts."

"Oh, I wanted to kill her. Shoot her in the head or strangle her and bury her out back."

"She did have one redeeming quality, though," Eric admitted.

Paul smiled. "That car was hot."

"Except for the paint job, it was sweet." Eric agreed.

"Needs to be black with flames."

"With cherry bomb glass backs," Eric added.

Paul pointed his index and middle fingers at his eyes and then at Eric's eyes and repeated the gesture. "You and me, Man, you and me. Right here."

Eric shrugged. "What can I say? Great minds think alike."

"And then there's the two of us." Paul waved Eric into the house. "Come on in."

Eric followed Paul into the house, the vase and flowers catching Eric's eyes like the hot pink tights on the woman who said it just absolutely had to be in the foyer. It was anything but masculine. It wasn't exactly feminine either. Flamboyantly ugly was perhaps the best description Eric could think of. Ming? There was no way any self-respecting Chinese artist, or any artist for that matter, would have thrown such an exquisite piece and then adorned it in yellow, green, brown, and gold with a more than ample splash of pink.

"I'm afraid that later tonight that vase will be the unfortunate victim of a drive-by." Paul shivered and walked into the living room. "Let me give you the tour."

Eric was glad to see the rest of the house was much more masculine. If Pottery Barn had a section entitled The Batchelor Pad in its catalog, Paul's living room would be featured. Sleek and modern black leather and chrome sofa and loveseat sat around a chrome and glass coffee table. A black, tan, and chocolate area rug lay beneath the coffee table. Matching end tables supported light green lamps which looked like pieces of modern art rather than light fixtures. The entertainment center, also black and chrome, supported a Sony sixty-inch flat-screen plasma television with a Bose surround system.

"I went ahead and ordered Chinese for lunch." Paul moved into the kitchen and Eric followed. "I didn't know what you liked so I got a plethora. Should be here any minute."

Paul went to the new stainless-steel refrigerator and retrieved a couple of beers as the doorbell rang.

"Perfect timing." Paul took a quick pull from his bottle, set it down, and headed to the front door.

Eric wasn't sure what to do. He wanted to help Paul if he needed it, but he didn't want to keep following him around like some lonely little dog. He shifted from his left foot to his right foot, staying in the kitchen, brought the bottle to his mouth, then went to set it down, then back up, stopped, and listened.

If Paul needs a hand, he'll ask.

Eric heard the door open and the thick accent as the young delivery man announced who he was. Eric choked on his beer as Paul's voice responded in Chinese. The young man's voice, now filled with absolute delight, now became a blur in the unintelligible language. Well, only unintelligible to Eric. The two men at the door comprehended each other quite well, as Eric heard the young man's peal of laughter.

The door closed and Paul appeared at the kitchen entrance brandishing two bags laden with Styrofoam and traditional Chinese box containers of food. He set the bags on the table and started pulling the containers out and opening them.

"Okay. We got Lo Mien...Moo Goo Gai Pan...Mongolian Beef...steamed rice...Kung Pao Chicken...egg rolls...fried rice...and last but not least, fortune cookies."

Paul went to the cupboards and drawers and pulled out plates and silverware.

The two sat down at the table and began dishing out food onto their plates.

"You speak Chinese?" Eric scooped fried rice onto his plate.

Paul nodded. "Cantonese." He bit into an egg roll.

"Why'd you learn that, if you don't mind me asking?" He took a sip of beer before tucking into the Kung Pao.

"Business," Paul said as he swallowed. "Sun Tsu said in his book *The Art of War* to know thy enemy. Same works for business. I mean the Chinese weren't the enemy, but I didn't like not knowing what they said to each other at the negotiation table." Paul stuck the rest of the egg roll in his mouth.

The conversation became sparse as they tore into the food. Eric was hungrier than he thought. It was nice to have an appetite again, Eric thought as he finished off his second egg roll. The food was good, the beer was good, and the company, well the company was great.

Paul sat back, finished the last of his beer, and patted his belly. "You know what this meal needs? Dessert."

Eric rubbed his stomach. He didn't think he could eat another bite and he had a thought of that Monty Python movie where the waiter tells the large guy to have a mint. They're wafer thin, the waiter tells him in a French accent. The big guy eats the wafer and explodes.

"What did you have in mind?" Eric's diaphragm groaned from the exertion of asking the question.

Paul smiled to himself. "Do you like stogies?"

Embarrassment tweaked Eric. He'd never tried smoking. Not cigars, cigarettes, pipes, or pot for that matter, and he had the feeling at this moment that perhaps he was less than a man. Why it would bother him at this moment he hadn't a clue. It'd never bothered him before. But his friend...friend? Yes, Paul was a friend, not a best friend or even a good friend, yet, but a friend. Eric had the strange sensation he was back in the pawnshop with Old Joe. Cigars, like guns and cars, should be something all guys should know, shouldn't it? Just hard-wired into the male DNA like the desire to get to first base by the end of the first date. He'd had no problem lying to Old Joe so why not tell Paul how much he loved cigars?

But he knew Paul would see right through him the moment he handed Eric one to light up and puff on. Eric wasn't even sure if that's what you did, puff. His embarrassment tweaked a little harder.

Yet Paul was so down to earth. He treated everyone he met as if they stood on the same playing field as he did. He didn't seem to care his car was worth more than most people's houses. Eric found he respected Paul, and respecting a man meant you told him the truth.

"I've never actually had one."

Paul sat up, ecstatic. "Cool. I'll be your first." He frowned. "That didn't come out right." Paul stood up and started clearing the table. "I'm not going to push you, but if you'd like to learn why God really gave us tobacco, I know this great little place in the city. It's got a walk-in humidor and an area where you can smoke right there. It's great."

"Sure." Eric stood up to help. There wasn't much to do. All the food was gone, and Paul had already gathered the containers up and dropped them in the trash can. Eric grabbed the plates and silverware and loaded them into the dishwasher. "Why not?"

Why not?

Why not live a little, Eric thought. It's not like cigars were gonna kill him. What was that old cliché? Eat, drink, and be merry for tomorrow we may die. Well that was a certainty in Eric's case, wasn't it? Wasn't it? Tomorrow he would eat a bullet. Definitely. Most likely. Why not indulge today?

"Excellent." Paul leaned against the counter. "We'll go into the city, smoke a few stogies, enjoy a cognac with the smokes, head over to the game, and grab a bite there."

"Sounds good." Eric slipped back into his coat.

"Sounds really good." Paul started moving for the front door. "I love a plan that includes cognac. And on the way, I've got an idea I want to run by you."

They reached the front door. Paul put on his coat and swept up his keys from the credenza now adorned with the hideous vase.

"What's that?" Eric was enjoying Paul's ideas. He always seemed to have one or two ready to pitch, and Eric was beginning to suspect that even if Paul wasn't loaded, he'd still be that way. It was in his genes. The tickets might not be courtside or on the glass, but there'd still be games and places to go to. Eric could imagine Paul getting excited about going into the city for a milkshake. He'd probably be just as excited heading to a bowling alley.

Paul buttoned up his leather coat. "You ever been to Vegas?"

Chapter 13

Eric settled back into the soft, and surprisingly wide, leather of his first-class seat, accepted the glass of Seven and Seven, and told the flight attendant he'd prefer the filet mignon. The Boeing 747 cruised smoothly through the friendly skies, made friendlier by the alcohol. He was on his third glass. Eric smiled as he took a sip, feeling the whiskey buzz thicken his skull. He could see himself growing quite comfortable with the lifestyle Paul was already accustomed to.

He looked over at Paul who was reading the New York Times. When Paul had mentioned Vegas to him, Eric had been wary. After all, how many guys invited other guys to Vegas on an all-expenses-paid trip? It seemed too much like that movie about the two gay cowboys, and Eric confessed as much to Paul. He just didn't swing that way and if that was what Paul was after, he was barking up the wrong tree.

Paul had laughed. "I'm not interested in your O ring, or any guy's O ring for that matter. I was flying out there on business with an associate. He's new and I was going to show him the ropes. But he had a death in the family, so his ticket and room are just going to go to waste."

A moment had passed before Paul spoke again. "Now if I'd surprised you with two tickets to Air Supply, then you could be worried."

Eric had laughed at that and accepted the invitation. But now, drinking Seven and Seven and eating filet mignon, he felt an uneasiness as a thought took hold of his brain. He had no real idea of why he was eating filet mignon and drinking whiskey in first class. He hadn't asked and Paul had never elaborated other than to say it was business. It was as vague as when he'd asked Paul what he did for a living. Imports and Exports was his answer, but that's as ambiguous an answer as the thirty-year-old guy who lives in his parent's basement and tells you after he delivers your pizza, he's an entrepreneur.

He looked over at Paul. "You never told me."

Paul looked up from his newspaper. "Excuse me?"

"What's in Vegas, besides Air Supply, Australia's greatest export?

"Second greatest." Paul shot back. "Or maybe third. Behind Hugh Jackman and Olivia Newton-John."

"Olivia Newtown-John?" Eric laughed.

"How about those black leather pants she wore in Grease?" He took a sip of scotch, appearing to weigh his words and the scotch before he swallowed. "Part of what I do is finding exotic toys for people who have exotic tastes and a lot of cash. In this case, the toys are guns."

Eric didn't like the sound of that. "Are you some kind of gun-runner? Am I gonna end up in jail?"

Paul shook his head. "Completely above board and legit. We're not helping third-world armies or tyrants get a hold of weaponry they shouldn't have. This is stuff that your average multi-millionaire can't just waltz down to the local gun shop or pawn shop and pick up."

Eric wasn't feeling any better. "Why do rich people need exotic weapons?"

Paul shrugged. "Some folks want a Hummer in the driveway for their neighbors to see. Others want boats or planes. These people want something they know for a fact no one, or very few people at least, have. They're not interested in using these weapons; they don't even want to flaunt them. They want to possess them simply for possession's sake. We make sure they've got the proper permits and registrations, help them find and allocate those weapons, for a fee."

"So that's what's in Vegas? Guns? Eric felt a rush of excitement he didn't quite understand. He'd never really been around guns at all. Had only purchased one in his lifetime, the one that sat in the glove box of his vehicle. He'd played with toy guns growing up, what boy hadn't, but he'd never really cultivated an interest in the real thing. He'd never gone hunting, skeet shooting, or even target shooting; didn't even have to watch every war movie that came out. Nor was there a lack of interest because Emily had been against it. They'd never discussed it; there'd never been a need. But now, the prospect of guns was exciting. There was something, he hated the cliché though it seemed to be true, manly about a room full of guns, and he wanted to be there.

Paul took another sip of scotch. "One of the biggest gun expos in the country. It's going on today and tomorrow. Have you ever been to a gun show?"

Eric shrugged. "No. He had a twinge of that whole less-than-manly feeling again like he should have at least gone to one gun show in his life.

"Well if you'd had, I would've said until this one no you hadn't. This is a gun show elevated to the Nth degree. There'll be more firepower in one room than some countries have in their entire military." Catching the awe-struck yet excited look on Eric's face, Paul added. "You interested in tagging along?"

Eric practically jumped out of his seat; only the constraint of his seatbelt, and the knowing look on Paul's face, the same look his father had when he announced to a nine-year-old Eric he was taking him to someplace exciting, restrained him. Eric quickly recovered. Fixing his face with a bored expression, he shrugged indifferently and said as nonchalantly as possible, "Sure."

Paul laughed then said in mock apology, "I mean, it's no gun show at the Cary fairgrounds, but it tries."

Eric sighed with knowing resignation. "I'm sure it will be...quaint."

"To say the least." Then Paul's face turned serious. "Just try not to laugh openly at the Second Amendment t-shirts on the Rambo wannabes, please. Remember I'm trying to scrape a living. Maybe even get an invite to represent a serious buyer at one of the more prestigious gun shows."

Eric put a pained expression on his face. "You ask a lot...but, if I can help you move up to the big leagues of the fairground gun show circuit I will."

Paul slumped in relief. "Thanks." He drained the last of his scotch, folded up his newspaper, and laid back in his chair. "I'm gonna catch a nap. Wake me when chow's here?" He closed his eyes.

"Sure." Eric drank his Seven and Seven and started reading the Robert Galbraith book he'd picked up at the airport bookstore.

The rest of the flight passed in relative silence. Eric woke Paul when the food came, but they didn't talk. The plane landed, they claimed their baggage, and set off for the Bellagio Hotel on the strip. Eric couldn't help but be dazzled by the lights. Of course, what really dazzled him was the thought of just how steep the monthly electric bill must be for the strip, and he expressed this thought to Paul, who just laughed and said nothing.

They checked in. Paul handed Eric a mag card for his room, a hundred-dollar bill, expense account he'd said, and told Eric to have fun and that he'd see him in the lobby in the morning for breakfast before heading to the expo. With that, Paul picked up his bag and headed for his room. Eric also decided to go to his room to drop off his bag which he did, dropping his bag and walking over to the window with the view of the fountains. A show was in progress, and he watched.

"Emily would have loved that." He spoke out loud without realizing it, without registering his voice, and without hearing the sounds of her screams filling his ears.

Still watching the fountain show, his right hand found the wedding band he still wore and began twisting it around his finger. "I love you, Emily," he said. "I miss you." He took a deep breath and let his eyes drift outward back to the fountains. He let out the breath slowly, feeling the air leave his lungs, and watched the fountains shoot colored arcs of water in silence.

After a few minutes, he decided he wanted to take a close look at what he could only think of as the most opulent mini mall he'd ever seen. He twisted the wedding ring once around his finger and set out to explore.

His explorations ended when he found a room in the casino with large and small screens covering the walls like paint, exhibiting every sporting event anyone might want to bet on: Horses, football, basketball, hockey, dogs, jai-alai, boxing; if there was any interest in laying a bet on the outcome, it was on a screen.

Eric sat down to watch the basketball game on the biggest screen, though he couldn't help but let his eyes wander around the room. This was sports heaven. Every fan should have a room like this. Of course, the universal remote would be as big as a laptop.

After the basketball game, came another basketball game, and on a small screen, a minor college bowl game started. He never moved from his seat, never had to. A waitress brought him a beer when he first sat down and a burger later in the evening. She kept him well-stocked in munchies and even woke him after he'd dozed off during the last few minutes of the ball game. He'd thanked her, looked at his watch, and realized he could use a good night's sleep.

He called for the tab and reached into his pocket for some money. He found the Franklin Paul had given him and had to laugh.

Come to Vegas and you don't even play the nickel slots.

He pocketed the hundred-dollar bill, promising himself to return it to Paul in the morning, and pulled out the cash he'd brought. He paid the bill and went up to his room, dropping on the bed and falling fast asleep. He was still sleeping when the phone on the bedside table started ringing. He picked the receiver up.

"Hello?" Eric said through what felt like a mouth of cotton. A pounding in his head was picking up in volume and intensity.

It was Paul. "Time to get up, get dressed, and meet me for breakfast."

"What time is it?" Eric rubbed at his eyes.

"Almost nine. So hurry up, I'm starving." Paul hung up.

Eric set the receiver back in its cradle, crawled out of bed, and staggered to the shower. The hot water felt great as it beat against his skull, massaging his headache. He showered, dressed in jeans, a blue sports shirt, and tennis shoes, and headed down to the lobby.

Paul was nursing a coffee he'd picked up from the espresso bar. He was dressed in black loafers, slacks, a t-shirt, and a blazer. Eric got the mental image of Paul's walk-in bedroom closet lined with rows and rows of black slacks, shirts, and loafers, looking more like a rack of men's wear at Macy's than a personal closet. Or maybe Paul just wore the same pair of clothes every day.

Paul downed the last of the coffee. "I'm feeling like pancakes." He tossed the insulated paper cup into the trash and turned for the breakfast buffet.

"Okay." Eric followed Paul into a room with so much food that the Big Boy himself would be ashamed of his own buffet if he were here to see this. Above the food was a banner announcing this bounty was all yours for just $64.95.

After breakfast, they caught a cab to the civic center for the gun expo.

"I'll catch up with you later," Paul said as he left him at the entrance. "Have fun."

Eric's 'bye' trailed off as he walked onto the main arena floor. It was filled with aisles and aisles of weapons, and not just guns. Knife and sword manufacturers had their wares on display, from one-of-a-kind custom jobs to exact replicas of the "Lord of the Rings" and "Blade" swords. One company had a mannequin wearing the latest in bullet-proof apparel quietly taking shots from different weapons to prove his indestructibility. Eric passed another booth where suppressers were for sale. The gentleman behind the case fired a pistol into a foam core target.

"All you hear is the click of the hammer," He was explaining to the impressed assemblage in front of him.

Eric continued on and found companies selling such accessories as gun cleaning kits, gun cases, and law enforcement paraphernalia. Then there were the companies he'd never heard of displaying weapons he'd never seen but learned from their posters and brochures how the United States military found them a valuable and effective tool on the battlefield. One vendor let him pick the weapon up and hold it. Eric had no idea what it did exactly, but it looked cool.

"Come on, Rambo."

Eric turned. It was Paul.

He suddenly felt foolish, like a kid strumming a guitar and lip-syncing to a record in front of an imaginary audience when his dad walked in on him. Eric quickly set the weapon down.

"You want to see some really cool stuff, follow me." Paul led him over to an area in the back of the arena. The booths here were somber, unassuming, even boring. No posters or emblazoned banners hung in this area, nor were there video presentations shouting above the din, exclaiming the glorious virtues of the products. Instead, stone-faced representatives stood beside their hardware, which spoke for itself. Again, Eric had no idea what he was looking at, but he was duly impressed.

"So what did you think?" Paul asked as he led Eric back out of the area and through the arena.

"I didn't know what to expect, but honestly, I liked it." Eric gazed over at a table where a man was showing a .38 snubnose to a guy. He reddened, quickly turning away. "I think I'd like to learn to shoot."

"It's a fun hobby," Paul was saying over his shoulder. "I could teach you if you'd really like to learn."

"You could?"

"Yeah. If you're going to be in this business, you've got to know what your customers are looking at and talking about." He stopped at a booth selling soft drinks and bought a couple of Diet Pepsis. "There's a great indoor range in the city. I've got a couple of pistols I was going to sight for the clients. When we get back to Chicago, you can come with me and I'll show you how to do that too." He handed a cup to Eric.

Eric took a sip. "Okay."

They stepped out of the civic center into the crisp afternoon. Paul pulled out his cell phone and a card for the cab agency and called for a ride.

"So what do you want to do tonight?" He asked as he placed his cell phone back in his pants pocket. It's New Year's Eve and we're in Vegas."

Eric felt himself deflate. He and Emily had talked about being on an island like Aruba for the holiday, toasting in the New Year with Mai Tai's on the beach. "To tell you the truth," Eric said looking at the sidewalk, "I'm not really in the mood to celebrate, but I don't want to be alone either."

Paul nodded. A moment of silence passed between them.

"Tell you what, why don't we find some quiet cigar lounge? We'll smoke stogies and have a cognac. Maybe they'll have a big screen we can watch the ball drop on."

Eric thought about it. He nodded "Yeah. Sounds good."

"Great." Paul looked at his watch. "Let's go back to the hotel. I want to eat lunch at Le Cirque."

Chapter 14

Eric pulled the trigger of the Glock 40 semi-automatic pistol several times, unloading the magazine in seconds. Holes littered the target from the erratic spray of bullets.

Paul was right, Eric thought as he looked down at the table holding the other handguns he'd already fired, the revolvers tended to be a little more accurate, but the automatics were a lot more fun. He looked over at Paul who'd just slammed in a magazine, locked, and loaded. Paul took aim, emptied the magazine into the target, dropped the magazine, slammed in a new one, and emptied that one in the time Eric had begun reloading the .38 snubnose Paul had brought.

A lot more fun and a lot faster.

Eric thumbed the cylinder release and dropped in six bullets. He twitched his wrist and the cylinder snapped back into place. As it did, Eric's brain caught up with his movement. He was holding a .38 that aside from the grip looked remarkably like the .38 still sitting in the glove box of his Expedition. He felt the hair on his arms rise from the gooseflesh. It hadn't even fazed him, much less dawned on him, when he'd picked it up and loaded it. His hands hadn't shaken today. His hands hadn't shaken at all as he'd learned to load and fire a Ruger .22 pistol, Beretta 9mm, 357 Magnum, Glock 40 semi-automatic, and, gooseflesh upon gooseflesh, the .38.

"You alright?" Paul had laid the weapon he was firing on the table in front of him and was staring at Eric.

Eric thought about it. Was he alright? He'd spent the evening holding and firing five different handguns without the first thought of using his head as a target. Not only had he shot the weapons, but he'd enjoyed doing so and was looking forward to coming back. And for never really firing a weapon in his life, he had a pretty good eye. He wasn't a deadeye, but he was fairly accurate and seemed to be a fast learner. The .38 was a fun shoot which was why he'd picked it up again. He liked its weight, the feel, and its look. It was a weird comparison, but the snubnose reminded him of an American bulldog. He'd always liked bulldogs, though he'd never owned one.

Well, he thought to himself as he looked at the .38, enjoying its weight and grip, maybe he'd get himself one of those as well. He smiled. *And I can name them both Snubby.*

"Yeah, I'm all right."

Paul nodded and then looked downrange to watch Eric's target.

Eric sighted the target and pulled the trigger. The bullet exploded from the barrel with a very big and satisfying bark as the .38 recoiled. Eric smiled. He was *very* all right. He aimed and pulled the trigger again. He repeated the process until the chambers were empty.

Paul nodded approvingly as he slipped off his protective earmuffs. "Not bad. Not bad at all."

Eric removed his earmuffs, admiring his handiwork. The target, the black silhouette of a human, was no longer a solid form. It now leaked light like a human would blood through holes in its head, chest, shoulders, and abdomen.

"Your guy is down for the count." Paul picked up the Beretta, popped out the magazine, and started to reload it. "You ready to go?"

"Yeah," Eric said, though he felt a slight twinge of regret at leaving. He ran a finger over the .38's grip. "Maybe we could come back next weekend."

"Sure." Paul slapped the magazine into the Beretta, chambered a round, checked to make sure the safety was on, and then deposited the firearm into his gun satchel.

Eric read the sign posted to the table.

Please ensure firearms are unloaded and safely stowed before leaving the premises. Thank you.

The Management.

Paul picked up the 357, looked at the sign, and then to Eric. "I treat every weapon as loaded because it is. He placed the handgun in the case. "What's the point of an unloaded gun? It's nothing more than a cumbersome paperweight."

Eric nodded, and picked up a handgun to reload, but not before glancing furtively in both directions before doing so.

Paul finished loading the last of the client's weapons back into the gun case, closed the lid, and locked it. Eric stood ready to carry the gun satchel in front of him. He'd waited patiently for Paul to finish with the weekend warrior weapons, as Paul called them, which he'd kept on a table away from Eric. He could look but not touch. Paul admitted he didn't even like touching them at this point, because if anything happened to them, it was all on him. "And a couple of them cost as much as my car."

They left the indoor range and walked the block and a half to the public parking garage, taking the elevator to the third level. As they stepped off the elevator, two shadows moved quickly from the darkness. Eric felt two hands shove him. He tried to keep his balance, but the weight of the satchel drove him into the concrete wall. Stars danced in front of his eyes as his knees buckled and he dropped to the pavement. A gleam of silver danced among the stars.

"Give me your wallets." An excited high-pitched voice behind the gleaming silver yapped like a Chihuahua. "Now, or I'll let you see what your guts look like."

As his head cleared, Eric was able to focus. Standing in front of him was a stick of a kid, not more than eighteen with long, stringy, greasy blond hair protruding from a greasy Cubs baseball cap with sparse thatches of blond on his chin and cheeks. He brandished a knife held confidently in his bony, dirt-smeared hands. His high tops, jeans, and army jacket were equally covered in grease and Eric couldn't help wondering if the guy had just gotten off work at some auto shop and was looking for some beer money.

Eric heard Paul say, "Easy, Man, I don't want any trouble."

A voice like a big dog boomed through the parking structure. "Oh, you got trouble, Dude. Big trouble."

Eric could now see a second man, much taller and bigger, dressed in Army fatigues and black Nike Air Jordans standing behind the Chihuahua in the Cubs cap.

As Eric watched Paul reach into his jacket pocket, he noticed a bulge in the side pocket of the satchel. Thankfully, Eric realized, Paul didn't believe in safely securing all of the weapons inside the gun case either.

"Hey." The stick thrust his knife in Paul's direction. The knife trembled slightly from the surge of adrenaline in its owner's bloodstream.

Paul's voice was unearthly calm and reassuring. "My wallet."

The skinny guy's eyes went wide as he saw the band on Paul's arm. "And your watch too."

"Okay. Just let us go." Paul finished pulling his wallet out and then unclasped the latch on his watch band. Sliding the watch off his arm, he held them up in front of him.

The greasy Chihuahua snatched them out of Paul's hand and then turned to Eric. "Now you." He motioned to the satchel with the knife. "What you got there?"

"Just court documents," Paul said. "I'm a lawyer."

"Documents, huh?" The Chihuahua was licking his lips. "Didn't sound like no paper, did it Hootch?"

The big dog of a man barked out a laugh.

Hootch? Like the dog in that movie?

Eric placed a hand protectively on the satchel, his fingers brushing the zipper.

"Give it here." The Chihuahua bared his teeth in an evil grin at Paul. "And I'm taking that suitcase too."

Paul stepped in front of the gun case. "I can't let you do that."

Eric's eyes snapped quickly to Paul. Paul was poised, ready to explode from where he stood like a bullet from one of the handguns they'd spent the night firing. But that's not what had Eric's attention. It was the steel in Paul's voice, cold, hard, and just as deadly sharp as the knife, the Chihuahua in the greasy Cubs cap was waving in Paul's face. The blade was swinging wildly in the young man's bony paw closer and closer to Paul's flesh, but Paul didn't flinch, didn't blink.

"There's over five hundred dollars in my wallet," Paul's voice couldn't have been softer or calmer if he'd been whispering at a funeral, "not to mention credit cards. And that's a two-thousand-dollar TAG Heuer watch. That's a pretty good haul."

Eric could hear the sincerity in Paul's voice. Not the sincerity in the voice of say, himself, pleading for his own life, but the sincerity of an unspoken and perhaps unwelcome promise. The dynamics of the situation had changed, but neither the greasy blonde nor the big dog behind him had the canine intuition to sense that.

But as the blonde started to move the knife to finally strike Paul, Eric shoved his hand into the outside pocket of the satchel and pulled out the pistol. He thumbed the safety off as he pulled the weapon up, gripping it in both hands as Paul had taught him, aimed for the blonde's chest, and pulled the trigger.

The young man's body jumped up and backward, twisting like he was showing off some *Matrix* move as the round from the Glock 40 entered his shoulder at an upward angle. His body hung in the air only for a split second before it dropped and hit the cement floor hard. Eric heard the stomach-churning crunch of teeth cracking and splintering from the skull by the impact.

"You shot him," the big dog spat stupidly at Eric. Fear and disbelief carved away at the big dog, reducing him to a helpless puppy. With a whimper, the man turned and started sprinting down the deserted level.

Paul moved calmly to Eric, pulled the Glock 40 from his hand, twisted towards the running man, pulled the weapon up, and fired one round. The back of the man's head exploded, and his body dropped like a sack of machine parts.

The blonde wailed, his eyes bulging with fear and disbelief. He tried pulling his hand up to his face, but his arm only slithered at his side like a snake missing its head.

Paul pointed the Glock at the man and put a bullet hole in his head. His body immediately went limp. Eric stared at the glassy eyes now staring into the abyss with that same look of disbelief and fear as blood spread from the sieve the man only a short time ago called his skull.

Paul quickly scanned the rest of the garage and cocked an ear to listen for the sound of someone coming to investigate. Satisfied the space was empty, he picked up his wallet and watch and pocketed both as he moved over to Eric and offered him a hand. "We need to go."

Eric took Paul's hand and hoisted himself up. He wasn't sure his legs would hold his weight, and though they trembled violently, they held. Paul unlocked the car, popped the trunk with his key fob, and threw in the gun case and gun satchel. As he closed the trunk, he tossed the keys to Eric. "You drive."

Eric stood staring at the man. How could he be so calm, he wondered.

Paul moved to the passenger side. "Let's move."

Eric obeyed, not because he had the presence of mind, but because the simple coldness in the eyes and voice of the man commanded him like some voice-controlled zombie. He moved to the Mercedes, opened the driver's side door, and climbed in.

"Start the car and drive," Paul said. He sat calmly disassembling the Glock.

Eric started the vehicle. "Where to?" His voice sounded flat and lifeless; the voice-controlled zombie had found employment as a cabbie.

"My house." Paul's voice had a different flat sound. His voice was coming from someplace of calm Eric had never known. His own hands were shaking as he tried to place the key into the ignition, but Paul's hands worked with peaceful deftness.

Eric finally managed to get the key into the ignition and turn it. The engine roared to life. Eric couldn't tell himself why, but he didn't want to hear Paul's voice again, so he quickly dropped the gear into reverse and backed out of the parking space. Before the vehicle had stopped rolling backward, Eric slapped the gear into drive and pushed on the accelerator.

"Easy." Paul never looked up from what he was doing, which looked like from the corner of Eric's eye he was removing a serial number or other identifying marks.

Eric didn't dare look at Paul. That calm, that dead calm, in his voice, Eric wasn't entirely sure Paul wouldn't simply reach out and kill him as matter-of-factly as asking him if he wanted a cup of coffee. Eric sat ramrod stiff facing forward, now and then stealing furtive glances at Paul from the corner of his eye.

Neither man spoke as Eric piloted the car towards Paul's neighborhood. As they passed over the Cortland Street Bridge, Paul touched the power window button, lowering his window, icy wind rushed into the cabin. Eric immediately began to shiver as he watched Paul fling a piece of the disassembled Glock out the window and over the guardrail where it quickly got lost in the darkness. Every ten to fifteen feet, Paul threw a piece of the weapon out the window, into a watery grave. When he finished, he touched the power window button, raising the glass and shutting out the bitter night.

The rest of the drive to Paul's house passed in silence and before Eric could think about anything other than those eyes, those glassy, disbelieving eyes, and how they had continued staring disbelieving even after death, the motion of his hand putting the car in park and cutting the engine brought him back to reality. They were sitting in Paul's driveway.

Paul pulled the key out of the ignition, opened the passenger door, and stepped out of the vehicle. He closed the door and headed towards the house, leaving Eric alone in the Mercedes. Eric sat watching Paul reach the front door, unlock it, and walk into the house as the heat slowly dissipated from the vehicle. As numbness began to creep into Eric's fingers and toes, he found the strength to open the door. The chill was on him like a wolf subduing its next meal, but it stopped before it reached his heart. It seemed to know there resided an iciness it could not defeat.

Eric stepped out of the vehicle and contemplated walking home, but then Paul pulled back the curtain and looked out at him. He had to know, had to know why Paul could have been so calm. Eric had shot a man to protect a friend, but Paul had shot a fleeing man in the back. Not only had he shot a man in the back, but he'd shot an injured man in the head, it'd been all too easy, like he'd done it before.

The door moved closer to Eric like one of those shots in a horror flick. He was standing still, but as he reached the door, he felt himself burst into the house. He looked to his left and found Paul standing in the den, waiting for him.

"How about a drink?"

Eric stood incredulously at the still-open front door. "Drink? Are you kidding me?"

Paul had turned and moved to the wet bar set up in the far corner. He set two tumblers on the bar and dropped ice into them from a bucket. "We've got a lot to talk about—"

"You think?" Eric interrupted.

Paul continued as he poured whisky over the ice. "I'm not sure where to begin." He nodded at the door. "Why don't you close that?"

Eric looked at the open door as if noticing it for the first time. "Yeah, sure." He closed the door and turned back to find Paul offering him a glass of amber liquid filling the tumbler to the rim. He shook his head. "I can't believe," he moved from the foyer into the den, unable to staunch the flood of words moving through his head, "I can't believe you want to have a drink...those guys are dead...they *are* dead, aren't they? I mean you blew that guy's brains out. I shot...self-defense...I mean...to protect. He was down. And the other guy...in the back...that's not self-defense. They have to be dead. Oh, my God. We're going to jail."

"Eric."

Eric stopped talking, stopped moving, and stopped breathing as he heard the icy steel in Paul's voice. The same icy steel when he told the greasy blond kid he couldn't let him take the gun cases. The dynamics had changed; that hadn't been lost on Eric.

"Sit down."

Eric obeyed, sitting on the loveseat.

Paul set the glass of whisky down on the coffee table in front of Eric. "Take a sip."

Eric picked up the glass and took a sip. The liquid was cool from the ice, but still burned the back of his throat as he swallowed.

Paul watched him quietly, but when he spoke his voice continued in that icy steel. "Now take a deep breath and let it out."

Eric did as he was told, and his head felt momentarily light.

"Now sit back."

Eric sat back, taking another sip from the glass he clutched unconsciously to his chest.

Paul took a breath, held it for a minute, searching his glass like a sentry watching the horizon, then let the air out of his lungs. He took a sip, swallowed, and looked Eric in the eye.

"My name's not really Paul."

Part 2
Chapter 15

Paul Stevens hadn't been born Paul Stevens. His real name was Drake Wetherford, a name that sounds exactly like what it is: high society. His parents, James and Stephanie, christened him Drake for that very reason. They wanted the world to know, and Drake to never forget, he was the cream of the socio-economic crop. That's also why the 'a' was dropped from the spelling of the last name to make it even more unique.

Drake, however, wanted nothing more than to forget, preferring the chaff of society. From a young age, Drake exhibited a penchant for all things not beholden to the Wetherford family crest and creed. At the age of five, his parents enrolled him in the very prestigious, and equally expensive, boarding school, Havenbridge.

Several governors, one U. S. President, and more than a dozen CEOs and COOs had been educated at Havenbridge. Almost all of the young men graduating from the school went on to Ivy League schools, usually graduating top of their class. James Wetherford thought on all this every night as he sat drinking his evening Brandy, planning his son's future, which of course included a Harvard law degree and a governorship, at the very least.

But these plans would crumble. By the time he reached the fifth grade, Drake was no longer attending Havenbridge. Nor was he attending any of the three other prestigious boarding schools and prep schools his parents had sent him to after Havenbridge. It had only taken a month for Drake Wetherford to be officially expelled, excommunicated, and any other word the school administrators of the last boarding school could think of that began with the 'ex' prefix. His behavior, they had argued, was beyond what could be considered normal even for a child in some public school and bordered, as the headmaster of the last private school had described it, on the psychopathically malevolent.

James and Stephanie had of course been worried about his behavior and expressed their concerns to James' grandfather. He listened patiently to his grandson and granddaughter-in-law prattle on about Drake's exploits over his brief tenures, such as braiding a little girl's pigtails together with glue, placing a live garter snake in the teacher's desk drawer, bringing a bar of Ex-lax to school and convincing several of the kids it was a candy bar, and of course, the unexpected fire drills which caused the sprinklers to activate, drenching the students, staff and faculty and destroying the computers, copiers, and fax machines. Drake's involvement was immediately suspected as no one else had shown up on those bright sunny days with an umbrella. James and Stephanie feared their son was a bad egg.

But a smile kept pulling at the corners of the old man's mouth. After the two had finally spent themselves, he asked them if Drake had exhibited that same behavior before or since attending these exclusive schools. They shook their heads but admitted that Drake spent more time over the years with his nanny. The nanny, however, had never mentioned any real problems with Drake but never failed to mention how Drake showed intelligence and precociousness she hadn't seen in the other small children she'd cared for over the years.

James smiled and told them not to worry, Drake wasn't a bad egg, he'd said reassuringly. "He just has a streak of his Great-Great-Uncle William in him." This revelation, however, did not have the intended pacifying effect but instead rocketed James and Stephanie from fear to absolute horror.

William was not a name mentioned often within the Wetherford family circle, not the later generations anyway, and these generations worked hard to ensure future generations didn't even recognize the name. Drake, like his cousins, was certainly never told about William. Had heard only very little of James, William's brother. The Wetherford name was synonymous with New Orleans high society and the more recent generations didn't like any hint of something less than pure New Orleans gentility in their stock. If it hadn't been for Drake's best friend, Paul, William and James Wetherford might have passed into obscurity.

Drake's great-great-grandfather, James, great-great grandmother, Mildred, and great-great uncle, William, had originally been from some Pennsylvania town long since deliberately forgotten to the family collective memory. This had been back before the Civil War. They hadn't been society then, just a couple of miners digging out a living.

Once the South was defeated and Lincoln launched his plan to rebuild, William had gotten the idea a fortune was to be made. He talked his brother, James, and his wife, Mildred, into heading south to Louisiana to the port of New Orleans. A couple of healthy, industrious, smart young men could make a killing, he reasoned, and if not, well then, they'd be no worse off than they were already slaving away in the bowels of the earth for other men.

So William, James, and Mildred left the open plains and rolling hills of Pennsylvania for the bayou of Louisiana. They rented a warehouse and the rooms above it and opened up shop, Wetherford Bros. Imports. William had been the dreamer, But James, as it turned out, had been the real visionary.

James was good with numbers and a fast learner, and he usually didn't make the same mistake twice. He quickly learned how to buy and sell on credit and turn a profit with little or no actual out-of-pocket expense to the business. But he was also honest, fair, and sociable. He wasn't an elitist and treated the impoverished as respectfully as the upper class. People liked him, as much as they could like a Yankee who'd come to exploit the South for personal gain.

He expanded the business into exports, land and waterway development, commercial barging, and hotels. People may have fussed over their dinner tables within the privacy of their own homes at the continued Wetherford exploitation of Louisiana, but the fussing was only half-hearted. Most people had the liberty to fuss at dinner tables in the privacy of their own homes because of the continued Wetherford exploitation of Louisiana. James insisted on hiring local and promoting from within. Like it or not, and most liked it, the Wetherfords were good for the local economy.

Sweetening the pot was Mildred, whom most in New Orleans believed had to have some Southern blood in her. Yankee women, they knew, just didn't come by that level of femininity naturally. Mildred had fallen in love with the people from the moment she set foot on New Orleans' soil, and even as the brothers were hanging up their shingle, she was throwing herself into bettering the local welfare. At first, her efforts were looked upon snidely as nothing more than a carpetbagger's con, but her quiet and tireless work as a foot soldier in all matters of civic concern soon won over even her most unwavering critics.

As the business grew so did her efforts. Believing it important for a community to participate in its improvement, she never paid for any of the buildings or programs outright but spearheaded fundraising campaigns and activities to get her fellow citizens involved. Though she did contribute most of the generous allowance James gave her to make sure her campaigns and activities were a success.

And she wasn't just satisfied with helping the local community. She helped rural communities improve their schools, expand their libraries, and share in the economic prosperity of New Orleans. However, she did find it was better to be a silent partner in these rural endeavors. The smaller communities could never bring themselves to trust not only a transplanted Yankee but a city one at that. All in all, however, she was well-loved in New Orleans.

William, like his brother and sister-in-law, liked doing for the community, but he was less concerned about fitting in with high society. He was more the *what-you-see-is-what-you-get-take-it-or-leave-it* type of personality and had no real interest in losing his blue collar. William liked to work. He liked rolling up his sleeves and getting his hands dirty. He liked a glass of whiskey or two or three or eight at the end of a hard day. He liked playing poker and dance hall girls. William wasn't any taller than the average guy, but he was solidly built. He didn't start fights, but he always finished them.

And he wasn't without his ideas. Moving to New Orleans had been his idea, after all, and he thought he'd never have a better one. But one spring evening as he watched the Mississippi River roll by, an old paddle steamer came floating lazily downstream.

William thought about his first time on one of those boats. He'd been transfixed by that large wheel turning and churning up the water propelling the ship forward, marveling at its ingenuity. He'd also enjoyed looking at the passing scenery and had thought every resident of a place should have the opportunity of seeing their home from this vantage point. He felt a pang of regret in his chest. He'd been so busy working hard and playing harder, he'd forgotten the simple pleasure of looking at something from a different point of view. He knew he wasn't the only person either.

But there was something else. William was restless. He was ready for something new. Not new, like picking up stakes and moving West, but different. He was ready to do something different. Something a little more...adventurous; something with a lot more dependence on himself rather than on his brother and sister-in-law.

He watched the paddle boat until he heard his stomach growl. He could hear the sound of a saloon piano playing faintly. He smiled. Usually by this time in the evening, he was in his favorite saloon, an empty plate before him, a half-bottle of whiskey in his hand, and a girl on his lap. He watched the boat paddle around the bend...and had a brainstorm.

He couldn't wait till the next day but ran to his brother's house at that moment to talk to him. He didn't want James to be involved; he just wanted his blessing and his investment. The idea had legitimate business potential, though not all parts of the plan were exactly honest.

James was, of course, unconvinced at the idea's legitimate moneymaking potential. More to the point, he questioned the integrity and morality of the idea. The idea was a simple one: Buy an old riverboat, refurbish it, and offer day and evening cruises of the Mississippi which included fine dining, live entertainment, and gambling, specifically, cards.

It was this last offering that had James worried. Card games involving liquor and money had a stigma rightfully attached to them. William had regaled him and Mildred with many a colorful story of a fight or murder over a card game he'd been involved in. James just couldn't see the lure to a family if gambling were going on and any money made by the boat on the dining or entertainment could easily be lost in the gambling.

James had already thought of that, and his solution was the one part of the plan he'd withheld from James. William would employ the best unknown poker players he could find to play and win at his tables. That way, people would believe everyone had a chance and regardless of the outcome the house would always win.

He also planned on buying only the best whisky on the market and only allowing one glass or shot an hour. His gambling employees would have one drink of whiskey an hour as well and then a glass of water. As they would be winning, he would count on the male ego of the other gamblers to follow their example. William understood that people, specifically men, were a lot less likely to start a fight if they were a lot more sober.

James succumbed to his brother's passion; always knew he would lend William the money even before William mentioned he wanted him as a silent partner. He lent the money to William with his blessings and his reservations.

William took the money, and the next morning purchased an old, run-down, barely floating riverboat. William knew doing most of the work himself, working like a bull twenty hours a day, seven days a week, he still wouldn't be able to open for business for more than a year. So he went out to the saloons, found the best carpenters and mechanics, and promised them free booze, easy winnings, and even easier women. The boat was finished in less than three months and was a complete success, allowing him to repay the loan in less than a month.

The paddleboat made William, and silent or no, James rich men all over again. But it wasn't until James' daughter, Lucille, who had more of her Uncle William in her than her father, that the riverboat made the entire family even wealthier than anticipated. It also became a family secret more scandalous than the family matriarch and patriarch being blue-collar Yankees.

One day, Lucille approached her uncle as he checked over the liquor inventory.

"Uncle Will, do you have a moment?"

William put down his pencil, rubbed his eyes, then picked up his glass of whiskey and drained the remaining. He poured himself a couple of fingers, then looked around.

"Your mother or father with you?"

Lucille shook her head.

William nodded, pulled out another glass, poured a finger's worth, and handed it to his niece.

She took the glass but didn't drink.

William took a sip. "What's on your mind?" He asked.

Lucille inhaled a breath, looked her uncle in the eye, and laid out her plan.

When she finished, William looked at her for a long moment. "Prostitutes?"

Lucille shook her head. "Independent contractors offering a service. Each one of these contractors will set her price for her services and we are simply landlords who charge a nominal fee for the space. If the contractor wants extra...amenities in the space, we will provide those for an additional fee, the amenity determining the price.

"Included in the nominal fee are laundry and cleaning services, but the contractors pay for their clothing, food, and drink. We'll also be guaranteed a percentage of each girl—...each *contractor's* earnings. The percentage will be tied to the length of the lease each one is willing to sign, but no less than fifteen percent and no greater than thirty percent."

Lucille also thought because some men preferred an ample backside while some men preferred an even ampler bosom, having a variety of independent contractors to suit a multitude of customer tastes could only improve cash flows. In short, Lucille wanted to take the power out of the Madame's hands and put it into the hands of each girl turning a trick, empowering each one of them, whether they liked it or not, to be entrepreneurs.

William listened to all of Lucille's ideas and plans, marveling at her audacity (loving it actually) before finally clearing his throat and saying, "I'm offended that you would suggest I turn my boat into a vessel of coital iniquity."

Lucille's eyes widened as her hand rose to cover her mouth. " And I'm offended that you would think I would suggest you turn your boat into a vessel of coital iniquity."

Their eyes then dropped to the bar top and studied it for several long and quiet moments.

Finally, William spoke. "So are we doing this?" His eyes were still on the bar top.

"That depends," Lucille replied, also staring at the bar top. "Are you going to tell my mother and father?"

William's eyebrows rose as he ran his tongue across his teeth. "You gonna tell my brother and his wife?"

Lucille rolled her lips between her teeth.

"In that case," William said as he leaned forward and grabbed the bottle of whiskey. "Mum's the word." He poured each a half glass. He took up his glass.

Lucille took up hers.

They looked each other in the eye.

"Cheers," he said as he winked with his left eye, then puckered his lips and crossed his eyes.

"Cheers," Lucille said as she winked with her right eye, then puckered her lips and crossed her eyes.

Clinking their glasses, they drained them in one.

"That's why you're my favorite niece."

"And you're my favorite uncle."

They set their glasses down and started planning.

It was on this boat that a young Randall Stevens went to work for William as one of his poker players. The Wetherford and Stevens families would be entwined through history from that point on. Some of that history was scandalous like the brief affair between Randall and Lucille which may or may not have produced a child. In truth, it had not, but the truth never could stand in the way of a juicy piece of gossip.

One truth, however, was never a rumor. Despite the affair between Randall and Lucille, the entwinement of the families always involved a Stevens working for a Wetherford. Never the two working together and certainly never a Wetherford working for a Stephens.

Randall was the great-grandfather of Paul Stevens Senior, a man who turned his green thumb into a thriving business. He was a hands-on landscape architect whom Drake's parents vulgarly referred to as the yard man. His son, Paul Junior, was Drake's age.

Wanting his son to follow in his footsteps, Paul Senior would bring the boy with him. He had hoped Paul Junior would take a shine to the job, which he did...except for the Wetherford Estate. Maybe it was because of the size of the house and grounds and the ongoing landscaping changes demanded by the Wetherfords who never seemed to know what they wanted except that what they currently had was not it. It was easy for Paul Junior to slip away from his father's side. That and this was the only job his father had where a boy his age resided. So not only could he slip easily away from his father, but he also had a cohort, a partner in crime.

One day, Drake thought it would be fun for Paul to sneak into the house, grab some snacks and play Nintendo with him. It wasn't hard to sneak. It was a big house.

Paul had grown bored. He wasn't into video games. He preferred to be outside making up games. He wandered into Drake's closet. He whistled. "Man, you've got a lot of clothes."

Drake winced; sure this is where the friendship ended. He paused the video game and joined Paul in the huge walk-in closet. "Yeah?"

Paul laughed. "Oh yeah." He stretched out a hand and fingered the sleeve of a suit jacket. "And you actually have suits. Not one, but...," Paul counted. "*Five* suits," he exclaimed incredulously. "Why do you have so many suits?"

"Don't you have suits?" Drake asked a little defensively.

"No," Paul replied. "I've got a blue blazer and a pair of gray slacks my parents make me wear to special occasions but that's it."

"Doesn't your dad have suits?" Drake asked.

"Well, yeah, but he's a grown-up. Grown-ups are supposed to have suits. It's like the law or something."

"So why's it a problem that I have suits?"

"It isn't, it's just...Dude, you're a kid. Kids are supposed to have a blue blazer and maybe one suit they get for Easter and outgrow by the next Easter." Paul came out of the closet. "Do you wear those suits more than once?"

"Yes," Drake answered, but then admitted, "I don't really mind suits, except the ties. I hate tying them.

Paul's eyebrows raised in disbelief. "Your parents make you wear a real tie?"

Drake nodded. "Don't yours?"

Paul shook his head. "Clip-ons."

Drake's mouth dropped open in astonishment. "They have clip-on ties?"

Paul couldn't help but laugh as he answered, "Yeah." Drake was reacting to clip-on ties the same way Paul had reacted when he'd been told how babies were made.

Paul would accompany his dad and play with Drake until his parents discovered this scandalous fact. James and Stephanie informed Paul Senior his services would no longer be needed and dismissed him.

But Drake's reputation as a malevolent bad egg preceded him and soon not a single private educational institution would accept Drake Wetherford no matter what endowments his parents promised. They were forced to enroll him in the public school system.

There he became reacquainted with his young playmate, Paul Stevens. James and Stephanie were not happy but found that Paul had a focusing effect on their son. His grades were better, he committed less mischief, and so they reluctantly approved of his friendship with the lower-class boy.

For Drake, Paul Junior was something he'd never had before in his life – a friend. And not just a friend, or even a best friend, but a brother. Someone who accepted him unconditionally, who listened to what he had to say, who didn't look up to him because of his family's money or down on him because of his mischief. A person who looked him square in the eye as an equal. Paul just didn't seem to care about the money, the house, or the prep schools. He just liked Drake for Drake. And Drake knew that. Cherished that. He didn't feel that from anyone else in his life, not schoolmates, teachers, family servants, and definitely not his parents.

Paul offered Drake something else as well. Drake had realized something about himself he'd never told anyone. Drake had a complete disconnect from life. Drake never felt like someone living his life, but more like a camera that watched life but didn't understand it. He didn't feel...anything. He didn't understand when people told them how they were feeling, especially his parents. When his parents would talk to him and tell him how they felt ashamed or disappointed by his actions and choices, he would simply stare at them. Sometimes, after watching a television show or movie in which a character would show remorse or pain or sadness, Drake would mimic that character's actions to his parents, and they would be supplicated. And sometimes they would be confused because Drake had perfectly mimicked the wrong emotion.

With Paul, though, he had someone he could observe in all types of situations and social settings. He could ask him questions and gain insight. It didn't help him feel anything, but he could understand better the feeling or emotion or action he was mimicking. And Paul always knew he was mimicking.

Once, while at a party, a girl was flirting heavily with Drake and as usual it went right over Drake's head.

"Dude." Paul punched Drake's arm. "What're you doing?"

"Huh?" Drake rubbed his arm.

"Krista's really into you," Paul said.

"She is?" Drake asked, not surprised, not curious, not anything. But that's what he'd heard Paul say when a girl had told him in the hall at school a girl named Jill was into him in a big way.

Paul rolled his eyes. "She's done everything but rip your clothes off." He leaned into Drake and spoke into his ear so only he could hear. "She asked me if you were gay."

Again, Drake didn't feel anything about this, but he knew being considered gay when you weren't, was supposed to be a bad thing. You were supposed to defend your manhood by either beating up the guy or bedding down the girl. He had no intention of beating up Paul. So he walked over to Krista.

On his way, he wondered what exactly he should do. Introduce himself? Ask her to dance? Offer to get her something to drink? Let her know he knew she was into him?

From the corner of his eye, Drake saw couples who were kissing. Making out.

Krista's eyes went wide as she opened her mouth to say Hi and instead received Drake's tongue. As his lips closed over hers, his arms slipped around her. Krista wrapped her arms around him as she returned the kiss.

Drake could hear whooping and wolf whistles and applause and people shouting, "Way to go, Drake," *and* "Get a room," *and* "Someone separate them before they suffocate."

Finally, Drake felt a hand on his shoulder and a familiar voice in his ear, "All right, Dude, I think you proved your point."

Drake hadn't thought he'd had a point to prove, except that he wasn't gay. Though, as he thought about it, why did he care if anyone thought he was gay or not? He knew he wasn't and that should be enough, shouldn't it?

But then he found himself behind the wheel of his 1956 Maserati A6 coupe with Krista beside him, Paul and Jill in the back seat, headed to a secluded spot to consummate his point. The car had been a gift to Drake from his parents for two very simple reasons. First, Drake had made it through his first two years of public high school without even a detention much less an expulsion. Second, and most important, the one-million-dollar price tag and sheer rarity of the car meant that no other rich kid in New Orleans was driving a 1956 Maserati. There was, after all, the Wetherford reputation at stake. And no matter who was behind the wheel, everyone had to know that person was a Wetherford. William, James, and Mildred would be rolling over in their graves.

Drake drove, constantly stealing glances in the mirror at Paul and Jill, at a loss as to what exactly he was supposed to do next and when. At the party, that had been easy, relatively speaking, he'd taken cues from what others were doing. But now...

Drake watched Krista furtively. She looked nervous and excited, apprehensive and impatient, all at the same time. She kept fidgeting with her hands, alternately wringing them, then folding her arms across her chest almost protectively, then running her fingers through her hair as she glanced over her shoulder. Then she would look at Drake and smile, a mix of flirtatiousness and nausea. But through all of it, Drake could tell everything she was doing was motivated by emotion.

That was a thing with Drake, he just didn't understand emotion. He wasn't sure if he'd ever felt emotion. He knew the emotional keywords and catchphrases; every child learns them as they go through that mimicking stage. But Drake realized he'd never moved past the mimicking phase. He *knew* the words, but he didn't *feel* the words. He *mimicked* the actions associated with the emotions. He wasn't *motivated* by the emotions.

Drake felt tired. This was too much work. He just wanted to be alone. Alone with Paul. Paul wasn't any effort. When Paul uttered his next husky direction, Drake responded with a flat, "No."

Drake waited for the protests from Paul, but none came. Instead, he heard Paul begin to dress as he told Jill to get dressed as well. She wanted to know why. She sounded overheated. Paul only told her he was taking her home.

Nothing else was said as Drake turned the car around and accepted directions from Paul to Jill's house. They dropped both girls off.

Paul climbed into the front seat.

Drake waited for Paul to tell him what an idiot he was. Ask him if he wasn't really gay.

Paul just said, "I think there's some leftover pizza in the fridge at my house."

They went to Paul's house, ate the leftover pizza, drank all the soda in the house, and fell asleep watching Paul's favorite movie, *The Big Red One*.

The next morning, Drake accompanied Paul's family on a visit to Randall Stevens. That day would change Drake's life forever. He could still smell the old man's tobacco as he sat on his porch in his rocker, lighting an old pipe, and pausing with a reminiscent smile before telling Drake about James and William Wetherford.

Chapter 16

Randall Stevens's gnarled, leathery fingers worked the tobacco deftly into the old pipe, as the old man stared hard at the young Drake Wetherford. Stuffing the stem of the pipe between his teeth, he lit a match and puffed like an old coal locomotive, spewing blue-gray smoke from his nose and mouth.

Drake eyed the man curiously. At first, he'd thought the old man had taken an immediate dislike to him, but when he looked into those surprisingly clear deep blue eyes, he found not anger but surprised recognition, like the old man couldn't decide if he were seeing a ghost or a long-lost friend who hadn't aged along with him.

The corners of the old man's lips finally curled into a smile that rippled across the wrinkles on his face like ripples across the surface of a pond. "You look like him you know." His voice was deep and gravelly. "And from what young Paul tells me, his looks aren't the only thing you inherited from him."

Drake was completely nonplussed. "Who do I look like, Sir?"

"Your Great Uncle William." The old man's eyes beamed.

Drake could feel his heart thump audibly in his chest. It was the first time someone outside his grandfather hadn't whispered the name without shame or embarrassment, let alone speak it proudly out loud. "My grandfather used to tell me that."

"Good man, your grandfather," Randall Stevens pulled the pipe from his lips, "I wanted to go to his funeral, but I knew your family wouldn't have approved. So I stayed here and smoked a pipe in his honor." He barked a regretful smoker's hack that sounded to Drake what the backfire from an old coal engine must sound like. "He had a small streak of William too, but he was a lot more like James."

Drake had moved to the end of his seat. Here before him was a man who'd known his grandfather, great-grandfather, and great-uncle. A thousand questions chased each other around his skull. His lips trembled as questions fell from his brain onto his tongue.

Randall Stevens seemed to understand. He raised a hand. "Easy there, young man. Don't run over an old man so early in the day." He puffed on his pipe in thoughtful silence. "I'll make a deal with you. Every time you come and see me, I'll answer a few of your questions, and tell you some stories of your family."

Drake's mouth went dry, and he simply nodded.

The old man nodded back and smiled. "Well, you're here, so let me start today by telling you how I first met William."

Paul Senior interjected. "Drake, I need to add a stipulation to this little deal you and my dad have made."

Drake jumped. He'd forgotten anyone else was in the room. "I'm sorry?"

"You gotta promise me you won't tell anybody what you hear."

"Why?"

Paul Senior. shared a strained look with his wife. "Let's just say your parents' influence can be far-reaching, and it isn't always...beneficial."

Drake's eyes narrowed as his voice tightened. He wasn't always on the best terms with his parents. Had started to suspect that their concern for appearance was covering up for a lack of substance in their civic, social, and humanitarian concerns. The contrast between the smiles and words spoken at press conferences and fundraising events was striking with the sour faces and unkind words spoken at home regarding the people at the press conferences and fundraising events. But all that was just nasty gossip compared to the looks and words spoken about the people these events assisted. Even so, Drake didn't want to believe his parents would act with malicious aforethought. Yet, as he looked around the room, it was evident that these people, who treated him like an equal not as superior or inferior, had been the recipients of just that. He could feel his nails bite into his palms as his hands clenched into fists.

"I'm sorry."

Paul Senior held up a hand. "Don't want an apology. I would just rather you not discuss with any Wetherfords what you hear from Dad. In fact, I hate to say it, but it might be better if you didn't even mention to your folks you were talking to him. I just don't think any of us could take being the nail again."

"I don't understand."

Randall Stevens chuckled. "It's an old saying. It's better to be the hammer than the nail. Your parents have made nails out of a lot of people in this town. They've just been clever enough to not be seen as the hammer."

Drake's fists clenched tighter. "That's not right."

"That's okay." The old man banged the pipe on the heel of his hand. The spent tobacco spilled onto the porch beside him. "If you aren't a nail at some point in this life, you will be in the next. There's only one hammer." His chuckle turned into a booming cough. "Now that's not the first time you want to be feeling like a nail."

"Dad, you okay?" Paul Senior's wife, Patty, wiped blood and spittle from the old man's chin.

"I've got a fresh pair of ears to hear my stories of the dearest man I ever did know." He grabbed a handkerchief from his pocket and mopped his face. "I haven't felt this good since…" His voice trailed off.

"Since what, Dad?" Patty ran a finger through the snow-white wisps of hair clinging stubbornly to the old man's head.

Grandpa Stevens smiled and patted her hand. "That's a memory not to be shared with women or children." He stuffed the handkerchief back into his shirt pocket and took a sip of the sweet iced tea sitting beside him. He smiled kindly at Drake. "Now, let me tell you a story."

Drake's hands relaxed as he swallowed hard.

"I first met William when I was a young man of nineteen, full of fire and vinegar. Didn't need anybody telling me what to do and too good for a regular job. I was God's gift to the ladies and a rattlesnake in a fight, or so I thought. I was a really good poker player so in the evening I would look for a game or two in whatever town I was in and at the end of the night I had a couple of days' funds for carousing and bumming around. Back in those days, you could live well on a few dollars, and I'd have more than a few.

"Well, this one night I was in Baton Rouge and came upon a game in this little gin joint. The players looked seedy but the money in the pot would set me up for a month of nice living and ladies. So I threw my hat in and sure enough, after a couple of hours I was ahead, way ahead. And the table wasn't so happy about that, except for this one guy who thought it was funny. He was the one guy who wasn't losing any money to me. This guy knew when I was bluffing, knew what cards I was holding, and I got the distinct impression he was letting me win when I did. He was big. Looked like he could drive nails with his fists. He was drinking as much as anyone else, but it didn't seem to me that it had much effect on him.

"The other guys at the table weren't as amused as this guy, and they let me know it. I wanted to go, but they wouldn't let me, they wanted one more hand to win their money back, but I kept winning. Finally, this one guy who was as shifty-eyed as a raccoon pulled a knife. That's when the big guy got involved. I didn't think a man that big could move that fast. Those guys didn't stand a chance. It was over in less than a minute. After the last guy dropped, he turned to me, offered me his hand, said his name was William and he had a job for me if I was interested."

The old man took another sip of tea and eyed Drake. He seemed to understand that the story wasn't all that extraordinary, how many bar fights had taken place over cards since Man had invented bars and cards, but for this young listener in front of him, hanging on every word, soaking up every detail of William, his flesh and blood, this was beyond fantastic. This was a story no one in the family knew, not even Drake's grandfather.

Drake had sat quietly through the story, though he'd wanted to interrupt the old man constantly demanding more details. But that didn't seem necessary, now he'd heard the story. He knew this old man would tell him more and he resolved to come visit him as much as he could, every day, if possible, if not, at least once a week. He looked at the old man and realized he was waiting for Drake to ask him about the job. So he did.

The man's lips curled into a mischievous grin. "Play cards on his gambling boat."

"How's that a job?" Paul Junior asked, just as caught up in the story.

"I was on a salary. What I won stayed in the house, but it gave the other players the idea they could win, and some did, and they'd return and lose. But William had a group of us that not even the dealers knew were working for him."

"That doesn't sound legal." Paul Junior shot a dubious look at his grandfather.

"May not've been," the grandfather said with a nonchalant wave of his hand, "but it certainly was lucrative." He smiled, revealing brown stained teeth, and winked at Drake. Drake thought Mr. Randall Stevens was just about the most brilliant man he'd ever met.

Drake went to see Randall Stevens the next Saturday, sneaking out before his parents woke that morning. He stayed the entire day, making lunch and dinner for the two of them. He promised the old man he'd come again the next Saturday, which he did, as well as the Saturday after that until he was going every Saturday. He would make lunch and dinner, and clean the old man's house. Even help the old man shave. His parents asked what he was doing, but he always evaded telling them the truth. They didn't push it. Drake's grades and behavior at school were improving, and he was the perfect Wetherford at home. Whatever he was up to on Saturdays had to be a good thing.

Once summer came, Drake went every day. Some days, he and the old man would simply sit on the porch sipping lemonade or iced tea and not speak, just watching the day pass by. On other days, the old man would tell one story after another about William. His favorite was the one that showed William's loyalty to his family.

One night William and Randall were in a bar having a couple of drinks, talking about hopes and dreams when a man down at the end of the bar started speaking unfavorably about his brother James. He also had some lewd comments about James' wife. William flagged down the bartender and asked for a full bottle of bourbon. The bartender eyed William, but only for a minute. He could hear what the man was saying, everyone in the bar could. He brought William the bottle and walked into the back room. William picked up the bottle, walked up to the man, and shattered it over the man's head. The smell of blood and bourbon permeated the bar. The bartender walked back behind the bar as William reached into his pocket, pulled out a wad of cash, and handed it to the bartender.

Some days, his friend Paul would go with him and the old man would teach them how to play cards, smoke cigars and pipes, and drink whiskey. Randall liked whiskey, and sometimes when Drake and Paul showed up, Randall would confess to having had a party the night before. On these days, needing time to confess his sins to the Almighty in exchange for feeling better, he'd send the two boys off fishing at the stream on his property.

One day, after a particularly successful afternoon, the boys were preparing their catches, catfish and brim, for dinner when Paul asked his grandfather, "So who comes to your parties?"

Randall's aged face stretched into a crooked grin, revealing his yellow-brown teeth, "Why Misters John Walker and Jasper Newton, of course."

"Jasper Newton?" Drake asked.

The old man winked, "Jack Daniel."

Paul's parents tried paying Drake for his caretaking duties, but he wouldn't hear of it, letting them know how insulted he was they would think he would take money from the people he considered his family. Randall Stephens had laughed, called him William, and told him not to break a bottle over anybody's head.

The old man was old, no one knew just how old, not even Randall Stephens, but they guessed he had to be over a hundred. In mid-July of that summer, his health took a turn for the worse, but he wouldn't allow himself to be taken away from his home. He and Death had played cards before and he'd won, but sooner or later, he'd told Paul, the house won. And when it did, he wouldn't be in some cold, sterile hospital room, but surrounded by his memories.

Drake was there the day the house won. He closed the old man's eyes, placed his pipe in his hands, and crossed them over his heart. He cried and then called Paul Senior. He stayed with the body till the coroner's van pulled away from the house. The Stephens thanked him for all he did and told him it might be better if he didn't come to the funeral. But Drake was going to be at that funeral, and he made sure nobody knew. After the funeral, he stole a bottle of whiskey from his parents' liquor cabinet and went to the old man's house. He pulled from his pocket the old man's pipe, a gift from Paul Senior, filled it with tobacco just like Randall Stephens had taught him, lit it, opened the bottle, took a swig, and sat down on the porch.

Chapter 17

The school year started the month after Randall Stephens passed away. Drake showed up most days physically, but mentally he was lost in the stories the old man had told him. He just couldn't concentrate, didn't care to concentrate, and disliked anyone who insisted he try harder. His general lack of interest in what authority had to say blossomed into full disdain. By Thanksgiving break, he'd spent more time in after-school detention than he had in P.E. class. He spent the first week after Christmas break at home for punching the coach in the face, breaking the man's nose.

Drake wasn't as violent with his other teachers, but he was no less insubordinate. He was sent to the Dean's office so regularly that the school secretary had a joke that Drake was even more dependable than an atomic clock to set her watch by. Sometimes he was sent to the Dean for things he didn't do but didn't deny when he was confronted. One fine Tuesday morning Drake was stopped by Mr. Maitlin the Orchestra teacher.

"What do you know about some bows that were burnt yesterday afternoon?" Maitlin bellowed as his fingers dug into Drake's shoulder.

Drake shook the man's hand free. "I know horsehair stinks when it's on fire." Drake had no idea what horsehair smelled like. Hadn't known that bows for violins were strung with horsehair. He hadn't even been in school that afternoon, he'd cut after lunch to go to the creek behind the old man's house, something he did every couple of weeks. He'd stopped in a McDonald's when he got back and heard Keith Duncombe laughing about lighting the bows on fire and how bad they smelled.

The Dean had wanted to expel him, but Drake's parents made a sizable donation to the high school football program, enough to purchase new uniforms and equipment, remodel the weight room and locker room, and refurbish the high school stadium in exchange for a three-day suspension.

Most teachers wanted to think Drake Wetherford was just hanging with the wrong crowd, but he didn't seem to hang out with anyone except Paul Stephens. And when he got into trouble, he was always by himself. Some wanted to blame his home life, but his parents were wealthy, apparently happily married, and Drake had been born with more than a silver spoon, he had an entire place setting.

The most frustrating thing about Drake Wetherford all his teachers could agree on was he didn't suffer from a lack of intelligence but motivation and focus. When Drake showed up and paid attention and turned in an assignment or took a test, he always aced it. There was no question in anyone's mind if he would just apply himself, he could write his ticket to the future. But no faculty member could reach him.

The only person who seemed to have any influence over Drake was Paul Stephens. His teachers felt Paul was a good kid and a hard-working student who fought tooth and nail for every C+ and B- he got. School was just not easy for him. The teachers took advantage of Paul's influence and would speak to him about some upcoming assignments that Drake needed to complete so he could pass. Paul always spoke to Drake and Drake always followed Paul's advice. Drake managed to pass his classes each semester and advance to the next school year until it was time to graduate.

It was a Friday night in early April and Drake was at the only place that felt like home to him, the Stephens's house. He was there most Friday nights and even if he wasn't he was still with Paul. Paul's mother had popped the boys a huge bowl of popcorn and brewed a gallon jug of sweet tea, her part of their Friday night ritual. There was only one part of the ritual Drake dreaded every time Paul slid a videotape into the VCR, hiding it from Drake's view and telling him it was a surprise, but not to worry he was going to love it.

"Nooooo," Drake groaned as the opening credits to *The Big Red One* with Lee Marvin appeared on the television screen. He threw a handful of popcorn at Paul. "Are you serious?"

"What?" Paul threw a handful of popcorn back at Drake. "This is the greatest film ever made."

Drake picked popcorn out of his hair. "I repeat the question. Are you serious?" Drake didn't mind the movie and had actually enjoyed the first few times they'd watched it together, but he just didn't understand Paul's enamored of the film.

Paul had seen it with his dad when the film came out in 1980 and had fallen in love with it. A year later he'd found a bootleg copy of it at a yard sale his mother had dragged him to. The video was a quarter and Paul had scrounged the car to find a dime, two nickels, and five pennies to buy it. It was a bad copy to begin with, blurry, and sometimes the picture didn't fit on the screen. The sound was touch and go and sometimes you had to read lips to figure out what was going on. By that April Friday night, however, the tape was only a ribbon of what it had been.

"You've seen this movie over a hundred times," Drake whined as he threw the popcorn he'd plucked from his hair back at Paul. "I know 'cause I've watched it with you every Friday night for the past year."

In truth, Drake didn't mind so much. Paul was his friend, his best friend, his only friend, and if it made Paul happy, well then, that was okay by him. This film, especially this worn-out bootleg copy, made Paul very happy. Paul wasn't a morose kid, enamored with history or even fascinated by violence, but this movie lit him up like nothing else could. The idea of being part of something bigger, something grander than himself, than his community excited him. Soldiers were like knights of old, devoted to serving and protecting their king and their fellow countrymen. They alone understood the truth that freedom wasn't free. In short, Paul was a patriot.

He found each funny moment just as funny as when he'd first seen it, the same with the sad moments and tense moments. He leaned forward in all the same places, back in all the others. Drake was fascinated by Paul's continuity. Paul, like the film, was the same story every time the video played.

What made Drake happy was the popcorn, the gallon jug of sweet-iced tea, and people who seemed to love him despite who he was. With his parents, it was all about the family reputation, and love and acceptance were delivered on a graduated scale of how well he upheld that reputation. At school, it was all about concentration and application, and the almighty grade. Teachers loved students who genuflected properly to the 'A' and were as repulsed as a television preacher talking about Satan and the fiery waters with the 'F'. Grades and perfect behavior were all schools were concerned about, not what was going on on the inside, just the outside. But here it was different. Paul and his family knew about Drake's full silver place setting and his screw-ups and didn't care about either. Not a flip.

But tonight, with graduation only a couple of months away, Drake didn't want to watch Paul watch the movie.

"You still plan on going into the service?" Drake faced the television, but his eyes were on Paul.

"Not service," Paul corrected as he took a big swig of sweet-iced tea, "Army."

Drake grinned. Paul's devotion to this movie was way out of control, he thought. He waited for Paul to take the bait which, of course, he did. Paul knew Drake well enough to know when Drake needed to talk.

"What about you? Are you gonna be a Harvard man or a Yale man?" Paul munched on popcorn, eyes on the television screen, but Drake knew he had Paul's complete attention.

"Don't forget Brown and Oxford."

"Oxford?" Paul put on an English accent. "Are you gonna turn into a bloody Brit? Start calling your underwear knickers?"

They laughed and threw popcorn at each other. What would I do without Paul, Drake wondered. Paul was his moral compass, Prozac, and Ritalin, all in one. Drake knew he'd have never made it through school, much less life, without Paul. Now his parents were applying to colleges for him, applications accompanied by sizable donations, though not a single college anywhere near Paul and his family. Drake didn't know what aggravated him more, his parents' plans for his life or the impending separation from Paul. How was he supposed to find his way in this world if his parents deprived him of his compass?

For Paul's part, he didn't like the idea of parting ways with Drake after graduation any more than Drake did. But Paul understood it for what it was. They were from two different worlds, and eventually, Paul knew, Drake's world would claim him back. Drake would go to an Ivy League school, get a degree in business or law, and keep the Wetherford family traditions alive and well for another generation. Who knows, maybe he'd even go into politics, become President, and Paul could have any traffic ticket fixed, he liked to joke to himself, or at least he could say he knew him when.

"I don't know." Drake shifted to face Paul. "What do you think?"

"I think you should shut up and watch the movie." Paul hit the Pause button on the remote and faced Drake. "What do you want?"

"What do I want?" Drake stared down at his hands. What did he want? He wanted his parents to get off his back. He wanted to forget he was a

Wetherford. He wanted to call his parents' bluff when they said they'd cut him off from the money if he didn't straighten up and fly right, whatever that tired cliché was supposed to mean. He decided to answer with a diversion.

"World peace, or if that's too much, whirled peas, I guess. What about you?"

Paul looked at the television and pointed. Lee Marvin was frozen on the screen. "I'm gonna be Lee."

"You don't want to go to college?"

Paul looked back at Drake. "Sure I want to go to college, but I'm just not college material right now. And even if I was, I gotta find a job anyway to pay for it. I ain't got the grades for an academic ride and I don't play a sport." He fumbled absently with the popcorn. "I'd love to go to Harvard or Yale or Brown, and maybe after a few years in the Army, I can sock the money away for community college or LSU." He smiled at his feet. "Or who knows? Maybe I'll make a career out of the military and let them pay for my schooling while I serve. Be one of those guys who retires after twenty years as an NCO with a doctorate or something."

Drake looked at Paul and realized he truly admired his friend. Paul knew who he was, knew his strengths and weaknesses, and was okay with that. He was comfortable with himself. Even liked himself. Drake had never liked himself and had never been comfortable in his skin. He felt a gnawing hollowness in his chest at the thought of parting ways with Paul, but a thought crossed his mind. It filled the hollow spot and spilled over until he could feel it surging through his veins as surely as his blood. But what would Paul think?

"Now I go back to my original question." Paul was looking hard at Drake. "What do *you* want?"

Drake cleared his throat and dropped his gaze to the floor, his tongue groping for the words. "I want to know if you'd like some company." He felt his ears, his cheeks, even his eyebrows, plume with the heat of embarrassment and he chastised himself. He wanted to see Paul's reaction, knew he'd be able to read it on his face before he said a word, but he couldn't pull his eyes up from studying the dirt on his Adidas sneakers.

If he'd been able to see Paul's face, he would've seen a cocktail of consternation and jubilance, with a chaser of pensiveness. Paul would love nothing more than to go into the Army with Drake by his side, but he'd also learned a thing or two from his grandfather. The old man had told Paul on more than one occasion that a true friend always put the friend ahead of the friendship even when it might cost him that friendship.

"I don't know if that's such a great idea, Drake." He sat up straight, squaring his shoulders. "I just don't know if you'd be able to cut it. I mean you're more frat boy than grunt."

Drake's eyes narrowed to slits just wide enough for the daggers shooting out from his sockets at his friend.

Paul wanted to flinch under that gaze, but he willed his body to stand his ground. He continued. "Look, I didn't mean it that way. I just mean, you've got a lot of opportunities, a lot of opportunities I'd love to have. Don't limit yourself by hanging out with me."

Drake couldn't believe what he was hearing. Was Paul giving him the shove off, saying that Drake was better off without him? It was like needing a blood transfusion and the only guy on the planet with your blood type was turning you down because he thinks you'd be better off dead than have his blood in your veins.

"Limit myself? Is that what you think I've been doing all these years? Limiting myself?" He thought back over the past several years. "You're the only reason I'm graduating and not dating my bunkmate in Juvie. Can you really see me in college? You think I'd last ten minutes?"

"Oh, you'd make it." Paul couldn't help but smile. "Though I don't know what kind of reputation the college would have after you finished with it."

Drake couldn't help but smile as well. "Not to mention how many buildings would be left standing."

Paul raised a hand. "Two. The cafeteria and your favorite sorority house."

Drake laughed. "See, I could use the demolitions training. All I need is the sorority house. They have kitchens, you know."

Paul eyed Drake thoughtfully. "Well, people do like a president whose served in uniform. That'll help with my tickets."

"What're you talking about?" Drake laughed, though not sure if anything Paul had said was supposed to be funny.

Paul waved him off. "Okay." He said after a moment of contemplation, nodding his head and extending his hand towards Drake. "Let's do it."

Drake took Paul's hand. "Sempre Fi."
Paul dropped the handshake. "That's the Marines, you dope.

Chapter 18

Drake's father, James, tapped his crystal wine glass for everyone's attention. The dinner guests stopped their conversations and dutifully looked upon their host with rapt attention. It was two weeks after graduation and the evening of Drake's eighteenth birthday. His parents had insisted on throwing him a birthday bash and graduation celebration. Looking around the room, however, Drake saw little that resembled a bash or a celebration.

The guests, dressed in tuxedos and cocktail dresses, spoke in hushed tones as if they were at a funeral or wake and cast looks at Drake of polite disinterest or barely concealed amusement or even frowned as if seeing a dog covered in vomit whenever they bothered to acknowledge his presence. Of course, these were all his parents' friends, acquaintances, clients, and others they just wanted to impress. Paul, dressed in one of Drake's suits, was the only person at the party Drake had been allowed to invite. The music was not provided by a DJ and was not Rock or Pop, but chamber music elegantly played by a string quartet.

His father, glowing with pride and booze, smiled lazily at his dinner guests as he placed a hand on his wife's shoulder, who smiled glassily if not absently up through her husband.

"Thank you. As you know this little shindig..."

Drake snickered. His father always said things like that. He thought it was self-deprecating and therefore cute, like referring to the mansion and grounds as the little shack on the bayou. People always gave his father a courtesy smile or laugh, like they did now, but for Drake, it was like running a cheese grater across his nipples, and he wondered if felt the same for these people.

His father continued, "...is in honor of my son, Drake, grown to be a fine young man."

Some of the guests stifled their snickers with coughing and wine.

James Wetherford didn't notice. He smiled at Drake, and Drake wondered if his father could even focus on him. "Young Master Wetherford has received offers from a few, small unknown schools like Harvard, Yale, and Stanford. Even a little school across the lake..."

He was referring to Oxford University in England. Drake rolled his eyes.

"...would like him to grace them with his presence. Yes, the future looks bright for my son and I thought he could share with those of us gathered here in his honor to let us know what his plans might be."

Drake flushed, shaking his head.

"You haven't told them?" Paul said under his breath.

"No, I didn't," Drake whispered back. He looked at his dad and cleared his throat. "I don't think this is the right time."

"Now, Drake, don't be shy." He stroked his wife's neck. "Your mother and I would like to know what you've decided to do. Is it Harvard?"

Drake shook his head.

"Yale?" His mother offered.

Drake shook his head in her direction.

"Oxford, is it?" James sounded relieved.

"None of them."

James smiled. "Brown it is." He raised his glass and gestured for the other dinner guests to do the same.

"I'm not going to college, Dad."

The room grew deafeningly quiet, and the dinner guests froze into statuettes only letting their eyes dart back and forth between their host at one end of the table and the young guest of honor at the other end.

James Wetherford's face darkened as he set the wine glass down with a trembling hand. The glass tipped and the crisp white tablecloth blushed crimson. "What are you going to do?"

"I'm going into the Army with Paul."

James' eyes drew a bead on Paul like a laser sight and Paul shrunk into the cushions of his chair.

Stephanie, Drake's mother, gasped and sunk into her chair, very melodramatic Drake thought.

James looked back at his son. "No."

"Excuse me?" Drake asked.

"No, you're not going to join the Army with Paul. I won't allow it." His hand was no longer on his wife's shoulder but clenched into a fist.

"You can't stop me." Now Drake was on his feet.

"I won't allow you to hurt your mother like this." James thrust a finger in Stephanie's direction.

"What's mom got to do with this?"

"Can't you see what this is doing to her?" James nodded at Stephanie.

Drake looked at his mother. She did look nauseated.

"But—"

James interrupted. "I don't want to hear it. You're not joining the Army and that's final."

"But I've already joined up." Drake blurted it out fast, and he could see it hit his father in the gut like a cramp from bad seafood. But he felt good, and he continued. "I signed on the dotted line this morning. I leave in three weeks." He paused before adding, "With Paul."

James slammed his fist down on the table. "How dare you. How dare you turn this matter into a public spectacle."

The dinner guests knew they would be talking about this for the rest of the summer, maybe even into the fall. But right now, they kept as quiet as a lioness selecting the weak or the injured from the herd for the next meal. Or hyenas, pacing and pawing the ground, quietly snickering, waiting their turn to sink their teeth into the carrion of James and Stephanie.

Drake looked his father in the eye. "That was never my intention."

James raised an incredulous eyebrow. "Oh, really? What *was* your intention?"

"To never tell you at all."

James and Drake stared hard at each other like a game between two kids to see who would blink first. The table, the guests, even Stephanie, lay unseen and forgotten as the two men stood motionless.

Stephanie's face crinkled as if she too could see a dog covered in vomit as she looked between her husband and her son and the dinner guests. How on earth could they, James and Stephanie, recover? She wanted to stand up, walk right over to her son, and slap him...what was it she'd heard her mother say..., into next week? Yes, that was it. She wanted to slap Drake into next week. How could he do this to his parents, after all they had done for him? They'd covered a multitude of his sins with dollar signs, but now he'd made it personal.

In front of our friends.

And the look on her face, the one Drake had become so accustomed to over the years, the look of disappointment soured to a black, sorrowful regret, regret that this young man ruining everything she and her husband had worked so hard for was ever born.

Drake saw the look on his mother's face and knew it for what it was. He expected his heart to break, his knees to weaken and his spirit to fold. But they didn't. Instead, he felt the burden of his name, of his family history slough off him. He nodded a quiet acknowledgment and goodbye.

James was not ready to say goodbye, to regret the birth of his only son. His mind searched, groped, and scratched like a man sliding down a cliff to the jagged, watery death below for any plausible reason as to why this was happening. He brightened as a snatch of root jutting from a cleft caught his mind.

"Look, Son, if you're thinking of this as a stepping-stone to politics, I applaud you, but there are better, easier ways of going about this. Senator Barton is a good friend. I'm sure we could arrange for you to attend West Point or Annapolis."

Drake shook his head. He opened his mouth but closed it again. There was no use speaking. His parents had never understood him, had never understood he'd never been enamored with the Wetherford legacy his parents' generation was trying to create, believed you truly treated people like you wanted to be treated, had never understood just how much of the original Wetherford blood flowed through his veins. He turned to Paul. "Let's get outta here."

Paul stood up. "Are you sure?"

Drake, didn't glance back at his parents, didn't need to; just nodded. They turned and started to leave.

James' voice boomed out. "Drake. You leave. You do this and you're cut off. The money, the cars, the name. Everything."

Drake stopped. How cliché, he thought, how incredibly tired and cliché. That's all his father was, just a tired cliché. Maybe under other circumstances, this realization would have hurt or made him angry or even annoyed. But right now, he felt nothing, neither sadness nor happiness, not even numbness. He just knew like he'd known nothing else in his life that it was time to go. He turned to his father.

His father, misinterpreting Drake's body language, smiled triumphantly. "I see you don't hold my money in contempt."

Drake smirked. "No, Dad. Just you." With that he turned on his heel and walked straight out of the house, his father screaming after him.

"You're done, you hear that, you ungrateful little brat? You're cut off. You're no longer my son. You're. *Cut.* OFF."

Drake didn't flinch, just walked out the door, straight to Paul's vehicle, and stood by the passenger door. "Can I crash at your place?"

Paul smiled. "No. But you can stay at my place. I'm sure Mom and Dad won't mind."

They got into the beat-up little Toyota Tacoma and drove off. Drake didn't hear the rest of his father's railings. Nor was he there when Leonard Chapman, the family attorney, came quietly up to James Wetherford, took him gently by the elbow, and led him silently out of the dining room and into the study.

"You can't do that," Leonard said quietly as he shut the door. He moved over to the liquor cart and poured two tumblers of scotch and soda.

"Can't do what?" James was furious. It just seemed to him everyone had lost their mind, telling him, James Wetherford, what they were going to do and what he couldn't do. It was mutiny and he felt the urge to grab Leonard by the scruff of his neck and toss him right of his house on his ear, giving him a swift kick in the can as he did.

"Cut Drake off. You can't do that." Leonard sipped from his glass and offered the other to James who waved him off. "Go on, take it You're gonna need it after I finish." He motioned for James to sit.

James took the drink, suppressed the urge to throw it into Leonard Chapman's face, and sat down on the Corinthian leather couch.

Leonard took another swallow and sat down in the matching leather armchair opposite the couch. He was a quiet, unassuming man, but he knew how to command a courtroom, or any room for that matter. He took another sip of his drink.

Setting his untouched glass down on the small, finished walnut coffee table, James shot daggers at his attorney. "Why can't I do that?"

"Your father," Leonard said, setting down his glass. "Or more specifically, your father's will. Your father was afraid something like this might happen and so he made provisions to guard against it."

"I was at the reading of my dad's will. I've even read it for myself. There's nothing in it about this."

"That's where you're wrong." Leonard folded his hands in his lap comfortably. "Have you ever heard of a reversion?"

James shook his head.

Leonard nodded. "I didn't think so. It's a clause in a will that allows for items passed on by inheritance to revert back to the direct heirs of an estate."

"I don't remember any *reversion* in his will," James spat.

"The reversion is in a sealed addendum which your father certified and then sealed before a judge." He paused to let this statement sink in. "Technically, I'm in contempt for revealing this to you, but in the light of recent events," he nodded towards the dining room, "I think it best you know this now."

Leonard didn't speak but let the silence passing between them sober his client further. James sank into the couch even more pathetically than Paul had sunk into his dining room chair. A contempt charge was worth this moment. Disbarment was worth this moment, Leonard realized.

Leonard Chapman was a third-generation attorney and a second-generation Wetherford family attorney. His father had been hired by James Wetherford's father and when Leonard had graduated from Tulane Law School, he'd gone to work for his dad. When his father retired, he took over the family business of taking care of the Wetherfords. It was a financially and spiritually rewarding job until James and Stephanie assumed the throne of the Wetherford hierarchy.

Now Leonard took care of the family business for no other reason than protecting Drake's interest. His son, currently a Captain in the Army's Judge Advocate General's corps, would not take over the family business. Leonard wouldn't allow that, not after what he'd seen tonight.

He decided he wanted another sip of scotch before he continued. "Your father's addendum contains a reversion and a trust. The trust is to be available to Drake upon his eighteenth birthday. The original principal amount, five hundred thousand dollars, was invested in a very well-rounded portfolio. The trust was set up when Drake was three years old and has grown into a rather substantial amount of money. Your father invested very smartly.

"The reversion states that if you and Stephanie disown Drake, your inheritance reverts to James, or more specifically the person named as his sole beneficiary, Drake. In short, Drake has, as of this evening, become heir to *ninety* percent of all things Wetherford, or approximately 1.3 billion dollars which will be given to him on his twenty-first birthday. The remaining ten percent will be divvied among you and the other Wetherfords. If you and Stephanie, however, wish to fight for that ninety percent, your father's addendum states your portion of the inheritance will be reduced to a monthly stipend which will allow you to survive, but not continue in your current lifestyle."

James melted into the Corinthian leather and Leonard had to bite his tongue to keep from smiling. Disbarment and jail time for contempt were definitely worth what he was witnessing. The mighty James Wetherford looked ready to wet his pants, suck his thumb and cry for his mommy. Only one thing left to do.

Leonard stood and inhaled a very satisfying breath. "The addendum charges me to watch over Drake Wetherford's affairs until Drake deems my services no longer necessary." He reached over and picked up his scotch and soda. "As for my services to you and Stephanie, I no longer deem them necessary."

James stirred at this last statement. "You can't do that." His voice squeaked.

Leonard smiled, drained his tumbler, and set it down. "Yes, I can." He turned to leave, stopped, and turned back to the couch. "My compliments to you and Stephanie for a very memorable evening."

James watched Leonard turn and leave the study. He sat there, not moving, till the sweat from the ice on the glass, like his own grand opinion of himself, completely evaporated.

Chapter 19

The Blackhawk helicopter banked left, and the contents of Drake's stomach lurched upward. Drake swallowed hard and grimaced from the burn in his throat. He looked over to Paul who lay relaxed against the bulkhead, eyes closed, head bobbing, headphones blasting what Drake couldn't hear, but he was pretty sure was *The Devil Went Down to Georgia* by Charlie Daniels or *Swamp Music* by Lynyrd Skynyrd. Both tapes were as worn out as his tape of *The Big Red One*.

It was Paul's ritual and Drake marveled at his ability to sleep on a helicopter. Drake could never sleep on his way to a mission. He was always too hopped on adrenaline to sleep. His ritual was to swallow lunch back down, marvel at Paul sleeping, and think back over their past together in the Service.

Three weeks after he walked out of his parents' dinner party, they'd caught the six A.M Greyhound bus from New Orleans bound for Columbus, Georgia, and Fort Benning, the home of the Army Infantry. Drake had thought Louisiana had been hot and humid, but, Georgia or the military, or both, had a stockpile of humidity stored at Columbus. Humidity and red clay.

As they stepped off the bus at the Greyhound station Drake opened his mouth to ask Paul how they'd get to the base or post or fort, whatever it was called, when a man dressed in Army fatigues and a sour face pointed at him and Paul and threw a thumb over his shoulder at the school bus painted green parked behind him. How this man knew who they were he wasn't sure. In the weeks to come, Drake would become convinced all NCOs could read minds and knew the future better than any fortune teller.

On the bus, twenty young men sat all looking the same: a shot of exhilaration chased by a pint of dread. They found a seat together and sat down, remaining quiet. A few more dreadfully exhilarated young men climbed onto the bus and did the same. Finally, the sour-faced man jumped on the bus, tapped the driver's shoulder, and turned and faced forward as the bus stuttered away from the curb.

Slowly, the tension, mixed with the feeling of being on a school bus headed for a field trip, loosened the young men's tongues and they began to talk, introduce themselves, and even laugh. The soldier standing beside the driver never sat or turned around. They were all complete non-entities to him. As the bus passed through the main gate, the conversations died down and every eye was gazing out the windows trying to take in every sight.

The bus squeaked to a stop and the soldier jumped out as the bus driver opened the door. The young men got up and started to exit the bus as a man who looked more like a shaved gorilla in fatigues marched up to the bus. His arms, the diameter of Drake's waist and painted with tattoos, reached up and grabbed the first man coming off the bus who'd made the unfortunate mistake of turning back to say something to the guy behind him, and threw him to the ground.

"Who told you you could talk on my bus?" The man screamed, spittle covering the next man. "Get off my bus."

Drake, who'd thought of embarrassing Paul by yelling Sempre Fi as he got off the bus, thought the best thing he could do was keep his mouth shut.

The man was still screaming, pushing, pulling, and generally abusing this group of recruits as he started to march them off to only God knew where, Drake surmised. Drake had trouble understanding the man most of the time, which was something the screaming gorilla found to be rude on Drake's part. Drake whispered to Paul as they marched.

"What have you gotten me into?" This was, after all, Paul's fault.

Paul turned his head slightly and whispered, "Do you trust me?"

Drake nodded. "Yes."

"Then shut up," Paul hissed.

Drake did shut up and found that wasn't any better. The gorilla was like a teenager, never happy about anything, no one moved fast enough, and the entire world revolved around him. And he never went to bed.

Finally, Drake felt he was getting the knack of Boot Camp as it was ending. That's when Paul announced Phase Two of his career plan; jump school followed by Ranger training. Drake thought Paul was losing it, but he jumped on the bandwagon and out of perfectly good airplanes right behind Paul. From there they qualified for Ranger school.

Ranger training was the worst thing Drake had ever experienced in his life and he loved every minute of it. Paul felt the same way. What Drake loved the most was the camaraderie. He felt he was part of a family, a real family that didn't care about money but valued character and looked out for each other. The Rangers were impressed with the two of them and put them in an Airborne Ranger battalion upon graduation.

And now, two years after Ranger school, here they were on a helicopter. Drake thought of the T-shirt Paul had gotten him last year for his birthday. It had a skull with a Ranger beret on its head and underneath it read, "Rangers. Go to exotic lands. Meet new people. And kill them." And as the crew chief gave Drake and the rest of his team the two-minute sign, he thought of the card Paul included with the shirt and its inscription, "been there, done that, got the t-shirt."

Drake reached over and tapped Paul on the shoulder. "Rise and shine, Sleeping Beauty."

Paul yawned, turned off his Walkman, and stowed it in his gear. "Are we there yet?"

Drake rolled his eyes as the Blackhawk came to a standstill in mid-air. The crew chief was screaming at the five Rangers to get off his chopper. Drake and the others tossed out their repel ropes and exited the helicopter, sliding down the ropes to the ground thirty feet below. As the last man unhooked himself from the ropes, the Blackhawk pulled away and disappeared into the darkness, leaving Drake and the others in a country to remain nameless on a mission to remain classified.

Forty-five minutes later, Drake was on the radio explaining the mission had been compromised and he had wounded. It was Paul. While setting a perimeter, they had been engaged by the enemy. Paul had a flare in his hand that was hit by a bullet and exploded.

A Blackhawk set down in the landing zone and two crewmen with M-16s jumped out to cover the Rangers as they carried Paul onto the chopper. Drake and the others set Paul down on the deck of the helicopter. The two crewmen jumped back on, closed the doors and the Blackhawk lifted off.

Paul lay writhing on the deck, screaming. The medic on board stabbed Paul's thigh with a hypodermic full of morphine as Drake tried to hold Paul down, but the remains of his fatigue blouse and blackened, blistered skin slid off his body as easy as chicken skin on a drumstick at a bar-b-que, causing Paul to scream in agony. The rancid stench of burnt clothing, hair and flesh quickly filled the cabin. It was an evil smell, Drake thought, an inhuman, unholy odor, that burned in his lungs and caused his eyes to water. Several of the guys had vomited. Paul's left hand was gone, ending in a broken and burnt stub that looked more like a blackened tree branch after a forest fire than a human appendage.

Drake and the other Rangers were screaming at the medic to help Paul who lay screaming for Drake. The medic cursed as he pulled another hypodermic out of his bag and stabbed Paul's other thigh. Paul thrashed and then grew still. He looked up at Drake with glassy eyes.

"I guess the bear ate me this time, huh?" He smiled through crackled plastic skin, his eyebrows and eyelashes gone, so that he looked like some deranged maniacal doll from a bad horror movie.

Drake felt bile burn its way up to the back of his throat. "Next time you'll eat the bear." His eyes burned and he could feel hot wetness on his cheeks.

Paul said. "Don't worry about me. I don't feel a thing."

Drake watched as the life faded from Paul's eyes like a setting sun. He began to scream, a primal scream from deep inside himself that drowned out the rotors of the Blackhawk.

No one on the helicopter said a word. The pilot and his crew had seen this happen too many times for it to affect them. The other Rangers, like bikers, knew this could happen, would probably happen, but not to them or anyone on their team. They said a quiet prayer the best they could to whatever higher power they believed in or were willing to take a chance on in a moment like this, and then moved on. The problem with death is it always interferes with the delusion of immortality.

Someone, Drake didn't know who, had removed one of Paul's dog tags and stuck it in his boot, and as the aircraft touched down, the Blackhawk crew began to pick Paul's body up to carry it off the helicopter. Drake placed a hand on the crew chief's shoulder, stopping him. The crew chief nodded and waved the rest of his crew away from the body.

Drake and another Ranger gave their gear to the two remaining team members and set themselves to carry Paul's body. Drake positioned himself at Paul's head. Seeing the remaining dog tag, Drake ripped the chain from Paul's neck and pocketed it.

The crew chief placed a hand on Drake's arm. "You can't do that."

The look Drake shot the crew chief, eyes filled with icy fire, told the crew chief that Army regulations governing the deceased did not apply to him, not today, even before he opened his mouth. "You got the one in his boot."

The crew chief sat on his haunches for a moment before finally nodding. "The other one probably fell off in the jungle during evac." He moved away and started belching orders out to his crew.

Drake and the other Rangers exited the helicopter with Paul's body. Drake didn't remember handing off Paul's remains to medics, nor could he recall much of the next couple of weeks. Aimless despair, mixed with alcohol, cut out that part of his memory. He didn't remember calling Paul's parents three weeks after his death. He'd been restricted to his quarters and unable to get his hands on any alcohol. Without the purpose of getting drunk and the benefits of numbness, he found himself lost. He'd wanted to call Paul's parents but hadn't wanted to be drunk when he did. However, sobriety had been a state he'd been avoiding.

The first half of the conversation was a blur of greetings, condolences, and confessions. Drake rubbed his thumb over a photograph of himself and Paul. They were standing on a pier, Paul holding a huge fish. Paul was laughing at something he'd just said. What was it? Something about fish stories and a dad and son in an old general store and the dad's telling some whoppers and finally the son says to the father, "Why don't you drive for a while and let me spread it around."

Drake laughed a laugh that quickly caught in his throat. It was like laughing at a funeral. What would Paul's parents think of him? He cleared his throat, hoping they would think he was merely choked up. "I've got a picture of me and Paul on R and R. Taken right before we shipped out to—"

"Drake," Paul Senior interrupted, "Stop." His voice cracked.

Drake admonished himself. He was being insensitive to these people who'd been so good to him. He wasn't being very supportive. "I'm sorry. I didn't mean to upset you."

"No, Drake. That's not what I mean." Paul Senior took a deep breath and exhaled into the phone. "Stop living Paul's dream."

Drake stared dumbfounded at the pay phone hanging on the wall.

"You've got to find your own life now." Paul Senior's voice was warm and reassuring. "There's an attorney whose been trying to reach you. Leonard Chapman. But you haven't been taking his calls."

Drake rolled his eyes. "My dad's attorney."

"Not anymore. Now he's your attorney. He stopped by a couple a months ago hoping we might be able to persuade you to answer his letters and phone calls."

"*My* attorney?" Drake was nonplussed. "Did something happen to my folks?"

"No, no. They're fine. He just doesn't work for the family anymore. Something about your grandfather's will. I talked to him for about an hour. He's a good man. Look, Drake, he's not trying to get you and your parents talking again."

"What does he want then?" Drake didn't really expect Paul Senior to know. Lenny was a good man and a good attorney. There's no way he would betray attorney/client confidentiality, no matter what.

"Talk to him and find out."

It was a strong confirmation of Lenny's character. He'd obviously won over Paul Senior, and he had a pretty accurate shyster meter. "Okay. Do you have his number?"

Paul Senior rattled the number off and then said, "Drake, we love you like you were our own. You know that." He took another breath and exhaled roughly into the phone. "I don't want you to call us for a while. Not until you figure your own life out." With that he mumbled a quick "We love you" and hung up before Drake could reciprocate.

Drake said goodbye to the dial tone, hung up, and dialed Lenny Chapman, Esquire.

Chapter 20

Drake fumbled hanging up the pay phone, his hand just wouldn't stop trembling, and fingered the piece of paper in his other hand, the penmanship resembling someone either very old or very young. He'd found it hard to write down the numbers, the pen in his hand had been as big as a horse's leg or as thin as a toothpick, he couldn't really tell. Scrawled across the paper was the phone number to a bank, his account number and pin number, and a dollar amount. He realized he couldn't remember which was the account number and which was the dollar amount, they had the same number of digits. And that was just the cash. That didn't include the investment portfolio. Drake Wetherford was a very, very wealthy young man.

Lenny Chapman was overnight mailing him his checkbook and credit card which, along with the information he'd given Drake over the phone, would allow him access to his funds from anywhere in the world. Lenny had insisted Drake call the bank that afternoon and verify the account information and balances for himself, not just take his word for it, but Lenny had already passed Paul Senior's shyster meter. Drake saw no reason to question the man's character a second time.

Instead he pocketed the paper and requested the MP watching over him to escort him to his commanding officer's office. The man just nodded. The guard had been posted mainly to make sure Drake didn't head to a bar or end his life. The MP had allowed him to use the phone down the hall from his quarters and had been out of earshot but within eyeshot of Drake the whole time.

Drake walked ahead of the MP out into the sunshine. His skin prickled from the heat, and he squinted from the glare. It felt so good to be outdoors, and when the MP stopped at his HUM-V and cleared his throat to get Drake's attention, Drake pretended not to hear him, but kept walking. The MP rolled his eyes and followed on foot.

The walk from his quarters to the commander's office, just five or six minutes by vehicle, took Drake and his bodyguard almost twenty minutes.

Drake was in no hurry. The sky was too blue, the day too gorgeous, his bank account too large to really care.

When he reached his commander's office, he was greeted by a young man whose skinny frame, chubby cheeks, and wispy high-and-tight haircut reminded Drake of an emaciated squirrel caught with its first mouthful of food all winter. He'd been a secretary his whole short military career yet had all the fire and vinegar of a young man straight out of Ranger school.

"Sergeant Wetherford requesting—"

Squirrel interrupted. "The captain's on a call at the moment. Be with you in a sec." He nodded at the chairs against the wall. "Have a seat."

Drake sat down and motioned for the MP to sit down as well. He didn't. "Suit yourself." Drake leaned back and closed his eyes. He didn't know what his next move would be, but right now he knew he wanted out of the military. This had been Paul's dream and that dream had died with him on the helicopter.

The trouble was he'd never had a dream of his own. Paul's dreams, whatever Paul was doing for that matter, had always been enough for him. Paul had never told him what he *should* do or *ought* to do, never lectured him, never did anything but give his advice when asked and do his own thing. The fact that Drake followed wasn't Paul's fault. But sitting in that chair waiting to speak to his C.O., Drake realized he'd never had a dream of his own to pursue, except maybe getting away from his parents, which he'd always been able to achieve by following Paul.

"The captain will see you now." Squirrel shoved a thumb over his shoulder.

Drake stood up and motioned to the door. "Shall we?"

The MP shook his head.

Drake shrugged, walked to the door, knocked, and entered.

The captain's office was decorated in the classic Spartan military design, typical of infantry officers who aren't quite ready to admit their days in the field are numbered, that there career is transitioning from leading troops to pushing papers. He looked up and smiled.

"Drake, nice to see you up and about, not hanging between two MPs." He nodded to the chairs in front of his desk. "Have a seat."

Drake sat down. "I want out."

"Out of the Rangers?"

"Out of the military."

The captain nodded thoughtfully, leaned back, crossing his hands behind his head. "I followed a buddy into the Army too. Well, R.O.T.C., which is kind of like Boy Scouts in camouflage. Back in college. My buddy washed out, but I fell in love with it."

Drake could see where the man was headed. "I never fell in love with it, Sir. Not like Paul did."

"You're a fine soldier, Drake. I'd hate to lose you."

Drake just shook his head. "I'm no good for it now, Sir." Drake could feel the hot sting of tears as his vision blurred.

The captain swiveled his chair around to the window, taking sudden interest in the dust particles floating in the sunlight. Several silent minutes passed before he swiveled back to his desk and picked up the phone. "Get me Major Patterson on the horn." He set the phone back in the cradle. "Major Patterson's an Army shrink, but she's got an agenda. She'll help you get the psych eval and out with an honorable discharge. You won't have to worry about a Section Eight."

Drake nodded, knowing he really wasn't worried about a Section Eight.

"What will you do?"

Drake thought for a moment, but he found his mental process had the fluidity of a bowling ball. He shrugged.

The captain smiled. "Well, I guess you could always backpack across Europe."

Six weeks later, Drake found himself walking out the main gate of Fort Benning on Interstate 185, everything he'd owned in his Army duffel on his shoulders. He walked up the off ramp to Victory Drive, turned left, and got himself a room at the Colony Inn.

He sat down on the bed, took a deep breath, and called Lenny Chapman. A half hour later, he hung up, knowing Lenny would follow his instructions to the letter. The Stephens would shortly receive the deed to their home, the titles to their vehicles, and a checkbook to an account that boasted several hundred thousand dollars. It was all supposed to happen anonymously, but Drake knew Mr. Stephens was no fool, he'd know who was responsible.

That was okay. The Stephens would understand, and they would accept the money. It was just the polite Southern thing to do.

Drake stayed at the Colony Inn until his passport came and then, having found no idea or dream of his own, he hopped a flight from Columbus to Atlanta. From Atlanta, he caught a flight to Newark and then on to London Heathrow. He flew coach, everything still packed in his duffel. He figured he could get any gear and supplies he needed once he was overseas. England seemed as good a place as any to start hiking.

Drake never planned his trip, never even looked at a map. He just walked which ever direction the road or the trail or his mood took him. His travel, like his life, lacked a compass. He didn't take any pictures, collect any souvenirs, or keep a journal. Some places he visited three and four times, others he visited only once and never returned, not because he didn't find the place intriguing or beautiful but because his wandering never led him that way again.

He slept in hostels or under the stars mostly and ate in pubs, outdoor cafés, or purchased a day's worth of food from the local farmer's market. Sometimes he traveled with others, but mainly he kept to himself. He backpacked for two years, but was never able, even to this day, to recall all the places he'd been or the people he'd met. His backpacking ended at the beach in Terracina, Italy.

The sky was an eye-squinting blue, and the day was hot. He dropped his pack on the hot sand and it seemed a good place to leave it. Twenty minutes after he'd walked away from it, an elderly Italian transient (the local authorities always denied their existence) who'd been watching the pack waiting for Drake's return, sauntered up to the pack, looked both ways, picked it up, slung it across his bony back with all the ease of ownership, and slinked off to the shade and shadier area of Terracina.

Drake found a bar for the tourists, ordered a glass of ice water with lemon and then a beer and then a glass of whatever that guy over there was having. He never did catch the name of the drink, but it cooled his tongue and heated his muscles. In time the beach bartenders would just put one on the bar whenever they saw him approaching, but for now, he'd point at the drink and then at himself. Alcohol consumption has its own universal language.

After that first afternoon, Drake became a regular on the beach bar scene. That first night he'd passed out on the beach and woke up the next morning with an earful of sand, a mouthful of sandpaper and a head that felt like it'd just been sanded. He decided to walk it off and found some private bungalows. He wrote a check for two week's rent on one and ended up staying for six months. His days consisted of waking up much to his surprise in his bungalow. The bar staff would carry him home and pour him into bed. After waking up, he'd stagger back to the bar where he'd find a drink waiting and then he wouldn't remember the rest of the day.

This repeated itself for months until one day he staggered into the bathroom to relieve himself before going to the bar for his first liquid meal of the day. After he'd finished washing his hands, he thought he might run a razor over his chin. He stared at his reflection in stunned silence for a full five minutes. His face was bloated from the alcohol, the color of his eyes was a vibrant bloodshot. His body was by no means emaciated, but he looked more like a scrawny beach bum than a former physically fit member of the military's elite.

He thought hard about the past six months and realized most of it wasn't a blur, it was a void. Rubbing his forehead he looked hard into the mirrors of his soul and saw Paul. Paul had that familiar look on his face.

"Drake," he would say as his head shook and his eyes rolled not with anger or frustration but more of the tired patience of an old schoolmaster explaining the same thing over and over to a pupil who just isn't getting it. "You've been blessed. If I had your name, money, and looks I'd be seeing the world, getting a good education, and generally, well, taking care of myself. I'd treat myself to the good life. What's wrong with that as long as you don't flaunt it? You don't have to live to excess, but you've got an opportunity to do so much more than the rest of us. It really would be a shame if you didn't."

With that he gathered up the few things he had, left the key under the mat, and headed not to the beach bar, but for a restaurant for a strong pot of coffee, a pitcher of water and a hearty breakfast. As he ate, Drake thought long and hard and decided that Japan would be a good place to go. He knew he wasn't ready to go back to the States yet, knew it to be a very bad idea.

But Japan, that was a country he'd always been impressed with, a country steeped in tradition and discipline. Growing up, he'd read everything he could on Japan. He could still remember the awful admiration he had for the Samurai and their act of Hara-Kiri or the Kamikazes in World War II. These were a people who completely focused and ordered their lives. He needed that kind of structure, a structure not to be found in the consumption-mad, "what about me" culture of the United States.

So he paid his bill, got a taxi to the airport, and got a ticket to Japan via Rome and Frankfurt. The flight didn't leave for ten hours, but Drake had no desire to go anywhere. He hadn't made any friends, except for the bartenders whose friendship was directly proportional to the size of his bill and tip, so there wasn't anyone to say goodbye to. Nor had he visited any landmarks, he didn't know if there were any besides the bar and his little cabana. Instead, Drake bought himself a cup of coffee and waited.

Once in Japan, Drake decided the best way to reclaim himself was through the martial arts. He figured the rigors of training would not only tire him out beyond going out for a good time, but he would also find the same thing he'd found in the military: Discipline. He tried several arts before settling on Aikido. He loved the beauty of it, like dancing with the wind or the ocean. Every movement fluid, no abrupt gesticulations, or hard endings, just an ebb and flow that left his body and his mind rejuvenated. He'd never been a mystical man, but there were times when he felt he moved beyond the corporeal into some other realm.

He built himself a dojo and found a Sensei who agreed to take him on as his only student. Drake spent nine hours a day, six days a week for eighteen months, training. He had no idea of the destination, wasn't interested in attaining a Sensei level himself, he just wanted the journey. But Drake absorbed the art and the culture and after eighteen months, his Sensei bowed, said there was no more he could teach him, and left. Drake never saw the man again.

Drake found himself at a crossroads. Was it time to go back to the States, or stay in Japan? Or perhaps there was some other place in the world he should visit? What was he going to do with his life? Drake continued to train, to stay focused, he wasn't trying to evade the crossroads, he would never evade anything in his life again, he just decided to let his newfound focus and his old friend guide him. He had no idea the path Paul and Japan would lead him down as he went to a bar for a double Jack Daniel's on the rocks to celebrate Paul's birthday.

Chapter 21

Others in the bar may have glanced over to see some American sitting alone at a booth, but for Drake, Paul was sitting across from him just as real as the young man in the blue shark skin suit sitting across the club from him with a table full of hookers. The guy was loud, obnoxious, and rude, with a New York accent and a Wise Guy vernacular. He was talking big and throwing a lot of dollars around.

Drake had blocked the man out almost completely, but he felt the vibe of the place change as dramatically as if all the lights had just flipped on. He turned and saw the three men who'd just walked into the bar. Their suits and haircuts were high dollar, but Drake could tell as he watched them scan the bar, not leaving a chair or a shadow un-scrutinized, these guys were not high society. He had the feeling he was watching Yakuza.

The skinny man of the three standing in the center slapped the two others on the biceps and pointed at the New Yorker. A wicked smile pulled at one corner of his mouth and Drake could see the man was missing the top joint of his right thumb. The other two men nodded, adjusted their suit jackets, and walked towards the young American. The two men looked like sides of beef stuffed into suits too small, but they moved with a grace and lightness that impressed Drake. They wasted no motion, made no unnecessary movement, they were completely relaxed. The third man, the man with one fewer thumbnail than his colleagues, swaggered over with a very purposeful nonchalance.

As the three men arrived at the table, the hookers decided New York's money no longer had value enough for their services. They scampered away from the table and into the darkest shadows they could find.

"Hey," the American was saying as he put down his glass of sake, trying to track the girls around the men. "You squinty-eyes make better walls than windows."

The wicked curl returned to the skinny man's lip, but he said nothing. New York looked at a gorilla of a man sitting at a table next to his. "Would you mind clearing my view?"

The gorilla stood up and opened his suit jacket to let the Yakuza know he would be using his friends, Smith and Wesson, to help him clear the view.

The side of beef to the right moved so quickly the gorilla never got the satisfaction of seeing intimidation flicker on the faces of the men. He never had time to register the side of beef had pulled a Tanto blade seemingly from thin air and moving in some David Copperfield magical illusion had closed the distance and slit his throat where he stood, his hands still opening his jacket to show the revolver at his side. His hands left his jacket and revolver and clutched at his throat as he fell back into his chair, his shirt and tie now thick with his blood.

"Whoa," the young man was wiping a shaking hand at the gorilla's blood that had sprayed across his face. "Whoa, whoa." His eyes darted wildly from the lifeless gorilla to the three men. "Wait a minute, wait a minute." He stammered. "I...You...that is...I mean." His eyes fell upon a large stack of one-hundred dollar bills several inches thick lying on the table. "Maybe we can make a deal." He put his hand on the stack and pushed it towards the skinny man. "That's a lot of dead presidents. What say you forget you saw me here tonight?"

The side of beef with the Tanto drove the blade through New York's hand, the stack of bills and into the table. New York screamed.

Drake wished he could be like the other patrons in the bar, able to hide within the shadow of their booth or corner, deep into the hum of conversation and music blotting out everything outside their personal space. But he couldn't, and he wasn't exactly sure why. He didn't know this guy from Adam, wouldn't want to know a jerk like that, throwing his money around like some Wetherford in New Orleans. But there was just something about this that didn't sit right with Drake.

Perhaps it was the three on one aspect of the confrontation. It just wasn't fair. Obviously, each one of these men could have handled this New York punk, so why the need for a trio? It was overkill for the sake of show, he guessed. In any case, it wasn't right, and the blood of his great-great uncle ran thicker in his veins than he realized at that moment. He remembered the story Paul's grandfather told him about how William had stood up for him at the poker game, but before his brain could make the connection and tell him to stop, don't get involved, the jerk is probably getting exactly what he deserves if he's crossed the Yakuza, his body was already up, moving towards the table where New York stared at his hand pinned to the table, eyes bulging, sweat glistening on his face, dampening his matching blue silk shirt and tie, conducting himself with all the manliness of a little girl who's just watched her puppy get squashed by a cement truck.

"Excuse me, guys." Drake didn't really know what he was going to say or do for that matter once he had the three Japanese mobsters' attention. The side of beef with the tanto made that decision for him.

He pulled the blade from the table and New York's hand as the other side of beef and his boss turned. Drake saw the two men turn to face him, saw the side of beef thrusting towards his chest, the blade gleaming maroon-brown under the neon light. His brain bypassed the normal thought process, shorted out the fight or flight instinct, and simply told his body to move.

Drake stepped into the lunge of the blade, shortening the distance, then side stepped his attacker, allowing him to stab thin air. As he did so, his left hand reached up, grasped his attacker's thrusting wrist, and pivoting his body, threw the side of beef off balance and down to his knees. As the side of beef went down, Drake locked the side's wrist and drove the knife backward deep into his attacker's throat.

The side's eyes goggled as he felt the warm sticky fluid gush over his hand still holding the hilt of his knife. He looked up at Drake with all the realization of a game show contestant who could not believe he just lost the new car and trip to Rio for a toaster oven.

Drake's mind recorded the dying man's look while making another decision without consulting Drake. The other two men would have to die. He could not spend the rest of his life looking over his shoulder. The Mob, regardless of franchise, doesn't forget and it certainly doesn't forgive.

The other side of Japanese Beef opened his jacket and reached for the weapon holstered underneath. Drake pulled the knife from the dying man's throat, pushed the corpse to the floor and drove the blade up through this man's throat and into the back of the brain.

Drake reached into the man's jacket, drew the weapon from the holster, which was a Beretta 9mm, aimed and fired a single shot between the eyebrows of the third and last mobster standing.

For Drake, it all happened in slow motion, one man at a time with all the time in the world, but for New York, he'd heard an American's voice say, "excuse me," and then before he could put a face to the voice, his three party-poopers were dead on the floor.

Those immediately around the table, those who couldn't shrink into the shadow, couldn't help but turn at the sound of the gunshot, and stare dumbfounded at the American standing over the lifeless bodies of three former Yakuza. The crowd's purposeful oblivion was soon interrupted as what they were seeing finally registered on their liquored brains. One bloodcurdling scream was enough to spark a wildfire of screaming and stampeding.

Drake's mind hadn't missed the fact that every set of eyes in the place had been on him, recording his image, details about his height, weight, hair color, clothing, which would be filed and re-accessed later for the right price or motivation. He assumed the Yakuza could be very motivating. Drake placed the pistol in his waistband, pocketed the knife and pulled a shrieking New York to his feet.

"Come on. We gotta go." Drake scanned the nightclub for the closest exit, and finding it, pushed New York towards it.

"Stupid squinty-eyes," New York was shouting as he passed the three dead mobsters, stopping to kick them. He stopped, reached back to the table, grabbed the blood-soaked stack of bills, and pocketed them. "You messed with the wrong Injun."

Drake's mind decided to file that last comment away for future inquiry, but now was not the time. Something else was nagging him, a set of eyes he was overlooking, a set of eyes that wouldn't need motivation or bribes. This place surely had a set of eyes like that. Drake scanned the room again, this time seeing the dark cloudy globe protruding from the ceiling. There were four of them, at least four he could see. Well, those needed to disappear. He noticed an unmarked door beside the restrooms. Drake walked over, kicked the door open and stepped inside. Six monitors hooked up to six video recorders showed, and were recording Drake had no doubt, different points of view of the bar. Drake pushed the eject buttons with the small Kubotan he carried in his pocket, collected the six tapes, and turned to find New York staring at him, his tie now tied around his hand like an ace wrap.

"Who *are* you?"

Drake pushed past the man. "Let's go." He expected to see another gorilla of a man standing behind the door, covering the alleyway, smoking a cigarette, carrying a katana or a bazooka maybe, just waiting for the chance to whack whoever was unfortunate enough to walk through that particular door, and he wished he'd handed the tapes over to New York.

Whack? Drake shook his head. Who used the word whack other than cheesy wise guys in B-movies? Get a grip, Drake told himself, as he opened the door.

Light spilled out the door into the alleyway like a drunk. Garbage cans lined the wall across, their stench invading Drake's nostrils. But no one was there. Sometimes, Drake thanked the good Lord above, life ain't like the movies.

Of course, now that he'd established no one was waiting to kill the two of them, not just yet anyway, the next order of business was finding transportation away from the bar. No sense waiting for someone to show up.

"Keys." Drake stuck his hand out to New York.

New York's eyes bugged like a boy caught by his mother fingering through the bra section of the J.C. Penny catalog.

"You've got to be kidding me." Drake thrust the tapes into New York's chest. "I'll be right back."

Drake rushed back into the bar. The neon lights and smoky haze of the now deserted bar unsettled him. The music was still playing but the only bodies left wouldn't be dancing ever. And now that Drake saw the scene, he was glad he'd come back in. He followed quite traceable bloody prints in his and New York's shoe sizes. Half empty beer bottles, glasses, including his own of Jack Daniel's, were left on the tables, teeming with fingerprints and saliva. And lying on the floor, just out of the growing pools of blood, was the dog tag of Paul Stevens, the chain that had kept it around Drake's neck broken beside it. The authorities and the Yakuza would know the identity of everyone in that bar before breakfast. That just wouldn't do.

Drake picked up the chain and dog tag, moved to the dead gorilla and started rummaging through his pockets. He found his wallet and car keys in the outside pocket of his suit jacket. Drake then moved to the bar, grabbed a bottle of Ouzo sitting almost completely full, downed a swallow then poured the remaining over the yakuza bodies, then smashed the bottle on the table where New York had been sitting. Moving quickly he went back out to New York and grabbed the tapes out of his arms.

"What the—?"

But Drake didn't wait to hear the rest of what he considered to be a very cliché, stereotypical New York question. Instead he went back inside and grabbed another bottle of liquor from the bar. Pulling the ribbon from the VHS cassettes, he doused them in alcohol, and tossed them on to the three dead Yakuza. He then hurled miscellaneous bottles around the club, grabbed a book of matches, lit them and tossed them onto the bodies. The fire blazed on the bodies before him but followed the alcohol like a drunk with a twenty. Within seconds the entire club was ablaze.

Coughing, Drake rushed back out, and still moving, grabbed New York by the arm. "Which way?'

"Huh? Oh." He pointed to a white limo parked on the bottom level of a parking garage caddy corner to the bar. "Right over there."

Oh, this just gets better and better, Drake thought. "You just can't help but be ostentatious, huh?" He started moving towards the limo but stopped as three or four people crossed his path at a run. They didn't notice him or New York, but they were definitely moving toward the bar. Thank God for human nature, Drake thought as he looked around the corner at the front of the bar. Everyone from the bar, and anyone on the street within three blocks stood across the street in front of the bar. Smoke billowed from the front door like a furnace. One might've thought a full barroom brawl was taking place inside as glass and wood exploded from the heat. People do love disaster.

Chapter 22

Drake reached the limo and unlocked the doors as New York moved instinctively to the rear door.

"I'm not a chauffeur," Drake said as he ducked behind the steering wheel.

New York blushed as he ran around the car and threw himself into the passenger seat.

Drake started the car, put it into drive and, leaving the lights off, moved slowly towards the exit on the other side of the garage.

"I hate squinty eyes." New York held out his bloody hand. "Name's Ricky Patrelli. Of the *New Jersey* Patrellis."

Ricky had emphasized New Jersey, but its significance along with the name Patrelli was completely lost on Drake. He stared blankly ahead.

Ricky left his hand out there. "Did my uncle send you?"

"What?"

"My uncle. *Frank* Patrelli? Did he send you?"

Ricky overemphasized his uncle's name.

"Is that supposed to mean something to me? New Jersey? Patrelli? Uncle Frank?"

"You're an American, ain't you?"

"I've been out of country for a while."

"Must've." He thrust his hand in front of Drake's face. "I didn't catch your name."

"I didn't toss it out." Drake, ignoring the hand, pulled onto the street. He wasn't exactly sure why he didn't want to give New York, excuse me, New Jersey, his name, other than his gut told him it was better that this guy, Ricky Patrelli of the New Jersey Patrellis, was a marked man with none other than one of the most brutal of crime syndicates, the Yakuza, so the less he knew about Drake, especially after he'd killed three of their number, the better. "You got an address?"

"Yeah." Ricky pulled his hand to his chest and grimaced. "But first, take me to a hospital. This thing's throbbin'."

"No hospitals. They'll find you." Drake checked the rearview mirror for any signs they were being followed.

"Who'll find me?"

"Santa Claus and the tooth fairy." *This guy can't be this stupid.* "Who do you think'll find you? The Yakuza."

"Sounds like a motorcycle." Ricky fished in his pockets and pulled out a pack of Marlboro cigarettes and a Zippo lighter.

This guy is that stupid.

"Well they're twice as fast and ten times deadlier. You show up in a hospital and you'll be dead before the nurse asks you to stick out your tongue and say, 'ah.'" Drake spotted another parking garage and pulled in. "What do they want with you anyway?"

"I'm supposed to tell you what I'm doin' here an' you won't even gimme your name?"

Drake considered the question. "Fair enough." He put the car in park, pulled out his cell phone, and dialed a number.

"So if my uncle didn't send you? What were you doin' there?"

Drake shrugged as he listened to the ring. "Wrong place at the wrong time."

Ricky mumbled something that sounded like an expletive, but Drake couldn't hear and didn't care. On the third ring, the line was picked up.

Ricky sat listening to Drake place the call for a cab, but he couldn't understand a word of it. Drake made the call in Japanese, fluent Japanese as far as Ricky could tell. "You a squinty eye too?"

Drake could see Ricky tense out of the corner of his eye and began wondering where a firearm or two might be hidden in this limo. As soon as he hung up, he said quickly, "I've called us a cab. We need to get rid of this limo." Drake pulled out his shirttail and wiped down his side of the vehicle.

Ricky cradled his hand, whimpering. "Dude, I've gotta go to the hospital. This thing's really killing me."

"No hospitals." Drake was satisfied his prints were now gone from the limo's interior. "I'll sew you up."

"What're you? Some kinda doc?"

The question reminded Drake of a commercial he'd seen of a man in a white lab coat talking to the camera and holding some product he couldn't remember. But he remembered what the guy had said. He looked at Ricky. "No, but I play one on T.V."

"Huh?"

"Never mind." Drake pulled his sleeve over his hand and opened the door. "We really need to keep moving."

Ricky followed and they were soon walking down the two blocks to where Drake had told the cab company to meet them.

Maybe he'd seen too many movies or maybe he'd had a hunch, but he didn't give the cabbie their real names or the right address when the young man asked where to take them. Instead he gave him an address in the opposite direction, an address which he knew was close to a Metro station. He hoped it would be some place that would blend into the driver's memory. Ricky, on the other hand, wanted to make sure the cabbie knew just how bad his hand hurt. His version, though, differed slightly from reality as he let the cabbie know he'd hurt his hand breaking some squinty eye's jaw.

Ostentatious and oblivious, Drake thought, to not realize you're not in Kansas anymore, but in a place where the mob has eyes and ears everywhere. This wasn't the United States, but an island and it was a lot easier to be everywhere when everywhere was just 377,835 square kilometers, smaller than California. Drake wasn't on a first name basis with any Yakuza, hadn't met any Yakuza that he was aware of, except for the three tonight, but he knew enough that when you crossed them, your best bet was to disappear like Jimmy Hoffa.

Upon arriving at the address, which turned out to be a touristy Sushi restaurant Drake had heard of but never patronized and could not remember the name, Drake paid the fare plus a tip that was neither too much nor too little, two American males were more than enough to remember let alone two that under or over tipped. Not that that really mattered the way Ricky went on about his hand.

"You hungry?" Ricky asked as the cab pulled away.

Drake asked himself not for the first time why he'd gotten involved with this guy. He's what Paul would've called 'a first-class hemorrhoid, a real pain in the rump roast.' It always made Drake laugh when Paul would say that, 'rump roast,' and it made him laugh now to think of it.

"What's so funny?" Ricky was indignant as he cradled his hand to his chest.

How odd, Drake thought, how the brain works, thinking of that now. His hand slipped unconsciously into his pocket and his thumb brushed over the dog tag. "Forget about it."

Drake led Ricky into the crowd that herded along the sidewalk; not caring or remembering or noticing those in its mist who were not Japanese, effectively pulling a Jimmy Hoffa, disappearing into thin air.

They moved with the flow of the crowd two blocks up from the restaurant and into the Metro station. They hopped a train and got off at Azabu Juban Station, the last before Drake's apartment, a luxury hotel called Azabu Towers.

The hotel, a modern ten story building in brown brick with tan balconies, resembled nothing of the culture in which it was built. Inside, however, Azabu Towers was distinctively Japanese: simple, utilitarian, uncluttered with no indulgences. It was new, clean, and modern. The front desk was white marble with chrome trim, and across from the front desk, like an ever so slight tip of the hat to their past, a small Zen Garden stood by itself. It was as if the Towers wanted its patrons, which were primarily American businessmen and women, to feel as if they were getting themselves a little bit of culture by staying there.

The effect, however, was lost on Ricky. "Now that's stupid," he said as he grimaced at the tree in the middle of the garden. "Why would you muck up a perfectly good floor with a sandbox?"

Drake didn't respond but moved directly to the stairwell. Since leaving Azabu Juban Station, they had not encountered anyone, but Drake saw no reason to push his luck. Besides, he thought, as he began to climb the stairs, no sense being a fish in a barrel, which is just what the elevator would feel like right about now.

Ricky whined but followed Drake up the stairs to the fourth floor.

As they approached the fourth floor, Drake opened the door to the stairwell slowly, cautiously, and peered to his left, then his right, and back to the left again.

Nobody.

Drake motioned to Ricky to stay close and keep his mouth shut as Drake stepped into the hallway and then down the hall to his suite. The mag card moved in and out of its receiver on the door, and Drake opened the door as soon as the green light glowed, pulling Ricky in behind him.

"Home, sweet home," Drake said absentmindedly as he walked to the dining room table and emptied his pockets of everything but his wallet.

"Home?" Ricky was incredulous as he looked around the apartment. "You live here?"

"Not after tonight." Drake walked to the bathroom, pulled a first aid kit and sewing kit from a drawer, and returned to the dining room to find Ricky seated at the table thumbing through the items Drake had left there.

"I knew you had to be an Army guy." Ricky held up the dog tag with Paul's name and information. "Or were you one of them Navy Seals?"

Drake stood there contemplating what he should say, what he should do. His first inclination was to remove the dog tag from Ricky's dead hand after he snapped his neck. Instead Drake took a deep breath, relaxed, and set the first aid kit and sewing kit down on the table next to Ricky. "Something like that."

Ricky fidgeted with excitement. "I *knew* it. With all that James Bond karate stuff you did." His hand lay forgotten on the table. "So, Paulie, can I call you Paulie?"

"Not if you expect me to answer." Drake opened the first aid kit, pulled out a small bottle of Lidocaine and a syringe, some gauze, and a bottle of aspirin.

"So what were you Paul, Special Forces? Seals? I always thought I'd a been a whale of a soldier. Whaddaya think?"

Drake contemplated using the Lidocaine on Ricky's mouth but decided not to. He'd just use less than he normally would.

Drake thought about how to handle Ricky. He wasn't about to let him know more information about himself than necessary, but he had to offer a diversion so that Ricky wouldn't notice his thirst for information was going unquenched. The best way to do that with a guy like Ricky, Drake knew, was to stroke his ego.

As Drake opened the sewing kit and selected needle and thread, he thought of Ricky's hand harpooned to the table by the Japanese mobster's knife. "Oh, you'd have been a whale all right."

"You got that right," Ricky exclaimed and slapped his injured hand down on the table. He cursed between clenched teeth.

Drake sat down, grabbed Ricky's injured hand, and pulled it to him. The blood had dried the tie to the wound and Drake had to yank it off. Ricky screamed in agony as his injured hand clawed the tabletop and his other hand white-knuckled the back of the chair.

Drake went to the kitchen and returned with a bottle of sake. He opened the bottle of aspirin and poured three onto the table, opened the sake, took a swig, and handed it to Ricky.

Ricky picked up the aspirins with his good hand, popped them into his mouth and washed them down with the sake. He watched as Drake stuck the needle of the syringe into the bottle of Lidocaine. "Is that gonna hurt?"

"No more than the knife did." Drake thumped the syringe to get the air bubbles out. "I'm going to numb the wound with the Lidocaine and then use the sake to disinfect the wound."

Before Ricky could react to what he'd said, Drake plunged the needle into the wound, and injected a small amount of the Lidocaine. Ricky yelped as Drake pulled the needle out and hit the other side of the wound. Drake flipped his hand over and repeated the process in Ricky's palm. Ricky let out a few more expletives, his face red as a beet.

Drake picked up the bottle of sake and poured it over the wound.

"Holy—" Ricky bit his lip hard.

"Sorry." Drake wasn't, but he did wait a few more minutes before he started sewing the wound.

Ricky mopped his forehead. "So what did you mean by not after tonight?"

"I don't know if the fire destroyed all the evidence, I'm pretty sure it did, but I'm not willing to take that chance with the Yakuza." And then he added after a pause. "And neither should you." Drake tied off the final knot. "You're done."

Ricky lifted his hand off the table and admired Drake's work. "Nice."

"Thanks." Drake started packing up the first aid and sewing kits.

"You coulda been a surgeon." Ricky tried to make a fist. He grimaced as the pain shot through his hand and up his arm.

"Don't pull those stitches out. There won't be time to fix it." Drake stood up, stretched, went into the kitchen, and threw the two kits into the trashcan.

"So where are ya gonna go?" Ricky called from the other room.

Drake walked back into the dining room. "I don't know."

"Well, I gotta great idea." Ricky smiled revealing capped teeth, one in gold. "Why don't you come back to Jersey with me? Let me show ya my gratitude. Show you round New York, get you a girl or two. No hookers, mind you. Just classy chicks." He laughed. "I'd love ya to meet my uncle." He slapped his knee. "Boy, he'd get a kick outta you."

There was nothing Drake loathed more than the proposition of kicking around Jersey or New York with Ricky. Drake shivered at what Ricky's idea of a classy chick might be. His mind's eye showed him a woman with too much makeup and hair much too big and clothes too tight for her meaty frame reeking of cigarette smoke, cheap perfume, hairspray, and grease.

But another picture came to his mind's eye; that of Yakuza, tracking him down, capturing him, and torturing him for hours, maybe days, before finally killing him. Faced with that snapshot…

"I'd love to see the Garden State."

Chapter 23

The cab pulled to a stop at the curb in front of *Cuppa Joe's*.

"Get it." Ricky was saying as he paid the cabbie. "Joe owns the place and it's a slang name for coffee."

"Yeah," Drake said as he slipped out of the cab. "I got it."

Ricky had been doing this since they'd gotten on the plane in Tokyo, and frankly, Drake was ready to deck him. At first, when Ricky was telling Drake how a Bloody Mary without alcohol was called a Virgin Mary and "get it, virgin, cuz she ain't got no alcohol in her," and elbowing him in the ribs, Drake just thought it was nervous energy. But the guy kept doing it. Everything was a "Get it?" and Ricky was the world's foremost authority on "Get it?"

As he followed Ricky into the small coffee house, Drake took notice of three guys, not unlike the beefcake now lying cold in a Japanese refrigerator, and another guy wearing khakis and a sport shirt. These were Frank Patrelli's bodyguards, he was pretty sure, and Drake had a hunch they, especially the guy in the khakis, would never have let Yakuza get three steps into the coffee shop.

Frank Patrelli sat in a corner table, quietly sipping an espresso, a half-eaten chocolate biscotti lay on a saucer as he read the newspaper comics. He was not at all what Drake had expected. He was a gaunt looking man in his late sixties, about five foot nine but small in frame, no turkey neck or middle-aged spread about his waistline. His white hair was cropped tight on the side but longer and disheveled on the top. He wasn't frail, but looked diminutive, unassuming.

"Uncle Frankie," Ricky exclaimed as he walked up to him, arms extended.

Frank looked up, a long-suffering smile creeping across his face, and stood, extending his arms. "Richard, glad to see you home safe." He embraced Ricky, "And in one piece." He released Ricky, patted his back, and prodded his arms. "No bones broke. Still got all your internal organs?" His voice was thick with Italy, not New York or Jersey.

Ricky laughed. "Naw. It's gonna take more than a few squinty eyes to stop ole Ricky's clock."

Drake looked at the four bodyguards, who'd taken their eyes off of Drake at this comment just long enough to look at each other and then return to the only person in the room they did not know.

Ricky turned to Drake. "Uncle Frankie, this is the guy I was telling you about."

Frank nodded and extended his hand.

Drake took it, surprised by the grip of the older man.

"Pleased to meet you, Mr. Stephens." He motioned to a chair at his table. "I've heard much about you."

"Thank you." Drake smiled, not so much to be cordial, but because he liked hearing the name again, liked being called the name.

Frank sat, waving him off. "No, no. Thank you."

Drake was sure he caught a whiff of sarcasm in the gratitude.

Ricky bounced down into a chair at the table. "Paulie," he looked at Drake. "Sorry. Paul here's a regular Rambo—"

"Richard," Frank interrupted, "why don't you go into the kitchen and see if Isabella can fix you something to eat."

Ricky's face reddened. "But I'm not—" he paused, looking down as if he'd just been excused from the grown-up table and cast down to where the kiddies sit. But he got up and went into the kitchen.

Frank looked at Drake and Drake got the distinct feeling he was being weighed and measured, probed and dissected. "Would you like something to drink? Joseph makes the best espresso and cappuccino around."

"Cappuccino sounds wonderful. Thank you." Drake said.

Frank nodded to a man behind the counter Drake assumed was Joe, and then turned his attention back to Drake. "So. What were you doing in Japan, Mr. Stephens?"

Drake shrugged. "Just doing a little soul searching."

"And did you find it, your soul?"

Drake looked at the man across the table, smiling pleasantly, his eyes still calculating. "Maybe."

Joe brought a cup steaming with cappuccino and set it in front of Drake, then left.

Frank's eyes beamed. "One of my favorite words." He took a sip of his espresso. "It signifies a willingness to listen. But first, let me ask you another question. That was a quite impressive piece of negotiating you pulled off in Japan. Where did you learn to do that?"

Drake thought about lying, but realized this man would know, and he found he didn't want to lie to the man anyway. "I spent some time in the Army. Rangers. And received some training in Japan."

Frank smiled. "Well, you appear to be very good at solving problems. I could use an outside..." Frank paused, choosing his words carefully, "analyst who would be willing to come in from time to time to solve problems. You could of course free-lance, provided you didn't work for any of my competitors."

Drake sat dumbfounded. He knew what this man was asking. Not really asking, more like expecting. But Drake wasn't ready to go to work for the mob and certainly not as an assassin or muscle.

Frank sensed his hesitation. "Where are my manners? This is supposed to be a moment of gratitude and celebration. Don't answer now. But..." Frank took a bite of his biscotti and another sip of espresso, "I do have one more question that you really must answer immediately." He leaned in as if to discuss a secret plan with a co-conspirator. "How did you get my nephew to not call you Paulie?"

Drake laughed.

"I really hope you will stay around for a few days, let Richard show you the city, and this evening you can be a guest in my home for supper, huh?"

"I'd be honored Mr. Patrelli." Drake really did feel honored.

Frank smiled. "Please. Call me Frank. And I'll call you Paul."

Drake nodded.

Ricky returned from the kitchen munching on a sandwich and carrying another sandwich. "The pastrami's great." He offered the plate to Drake. "Want one?"

Drake looked over to Frank who only shrugged. "It really is good."

Drake took the sandwich. It really was good, but not near as good as the meal Sophia Patrelli, Frank's wife, prepared later that evening. There was pasta with red sauce and pasta with white sauce and meatballs the size of a fist on the table along with garlic bread and other dishes Drake had no idea of the names. And to wash all this good food down were bottles of Chianti all along the table, buffet, and counter tops.

It was enough food to feed a small army, and that's just what showed up. Every one of Frank's immediate family, sons and their wives and children and daughters and their husbands and children, and not so immediate, Frank's siblings and children, seemed to float in and out of the house. The air was thick with laughter and conversation and arguing. Who would ever believe these people were the mob?

Drake found himself in the middle of all this food and family and felt a warmth he hadn't felt in years. Not since, he tried to remember, not since he'd been in the Stephens' home, laughing over pot roast and mashed sweet potatoes and key lime pie in honor of his birthday, or eating pizza and watching *The Six Million Dollar Man* or *The Bionic Woman* or some other show he couldn't remember. He didn't remember the show, but he remembered the laughter and the food and the fun. This was as close, he realized, as he was ever going to get at recapturing those feelings.

Drake asked Frank what the special occasion was, half expecting to be told it was in his honor, but Frank just looked blankly at Drake and said, "It's Tuesday."

After the dessert had been eaten and the coffee drank, Frank caught Drake's attention with a wave of his hand, in it were two fat cigars. He nodded towards the backdoor of his brownstone and Drake dutifully followed.

Once outside, Frank closed the door, handed a cigar to Drake, looked around the small back patio then moved quietly to what looked like a box of garden tools. Frank opened the lid, pulled out a glass jug and held it up to Drake.

"Grappa," Frank said with satisfied triumph.

Drake stared blankly.

"Italian moonshine," Frank explained as he opened the jug and took a deep whiff. He closed his eyes in delight. "Made it myself. I've been waiting for a special occasion."

Frank reached into the box and pulled out two glasses.

"What's the special occasion? Tuesday?" Drake teased. He couldn't believe how comfortable, how happy he was with this man.

Frank shook his head. "You're acceptance of my offer." He filled a glass and handed it to Drake.

Drake took the glass. "How'd you know?" He hadn't known himself. Well, that wasn't true, not really. He'd known this evening he'd accept the offer. Paul was back, for the first time in years, Paul was back. For the first time in a long time, he felt like he had when he and Paul were on a mission. And he liked being called Paul. He was no longer Drake of the New Orleans Wetherfords, but Paul of the bad mamma jamma Stephens's.

Frank did not answer the question, but took a swig of grappa, rolling it around in his mouth in a very satisfied fashion. He swallowed. "Sophie likes you." He smiled. "If she was twenty years younger and you were twenty years older, well, let's just say I wouldn't be offering you a job." He pulled a zippo from his pocket, lit his cigar, and handed the lighter to Drake.

Drake lit his cigar. It was a Cuban, very expensive and very illegal. "Nice."

"Nice?" Frank feigned offense. "For a Cuban, it's either excellent or it's the stuff you fertilize plants with."

"Sorry." Drake took a couple of more puffs. "This is excellent. This is..." He searched his mind's databank of stored words, "Kokenn."

Frank laughed. "I like this word. What does it mean?"

"It's Creole. It means fantastic."

Frank repeated it several times, savoring the feel of it on his tongue.

Drake asked again. "So how did you know?"

Frank puffed on his cigar for a moment. He pulled the cigar from his mouth. "I have a hunch." He snatched a small part of the cigar leaf from the tip of his tongue and flicked it into the grass. "I've got a good feeling about you."

Drake had a good feeling about Frank Patrelli as well, or as good a feeling one could have of a mobster. But maybe that's why Drake had a good feeling about him. He knew Frank would never judge him for who he was or what he did. Drake could be exactly what Frank saw; mild-mannered Paul Stephens, connoisseur of such fabulous words as Kokenn, ex-Army Ranger, able to kill without guilt or remorse. Yes, Drake thought as he settled back into his chair, he could definitely live with what Frank saw.

The door burst open and out bounced Ricky. "Hey, you guys, the game's about to start."

Frank waved him off. "It's only pre-season."

"Hey, Paul," Ricky saw the jug of Grappa, downed his beer, picked up the jug, and tried to refill his bottle. "Do you know why they call them the Steelers? Cuz they *steal* the ball. Get it?" More Grappa hit the ground than made it into Ricky's bottle.

"Yeah," Paul said deflated, watching the puddle of his newfound favorite beverage on the porch, "I get it."

Ricky took a swig, "Grappa," then bounded back into the house.

Frank watched him go, then dropped his gaze to the same puddle Drake was staring at, his face wrinkled with disgust. "At times like this," Frank looked up to Drake, "I wish you would've just finished your drink."

"Me too."

Frank smiled, stood, and offered his hand to Drake.

Drake stood and took his hand.

"Welcome to the Family, Paul Stephens."

Part 3
Chapter 24

"You work for *the Mob*?" Eric sat glued to the edge of the loveseat. He wanted to throw the glass of whisky into Paul's, or Drake's or whoever this guy was, throw it right into his face and leave, run, do not pass go, do not collect two hundred dollars, but run as if his life depended on it and it just might.

"Not anymore." Drake finished off his drink. "I freelance now."

He said it just as matter-of-factly as if he were telling someone he'd been a journalist but stopped working for the Man and decided to go into business for himself. Eric stopped to think about that. He now had a very new, very real appreciation for that term, hired gun. Still, phrases like 'working for the Mob,' and 'freelance' skirted a very real and dangerous truth.

"You kill people for a living?" Eric couldn't hide the incredulity in his tone and wondered if this might not offend the man he was talking to and what that might mean, but he continued. "You *kill* for money."

Drake moved to the bar and began pouring himself another drink. "If it makes you feel any better, they were all bad people."

Laughter spilled out of Eric like a waterfall. The statement hadn't been funny, hadn't meant to tickle his funny bone. If he'd been sitting on his couch watching the television or eating popcorn in the cinema watching a dark comedy about a hitman like *The Whole Nine Yards* with Bruce Willis, he imagined he would find the line quite funny. He could even hear Bruce Willis saying the line in his head and it was funny. In a movie. But not now, not here. And yet, he laughed. He laughed with nervous energy, exhaustion, and sheer adrenaline. He laughed until a thought popped into his mind. Who decided if these people were bad or not?

Eric felt an icy fingernail rake up his spine to the bottom of his skull. Every hair on his head bristled. "Did-?" His throat was dry, and the word came out more of a whisper. He cleared his throat. "Did someone hire you to kill me?"

Now it was Drake's turn to burst into laughter.

Eric stared at Drake with a mixture of terror and anger. "What's so funny?"

"Who could possibly gain from your death?" He moved over to Eric and took the glass from his hands. "And, quite frankly, I don't come cheap." He refreshed Eric's drink. "Despite what you're thinking at the moment, I'm not sick. I don't get to know a mark before I kill them." He offered the glass to Eric.

Eric quietly took the glass and set it down on the coffee table.

"What're you thinking?" Drake asked, watching Eric closely.

Eric thought for a moment, then spoke, not looking up. "I don't even know where to begin. My wife's dead, my son..." Eric's voice caught in his throat. Over the past few weeks, he'd been able to begin accepting his wife was dead. It was tough, the hardest thing he'd ever done in his life, but he'd never move on with his life if he didn't. And Emily would've wanted it that way. She would've wanted him to be happy. But his son. There was something unnatural in that. Children weren't supposed to die. Parents weren't supposed to bury them. And though many men don't make any kind of a connection with a child till it is born, Eric felt the loss in a very real, palpable way.

Eric could still remember how the sun seemed to pale in comparison to Emily's vivacity, she glowed as if the baby growing inside her was a huge light shining through her pores, her hair, her smile. But there was something else; it alighted in her eyes, a pride. She was carrying her husband's child, his family lineage.

He'd been grateful for that look. He'd never understood how much Emily loved him until that moment. She was the mother of his son, his *son*. That day had been spent in the philosophy and responsibility of what it meant to have a firstborn. The next day was spent buying his unborn son a football he'd never get to play with, never get to imagine he was catching the game-winning touchdown.

Drake was asking him a question.

Eric looked up. "Hmm?"

"Your wife was going to have a boy?"

Drake seemed genuinely interested, but Eric found he had no desire to talk about it with him. Instead, he offered a curt nod, picked up the glass of whiskey, and downed half the glass. He felt it dribble down his chin, and he wiped at it before talking. "Like I was saying, my business is in the toilet, and the first real friend I have in years is a Mafia hitman."

"Freelance hitman." Drake corrected.

Eric laughed. "Pardon me. Freelance hitman."

A silent moment passed.

"Thanks." Drake stared into his glass.

"Eric looked up. "For what?"

"For calling me a friend."

Another silent moment passed between them before Eric finally summed up the courage to speak his next thought. "Why me?"

"Huh?"

"Why would you want to befriend me? I mean, my life's pretty ordinary, boring even, not counting the last six, seven months."

Drake sipped his drink thoughtfully. "My life isn't boring. And it's definitely not ordinary. I can't trust anybody. *Anybody.*" He looked like a kid new to a school halfway through the semester being introduced to his new classmates. "I just wanted a chance to have some kind of normalcy. You know, hang out with the guys. Have fun. And I just had a good feeling about you. I felt we clicked." Drake cleared his throat. "Well, look it's late. Why don't you crash here tonight, and we'll figure out what to do next in the morning."

Eric wanted to protest, but as he stood, his head began to spin from the alcohol and the lateness of the hour. So instead, he nodded and trudged off down the hall to the downstairs guestroom.

He closed the door behind him and sank onto the bed. He felt drugged. He kicked off his shoes and stretched out, wondering how he would ever get to sleep. He'd killed a man and watched another man die in cold blood. The man may have been one half of a mugging duo, but he'd turned to run and Drake had shot him in the back. He'd left the scene of the crime, and now he was crashing in the home of a hitman. Could his life get any more surreal? Could this night get any more horrific? It was his last thought as his body, filled with the weight of sleep, sank deep into the mattress.

Drake floated at the corner of Westcott and 17th Street. He knew it to be a dream, the same dream that'd haunted his sleep once or twice a week, ever since...

He'd once heard you could train your mind to seize control of a dream and then bend it to any outcome you wanted. He'd tried it before on other dreams and had been successful, but not with this dream. He'd never been able to change this dream. Like a car accident, you knew it was obscene to watch and yet you found yourself pivoting to get the best possible view, he would watch this dream unfold with an unblinking stare in all its grotesqueness just like he had the last time, and the time before that, and the time before that, and the time...

In this dream, all five senses worked, not at the beginning of the dream, when he was floating at the corner of Westcott and 17th, but as he moved down 17th towards the house. He wanted to turn, run back to the corner, but he kept moving towards the house. And then he was inside the house.

The interior always surprised him, though why he didn't know. It was always the same; spotless, clean, not like the house of a bachelor, but like a model home or a home the owner was ready to put on the market. And yet, an odor, one that wasn't natural to the living, permeated the air. It was faint, like the scent of a flower or perfume that wafts for a moment in the space its wearer was just in. Only, it didn't fade, but grew stronger. He tried to turn his head, his body, back towards the front door, but his body started moving towards the one room he would trade his life not to enter, the kitchen.

As his body floated to the kitchen, the sound of wailing, those of an infant, started, not suddenly, but fading in like a stereo volume knob being turned up slowly. He could feel gooseflesh creep from the top of his skull down his back and arms. He tried to move his hands to cover his ears, his eyes, reach out and grab something to keep him from entering the kitchen, but his hands wouldn't move from the sides of his body. His eyes wouldn't blink, let alone close.

He passed into the kitchen and here the infant wailing was deafening. The room temperature was roasting, like standing too close to a wildfire on a hot summer's day. The heat was emanating from the stove, yet there was no flame anywhere in, on, or around it.

His heart was pounding in his chest like a hammer beating iron into submission. The unnatural scent was growing stronger. It was the unmistakable rancid stench of charred flesh.

He wanted to vomit, could feel the hot sting in his throat as bile crept up into his mouth. And now the wailing filled the air like a sonic boom, ringing in his ears and skull and teeth, as the owner of the unholy scent and the owner of the wailing appeared before him. It was a woman, her clothes hung in charred tatters, revealing blackened skin bubbling with red blisters leaking clear, shiny fluid. In her arms was a baby, not a fetus or embryo, but a fully developed infant. The baby's skin wasn't blackened or bubbling with blisters but melting. Not just the skin, but the entire baby was melting like a wax form would. The toes dripped and splattered on the kitchen tile.

The woman squeezed gently the baby's hand which squished like a melted chocolate bar between her fingers. She looked up from the infant dissolving in her arms to him. There in the eye sockets where her eyeballs should have been, were gelatinous puddles crisp on the edges. She raised her hand, the skin hissed like gristle on a grill, the blisters burst violently, showering him in the clear, sticky serous, and pointed an accusing finger at him. She opened her mouth to speak and the deafening sound of fire raging uncontrolled issued forth.

Drake sat bolt upright, his heart still pounding like a hammer beating steel. His body glistened from the sweat. He looked wild-eyed around the room, making sure he was in *his* room, alone, no longer standing in the kitchen facing his accuser, the only mark who had the right to accuse him, because she wasn't a mark. She was an innocent. The only person he'd killed who didn't deserve it.

Drake got out of the bed and stood on legs made of rubber. He ran a hand through his hair as he staggered into the bathroom, flipped on the light switch. The sixty watt was blinding and his eyes squinched shut in pain, but it was better than darkness. The darkness brought shadows.

He turned on the water faucet and splashed his face and head with cold water. As his eyes became accustomed to the light, he opened them and caught his reflection in the mirror. His eyes dropped quickly. Just like the nightmare, this part immediately following it was always the same.

I should have known.

Not only was hindsight twenty-twenty, it came fully automated with bells, whistles and flashing red lights. Drake had always prided himself on the fact that he'd never killed an innocent, a non-combatant. He'd turned down jobs because there was a risk of collateral damage or because the mark was just some poor shmoe who'd been at the wrong place at the wrong time and seen something he or she shouldn't have seen. It wasn't their fault, and they were just doing their civic duty in appearing in a court of law and telling the jury of their peers what they had witnessed. That was not a good enough reason to kill someone, not for Drake. There was always someone out there willing to take those risks or kill for that reason, and so the jobs had been done, but not by Drake. He knew he could face himself in the mirror any time.

And now here he was, afraid to make eye contact with the image in the looking glass.

I should have *known.*

This time he said it out loud, and the sound of his voice caused him to jump. He turned off the faucet and looked around the bathroom, afraid Eric or someone had heard him and would now ask the inevitable question, "What should you've known?"

He should've known as he drove up to the house in the A/C repair van and saw the newly manicured lawn and fresh coat of paint on the exterior that something had changed, the intel was wrong. When he'd driven by the house a few days before, the yard hadn't been a jungle, but it hadn't been neat either. The grass had needed mowing and weeds needed pulling from the flower bed, but that day, the lawn looked immaculate. And he could still smell the fresh paint on the exterior.

In the nightmare, he's always surprised at the interior of the house. He knew it was his subconscious playing with him. He'd been inside the house, had even remarked to himself as he moved through the house how much it looked like a model home, or a home ready to be put on the market. And still he hadn't given it much thought. Now awake, looking back, it screamed to him.

And several nights a week, every week, since that day, she appears in his dreams with her baby to accuse him, to point out what should have been so obvious to him. He had survived as long as he had, had been as successful as he had, had been able to look himself in the mirror because he had always paid attention to the details no matter how minute or seemingly insignificant. She pointed a finger at his laziness, at his carelessness.

You should have known.

An innocent was dead. No, he corrected himself, two innocents.

This was the part of his life he'd withheld from Eric, that and the fact that the trust fund his grandfather had left him, made him one of the richest young men on the planet. He wouldn't have been able to tell anyone why he'd withheld the latter from Eric. Instinct told him it was best if Eric assumed his good fortune was just one of the perks of his profession. Drake felt the reason for omission of the former was more than obvious.

Drake took a deep breath and looked at himself in the mirror, and not for the first time, watched his reflection blur. He let himself collapse to the bathroom floor and sob, face buried into hands, his body rocking gently. He spent the rest of the night on the cold tile of the bathroom, rocking, weeping, condemning.

I should have known.

Chapter 25

By the time Eric stumbled into the kitchen feeling like he'd been hit by a vehicle and left for dead, Drake showed no signs of the night before. He leaned against the counter sipping what smelled like a banana-berry smoothie made with year old bananas and rancid berries.

"Morning," Drake said in a sing-song tone.

Eric grunted a response which Drake couldn't understand. Eric moved slowly to the coffee maker, picked up the pot, and poured a generous amount into the oversized mug Drake had left out for him. He added creamer and sugar and took a long swig before turning to Drake.

"What on earth is that?" Eric was grimacing and pointing to the smoothie. "It smells awful."

"Energy shake. Guaranteed to cure hangovers and whatever else that ails you." He extended the glass to Eric. "Want one?"

Eric got a better whiff of what he was now sure was the liquefied version of a compost heap and pushed the glass away. "No thanks. Coffee'll be fine."

"Suit yourself." Drake took another swig. "But you'll do better drinking water. Water dilutes the alcohol while it hydrates."

Eric nodded weakly and took another sip of coffee. He looked around the kitchen. "You don't happen to get the paper, do you?"

"Yeah, but I haven't gone out to get it yet." Drake finished off the smoothie with a grimace and immediately washed it down with a long draw from his own coffee cup.

"Mind if I?" Eric pointed towards the front door.

"Suit yourself," Drake responded. "But it won't be in there."

Eric stopped. "What won't be in there?"

"What you're looking for." Drake sipped his coffee and began rinsing out the smoothie glass in the sink.

Eric shook his head, and, deciding he wanted to check anyway, set down his coffee cup and left the kitchen.

Drake didn't turn as he heard Eric close the front door and start tearing through the paper. He set the glass in the drainboard, picked up his cup, drained it, and then set about making himself another cup. "Anything?"

Eric re-entered the kitchen, thumbing through the paper. "There's nothing here."

"I didn't expect there'd be." He turned and leaned back on the counter. "Two punks who ended up on the wrong end of the gun this time, who's gonna care? Certainly not the papers. There might be a blurb on the evening news tonight, but with no leads and the only victims, crooks. Most people will simply think they got what was coming to them and want to know the scores."

Eric put down the paper. He took a tentative sip of his coffee.

"Something on your mind?" Drake stayed leaning against the counter.

Eric stared into the coffee cup hard, as if trying to see the bottom of the mug through the coffee. Since last night he was having trouble with how to look at himself. He'd shot a man. In self-defense. And yet, that just didn't seem like a good enough reason. He'd *shot* a man. And he didn't know if he should be ashamed or have an improved opinion of himself. It was like joining the Mile High Club. Everybody knew about it, had plenty of opportunity to join, yet something held them back. Eric knew what that something was. Getting caught.

Of course, getting caught joining the Mile High Club wasn't nearly as severe as getting caught killing someone, even if the guy was a scumbag. So a flight attendant might catch you, what was she going to do? Open the door and throw you out of the plane? Sure, maybe she'd report you to the captain, who'd call it in, and the airline would let you know that after the flight landed you were no longer persona grata on any of their fleet, but that was pretty much the extent. Probably she'd, or he, sneer and make some condescending remark as she got 13A another bag of pretzels to help him finish his Diet Coke, and that'd be it.

What does sex on an airplane have to do with shooting a man?

Eric shook himself. He kept doing that. He'd start to think about it, to try to reason through it, and then he'd run off on a tangent that sounded more like rationalizing and justifying than understanding.

"Eric?" Drake was saying. "You okay?"

"I-" Eric paused, not sure what he wanted to say. He didn't want to be rude, but he just wanted to leave. He wanted it with every fiber of his being. He wanted to leave under some pretense, any pretense. But he just couldn't lie to Drake. And so he didn't. "I gotta go."

Eric pushed away from the kitchen table and called "I'll see ya," over his shoulder. He thanked God his car was here as he moved quickly out of the house. He pulled his keys from his pocket, opened the door, climbed inside, fired up the engine, and sped away like a man taking his expectant wife to the hospital.

He didn't even think where he was going, just drove. Like a robot on an assembly line, he followed a pre-programmed set of instructions and found himself sitting in the road in front of his house, not in the driveway, just idling in front of the house as if he were the world's worst, most obvious burglar casing the place.

It was the last place he wanted to be, that house. That house belonged to a happily married couple expecting their first child. They've turned one of the upstairs bedrooms, the one right next to theirs, into a nursery. The room's painted yellow, a nice, neutral color that seems to work with either boys or girls. And besides, it's a baby, not a teenager, so the room could be painted black, and the kid wouldn't care. But it's a nursery, and it's their first child and they'll definitely have a second, maybe even a third. The more the merrier, the couple would laugh and say as they painted the eggshell white walls yellow and thought up baby names (the doctor could be wrong after all) from the conservative, Jonathan or Michelle, to the boring, David or Lisa, to the absurd, Rutabaga.

He had no business being in that house. He didn't belong. That young family belonged, but he didn't.

But he had to be somewhere. Anywhere.

Eric pulled out his cell phone and dialed his sister's number. She answered, sounding frazzled, on the third ring.

"Hello?"

Remembering something his old mentor used to say, "Smile, cause people can always hear you smile," he put the best smile he could on his face. "Hey, Sis."

He could definitely hear Jennifer smile as she exclaimed, "Hey."

He couldn't believe how good it was to hear her voice. "What're you up to today?"

Jennifer exhaled heavily. "Just trying to subdue the Barbie Army insurrection."

Eric couldn't help but laugh. He could see his niece's collection of Barbie dolls with flattops.

"What about you?"

"Well, it seems my day is free. I thought maybe I'd drive up and take you and the girls to lunch."

"Lunch? Out? Real food? Adult conversation?" She seemed to relish each word like cool water on parched lips. "How soon can you be here?"

Eric searched the house room by room, in his mind, one last time for himself, but he wasn't there. Only the happy family. Eric pulled away, wondering if he'd ever be able to find himself in that house again, knowing the odds grew smaller and smaller, like the reflection of the house in his rearview mirror.

"I'm on my way as we speak."

Eric rang the doorbell and listened to the mayhem inside.

"Mommy, Uncle Eric's at the door," Julie yelled over the sound of something exploding on the television.

"I don't wanna wear shoes," Jody screamed.

"Jody, you were wearing your shoes. You just had them on the wrong feet." Jennifer said in exasperation.

"They fit better." Jody protested.

"No they don't." Jennifer raised her voice. "Just a minute. Julie, turn the T.V. down, please. You want to go deaf?"

"What?" Julie shouted.

If Julie had been older, Eric would've sworn the kid was being a smart aleck, but he didn't think she was that clever. Yet.

"They do too." Jody was disagreeing.

"No, they *don't*."

Eric was laughing now. His sister was now having a "yes they do, no they don't" argument with a child. The woman definitely needed a little downtime. He rang the doorbell again.

"Mom," Julie screamed. "Door."

He heard his sister scream at Jody to leave her shoes on the proper feet, at Julie to turn down the television and don't make her say it again, and at him that she was coming.

Jennifer opened the door. "Eric," she cried. She gave him a big hug.

"Hey, Sis." Eric embraced her. "How you doin'?

Jennifer released him. "Oh, you know. You've gotta love the swamp rats."

"Why's that?" Eric smiled.

"It's God's way of making sure they make it to eighteen." She stepped back and looked over him, a perplexed yet pleasant look on her face.

"What?" Eric looked over himself. "Is my slip showing? Something offensive in my nostrils?"

Jennifer laughed. "No. You're just..." her voice trailed off. "Different. Happy."

She smiled. "I like it."

"Uncle Eric," Jody squealed as she gave him her traditional bear hug around the legs.

"Hey there, JoJo." Eric rubbed a hand over her head.

Jody looked at him, her face screwed up indignantly. "I'm not JoJo. I'm Jody."

"Oh, I'm sorry. My mistake." He touched her chin. "Hey there, Jody."

She gave him an approving smile and buried her head into his thighs.

Julie walked up, seemingly bored with the whole day. "Hi, Uncle Eric," she yawned.

"Hey, Jules." Eric waited for protestations but received none. "Everybody ready to eat?"

"Yeah." Jody sounded like she'd just been asked if she wanted an ice cream sundae for lunch.

"Sure," Julie answered with indifference.

Eric looked at his sister, who smiled. "Like I said, you gotta love the swamp rats." She closed the front door. "Do you mind if we take my car," she said as she locked the deadbolt. "It's easier than moving the car seats."

"Oh, yeah, sure." Eric followed his sister and nieces to the minivan parked in the driveway. He helped his sister buckle the girls in, and then climbed into the driver's seat at his sister's request.

"So," Eric said as he buckled himself in and turned on the engine. "Chuck E. Cheese's?"

The girls screamed in delight.

"I'll kill you right now." Jennifer responded.

Eric laughed and held up his hands. "Okay, okay. So where do you want to go?"

"Olive Garden."

Forty-five minutes later they were seated at a table, meals ordered, and Julie and Jody arguing over the crayons.

"You've each got the same colors, you little heathens." Jennifer yanked the crayons away from each girl.

"We're not heathens, Judy rebuked her mother. "We're Americans."

"Give them back," Julie demanded.

"Excuse me, little lady." Jennifer's voice had that tone which says, *I'm sure I must've misunderstood you, because if you said what I think you said, I'm gonna have to blister your little bottom right here in front of God and everybody, and you really don't want that do you?* It's the tone all adults develop once they have children and works right up until the time those children hit puberty. It worked today.

Julie backed down. "Mom, may we please have our crayons back?"

"Are you two gonna stop fighting?" Jennifer held up the crayons.

Julie eyed the crayons hungrily. "Yes."

"Yes, what?" Jennifer demanded.

Julie rolled her eyes a little. "Yes, *Ma'am*."

"Yes, Ma'am," Jody chimed in.

Jennifer laid the crayons down in front of the girls.

Each snatched up a different colored crayon and went to work on their placemat.

The waitress arrived with Sprites for the girls, and a small carafe of sangria with two wine glasses.

Jennifer thanked her as she grabbed the carafe and filled her glass halfway. She looked up to Eric, the carafe still poised over her glass. "You are gonna drive us back home." It sounded more like a plea than a demand or request.

Eric nodded. "Of course."

Jennifer smiled and filled the glass to the rim. She filled the other glass halfway and set the carafe down. She picked up her glass, took a long sip of the sangria, smiled, set down the glass, leaned into Eric, and fixed her eyes on his. "So what's going on?"

Chapter 26

Eric filled his mouth with sangria, but didn't swallow, as he contemplated how to answer. What was going on? Really. He wasn't sure, but he knew he wasn't the same man who'd come up for Christmas. Nor was he the same man who'd gone target shooting the day before with Drake. Or should he still call him Paul? Probably Paul. In any case, he was different. He *was* happy.

But why, he wondered. Why was he happy? Last night, this morning, during the drive up to his sister's house, he'd been in a moral dilemma. Not so much about killing the guy last night, he'd realized. That had astonished him. Like everyone else, he'd said he could've killed the guy who'd cut him off then flipped him off once or twice before in his lifetime, and like everyone else, he'd said it but never done it. Like everyone else, he knew he could kill someone trying to harm a loved one, and like everyone else he'd said he could never kill someone in cold blood.

But hadn't he? Eric hadn't known it at the time, but Paul could've killed those two guys. He hadn't needed Eric to protect him. And the guy wasn't advancing on Eric, he'd been moving towards Paul. So if one looked at it reasonably, he'd killed not in self-defense or in defense of another, but in cold blood. And what astonished him was that he was okay with that.

What was really bothering him, he realized, was what to do about his friendship with Paul.

"Well, I've met someone."

"Met someone?" Jennifer leaned in closer.

"Not like that," Eric explained. "A guy."

"You met a guy?" Jennifer sat back; her face screwed up with incredulity. "You lose your wife and turn gay?"

"No, no, no." Eric took another swallow of sangria. "I didn't turn gay." He'd put the emphasis on the word turn and knew by the way his sister lifted her left eyebrow and folded her arms under her breasts exactly what she was about to say.

"So you've always *been* gay?"

He was right. "Boy this is coming out all wrong." He rubbed his forehead.

"Mommy?" Jody asked, looking up from her drawing of a clown, his face all purple and blue like a bruise. "What's gay?"

"It's when you like watching movies with guys." Julie sounded just like her mother, not looking up from her drawing of the same clown, only his face was white with a purple mouth and hair."

"That's not gay," Jennifer responded, not taking her eyes of Eric.

"That's what Daddy said." Julie retorted.

"Mommy likes watching movies with Daddy. Does that make her gay?" Jody's voice carried and several patrons turned from other tables to stare at their table.

"No it doesn't," Jennifer said. "When did Daddy tell you that?"

Julie looked up from her clown. "Last week. We were watching T.V., and the guy told this other guy he was gay, and I asked Daddy what that meant, and he said that's what it meant."

"I'm not gay," Eric said above the fray, causing a general hush about the room.

"But what if you really liked the movie and you didn't want to watch it by yourself?" Jody asked.

Eric could hear chuckles from around the room as more people turned to stare at him.

"Jody," Jennifer said as she picked up a crayon and handed it to her daughter, "why don't you give your clown matching bruises on his hands and feet?"

Jody's lips curled in a wicked smile as she took the crayon and busied painting contusions on her clown's hands.

Jennifer turned her attention back to Eric. "So. Tell me more about your boyfriend."

Eric cast her a warning glance.

Jennifer held up her hands. "Okay. You were about to tell me about your, uh, movie buddy?"

"Look, if you don't drop this gay thing, I'm not gonna talk to you at all."

"Oh, lighten up fancy pants."

Eric rolled his eyes. Same ole Jennifer.

The waitress arrived with salad and the girls' meals. The girls threw the crayons aside and tucked into their grilled cheese sandwiches as if they were steaks, or more apropos for small children, McDonald's cheeseburgers.

Jennifer finally told the waitress there was enough fresh grated cheese on the salad only after it disappeared under a blanket of parmesan. She dished salad for herself and Eric. "So out with it."

"Do you remember that house I sold at Christmas?" Eric forked salad into his mouth, grimacing a little from the cheese. He swallowed. "That's the guy."

Jennifer took a satisfied bite of salad and then gave Eric a look to continue.

"Well, he's new to the area, didn't know anybody. He had an extra ticket to a Bulls game and called me up." Eric took a bite of salad and added. "Courtside."

Eric wasn't sure why he had to tell her that, but it felt good to brag. "He invited me a couple of days later to a hockey game."

"Hockey? You?"

"I like hockey. And these were on the glass." Eric said defensively.

"Courtside seats. Seats on the glass. What's this guy do for a living? I wanna date him."

Eric ignored the jibe. "Anyway, we went out for a couple of meals and then he had to go out of town on business and asked me to go with him."

"Where?" Jennifer asked through a mouthful of salad.

"Vegas."

There was that eyebrow again. "Okay," Eric conceded, "I'll give you that one. No actually it was pretty cool. It was a gun convention."

Jennifer stopped chewing. "Gun?"

"Well, that's what he does for a living. Imports and exports exotic weapons."

Eric hated lying to his sister, but what could he do? It wasn't safe telling her Drake, or was it still Paul, killed people for a living. And even if it was safe, if it was okay, what was the polite way of saying it? Hitman? Assassin? He remembered an Army recruiter coming to the high school one time when he was a senior, telling the young men that when people asked him what he did for a living, he liked to say he was in population control. Somehow, he didn't think that any of these would have flown with Jennifer.

Jennifer swallowed. "And is *he* gay?" She took a large draught of sangria.

"No. I think he was just lonely. And to be honest, I think he felt sorry for me. He knew about Emily. He'd contacted another agent trying to reach me and she'd told him what'd happened." Eric took a bite of salad and chewed thoughtfully. "I guess he felt we were kindred spirits."

"Hockey, guns, weekend trips to Vegas," Jennifer said with a playful smile on her face. "Who are you and what have you done with my brother?" She set down her fork in the salad bowl and pushed it away from her. "Seriously, though, it's really great to see you happy." Her eyes moistened and her bottom lip trembled ever so slightly. She looked away, blinking furiously. "You really had me scared."

Each word had come out of her mouth deliberately, pointedly, just above a whisper. She looked at Eric dead in the eye. "After I left your house that last time, I honestly didn't think I'd see you again."

Eric could hear the pain in her voice; see it in her eyes, on her brow. He felt a pang in his own heart. What was it Jennifer would always say whenever someone around her was brooding? *Pity party, table for one.* And that's exactly what he'd done. He'd been so wrapped up in his own loss, in his own pain, had become so caught up in his own self destruction; he'd forgotten that others were feeling loss and pain watching him. He felt his face flush with shame. "I know. I'm sorry."

Jennifer shook her head and wiped quickly at her eyes. "I'm just glad you're back."

"Me, too."

Jennifer, stealing a glance at her daughters to make sure they didn't see Mommy cry, shook off the soberness of the moment and smiled brightly as the waitress brought their meals. "Anyway, I'm just glad you've got a friend of your own for a change."

Eric waited patiently as the waitress piled what Eric was sure had to be the restaurant's remaining supply of parmesan cheese on Jennifer's shrimp Alfredo and walked away before saying anything. "What do you mean?" He shoveled an enormous forkful of lasagna into his mouth.

Jennifer offered the girls each a bite of shrimp. "Well, you never really had a lot of friends growing up and it seemed after you married, all your friends were Emily's friends." She slurped some of the linguine and shrimp into her mouth and swallowed. "This new friend of yours, he's been really good for you. What'd you say his name was?"

Eric held up a finger to signal he needed a minute, or more, to finish chewing what he realized might've been too large a bite. He also found himself biting his lip before saying something snide like, "I didn't." He was definitely back, and it was definitely within the old repartee between him and Jennifer. But it seemed a bit too secret agent man, a little too James Bondish, and Drake/Paul was a man, not some fictional character in a story existing only in the mind of a writer or a reader.

Yet how could he answer Jennifer's question when he hadn't made up his own mind what he should be calling Drake/Paul? Maybe he should make up some generic name like John or Joe? Those sounded purposefully vague, stupidly coy, and downright insulting to his sister's intelligence. They definitely sounded like he was trying to hide something, like his gay lover's real name.

So no made-up names then. But wasn't Paul a made-up name? No. Paul had been a real person, and as far as a lot of people were concerned, he still was. It was, however, just a name, a name of a guy who bought a house, and he hadn't gotten to know a name last night, he'd gotten to know a man. He wasn't talking to Paul Stephens last night. Drake Wetherford had let down his guard for the first time in who knew how many years.

And wasn't Paul Stephens a persona? A deadly persona, yes, but still just a persona? After all, Paul was a hitman. People who got to know him ended up dead and Paul had had plenty of opportunities to kill him. But he hadn't. That's because Drake wasn't a killer. Drake was a…friend.

"Drake. His name's Drake."

Jennifer wrinkled her nose. "Sounds a bit preppy."

Eric laughed. "Nobody says preppy anymore."

"Ostentatious, then?" Jennifer wrapped linguine around her fork.

"No, but that's what you're being, using big words like that." Eric stuck another forkful of lasagna into his mouth. He was feeling ravenous now.

"In that case, I want tiramisu for dessert." Jennifer finished off her glass of sangria and poured herself another one.

"Because you're ostentatious?"

"Because you're buying."

Chapter 27

"I probably should've called first," Eric said out loud to himself as he eased the Expedition into the driveway and pulled up close behind Drake's Mercedes. He cut the engine but didn't get out of the vehicle.

Jennifer had been right; Eric didn't have any friends, none really to speak of as an adult. Sure he had some close acquaintances, but not anyone he'd call a friend, let alone a best friend. He and Emily had friends, but that was he and Emily. He and Emily had John and Susan, Randy and Allison, Dan and Donna. Emily also had single female friends who came over for dinner, to watch a movie, enjoy a bar-b-que. Eric enjoyed all of these people, spent time with them, but never cultivated any deep, meaningful relationship one on one with any of them or anyone else, for that matter, outside of Emily. He just didn't feel the need.

Once Emily died, John and Susan, Randy and Allison, Dan and Donna didn't call to hang out. Sure they called to see how he was doing the first couple of months, offered hollow invitations for dinner, but they really didn't want him around. He was a reminder that there was something worse than death, those who had loved and been left behind to face this world again alone.

And of course, Emily's single friends didn't call. He couldn't blame them. He hadn't been their friend, just the man they had to tolerate because of their friendship with Emily.

Drake had become the first man Eric could honestly say was a friend by his own right. And now that he had a friend, the fear that he might've lost that friend by his actions earlier that day left him unable to move.

The cold was creeping fast into the car, however, numbing Eric's fingers and toes. He caught himself shivering and decided it was time to get out of the car. He hurried up the walkway to the door and gave it three hard knocks.

The door opened almost immediately, as if Drake had been by the door, waiting for Eric. Drake smiled broadly. "Come on in." He motioned for Eric to follow.

"Sorry, I didn't call first." Eric stepped into the house and closed the door.

Drake waved off the apology with a "don't sweat it" over his shoulder as he led Eric into the den. "I was just about to make Mojitos. You want one?"

Eric sat down on one of the loveseats. "Sure, if you'll answer a question for me."

Drake slid in behind the bar. "Shoot."

"What's a Mojito?"

"Mojito." Drake savored the word like a favorite food. "I just love that word." He grabbed a mixer from under the bar. "It's Cuban." He reached into the mini-fridge and produced a handful of diced limes as he made the drinks. "Limes...brown sugar...white rum...tequila...mix it up..." He pulled two tumblers off the shelf behind him and dropped ice into them from a small ice bucket. "Serve over ice...some mint leaves...top off with club soda..." He picked up the two glasses, walked over to Eric, handed him one, and sat down in the loveseat opposite. "And enjoy your own private siesta." He took a sip, closed his eyes, and sat back, pleasure washing over his face. "Mojito. *Moooeee Heeee Toooeee.*"

Eric wondered just how many *Moooeee Heeee Toooeee*s Drake had already had today as he sniffed at the concoction. It smelled cool, refreshing, and just a little bit dangerous, like the private siesta could end with a little kneeling before the porcelain throne come morning. He sipped tentatively and decided the siesta might be worth the worship.

They drank the first Mojito in silence, but it didn't take long for the liquor to loosen their tongues. Eric gave Drake a rundown of his own life over the course of several more drinks, and after the Cuban food arrived, Cubanos and fried plantains, Eric told Drake about Emily while they ate.

Or at least he tried, but when he went beyond the general, like he and Emily were high school sweethearts, to more personal information, like how much of a planner Emily was, mapping out their college careers at Northwestern and how she insisted they wait till they were married, something would happen. Drake wouldn't just steer the conversation away from the intimate details, he'd hijack the subject all together. Eric was just recounting Emily's excitement and how cute she was upon learning she was pregnant, when Drake just stood up, excused himself for the bathroom and walked out of the room.

Eric stared after him.

Okay, that was rude.

He finished the last of his Mojito and wondered why Drake would do that. He'd listened for several hours as Drake detailed his life and Drake couldn't give him a few minutes to talk about the most important part of his life. What was his problem? Drake had been in special ops, had conducted black ops, was now an assassin, surely he had the stomach to listen to him go on *like a chick*, a small sarcastic voice finished the thought in his head.

Of course, Eric thought, that had to be it. Drake was a man's man. Why would he be comfortable hearing me gush about a woman he never met, didn't know, and will never have the chance to. Come to think of it, Eric thought as he lifted the empty glass to his lips without thinking, Drake had never once mentioned having had a girlfriend much less a wife. Drake had absolutely no frame of reference. It was like Drake trying to talk about one of his missions when he was a Ranger, except that was interesting. Eric was positively boring him to the point he'd had to feign a full bladder twice now. He wasn't trying to be rude; he just didn't know how to politely tell Eric to shut up.

Eric remonstrated himself as he set down the empty glass.

I'm talking to a man about something that isn't pertinent to him.

When Drake returned, Eric decided, he'd deftly move the subject to something more manly like sports or guns or...what was on his mind if he wasn't going to talk about Emily; just how Drake did his job. He shifted in his seat. He had to be smooth. Casual. Nonchalant. Unassuming.

Drake walked back into the room and was sitting down when Eric blurted out, "So how many people have you killed?"

Smooth. Really smooth.

Drake stopped mid-sit. Eric gaped, aghast as he heard himself speak. "I mean, have you killed lots of people?"

Now would be a good time to shut up.

"I'm sorry?"

"I-I-I mean, d-d-do you-you keep, keep, you know keep a c-c-count?" *Oh my gosh, I'm Woody Allen.*

Drake chuckled as he finished sitting down. "Look it's okay, really. You can ask me anything you want to ask. If I don't feel comfortable answering, I just won't answer." He took a sip of his Mojito.

"Okay." Eric collected himself and took a deep breath. "So." He looked at Drake expectantly who just smiled serenely back as if Eric had just complimented him on his ability to mix drinks. After a moment, he raised his eyebrows, queuing Drake, but he didn't seem to notice. After another moment, Eric got it. "Oh. Right." Eric looked around the room, contemplating his next question. "When's, ah, when's the...uh...last time...you...ah..." he cleared his throat.

I'm freaking Woody Allen again.

"When'sthelasttimeyoukilledsomeone?"

Drake's eyebrows rose. "Sorry, I didn't quite catch that."

Eric took a breath and slowed down. "When's the last time you killed someone?"

The eyebrows settled. "You were there."

"I mean other than the garage."

"So do I." Drake sipped his drink.

This time it was Eric's brows rising in surprise then furrowing as he thought about Drake's last statement. Where else had he watched Drake kill someone? Had it been that traumatic that he'd blocked it from his memory? He'd had his fuzzy moments during the six months he'd turned to the bottle after Emily had died, but this was an absolute bust.

And the look on Drake's face at this moment was helping. His head, slightly inclined, his eyes opened wide, brows raised as if helping to pull up the memory from the depths of Eric's brain, and a smirk that said, "Come on. You know."

Eric met that smirk with a blank stare.

Drake took another sip of Mojito. "The Bulls game."

"Bulls game?" Eric repeated the words in his head, but still had nothing.

Drake continued to prod. "The corpse in the back of the ambulance. When we were getting into the cab."

And now Eric remembered. "That was you?"

Drake smiled and nodded. Eric got the idea the smile was more for Eric finally getting it than pride in his work. Not that Drake didn't take pride in his work. He was sure Drake had a lot of pride. He was good after all. He must've killed dozens of people over the years if not hundreds and he'd never been caught.

But where was this line of thought taking him? Who cared if Drake took pride in his work?

Eric shook his head to clear it. "But when? How? Why?"

Drake watched his drink as he swirled it, the mint leaves went round and round like a boat in a whirlpool.

Okay, not going to answer. That's not really important though, is it? That's not what I wanted to know ultimately, was it?

Eric took a sip of his own drink, pondered his next question, and didn't really care if he sounded like Woody Allen.

"What does it feel like...for you...killing?"

Drake didn't answer, but Eric got the sense it wasn't because he was uncomfortable, he was letting Eric explore his own question. Eric took another breath. "Do you feel bad? Remorse?"

"No," Drake answered without hesitation. "I'm very particular about the jobs I take, and like I said last night, the people I deal with are not saints. Their deaths are of no loss to society. They deserve what happens."

"But have you ever killed the wrong person? I mean, have you ever had one job that just didn't sit right with you?"

Drake had finally tracked Fabozzi down in Mexico. *Mexico*. How thoroughly cliché and unimaginative. But Drake reminded himself, Fabozzi was a wiz with numbers, not ideas. Still, it had taken him six months to track him down, hiding in a little hotel in a little village that was better described as a toilet. Fabozzi stood out like a sore thumb, like a gringo with a sore thumb. He didn't know the language, couldn't just blend in.

Drake flew into Mexico City Christmas Eve, spent the night on a little bus singing *Feliz Navidad* with the rest of his compañeros, arriving in the little toilet sometime after sunrise. The sun hadn't been up more than half an hour, and the heat was already sweltering. His shirt clung to his back as a river of perspiration flowed from his skin. Dust rose up with every footfall, but didn't settle, just hung in the air like gnats. The dry breeze offered no respite from the heat but felt more like a blow dryer held directly into the face, chapping the lips, and parching the throat.

Drake had only to ask one villager, follow the vector of the little señorita's filthy index finger pointing to the inn to find him. He was in his room, boxers and a tank undershirt, grimy with sweat and fear. Drake knocked on the door and placed the silencer up to the eye hole. He heard Fabozzi swear, a crash of what sounded like glass bottles, and then Fabozzi, coming to the front door. He could actually hear Fabozzi's heavy breath as he reached the door. He pulled the trigger once, heard the silent plink, saw a tiny hole explode in the door, followed by the unmistakable sound of flesh and bone hitting the floor as nothing more than dead weight.

But this would not suffice. He had to make sure Fabozzi was dead. Pulling his knife from his pocket, he popped the lock and opened the door. It creaked like a bad horror movie. Fabozzi like on the floor blood dribbled from where one eye used to be. Drake pulled the trigger two more times.

Drake walked out of the little village, rubbing his hands together like a man leaving a public restroom, but still unable to get the stink off his hands.

Drake reached over and picked up Eric's glass. "Looks like we could use a refill." He moved to the bar to mix more drinks.

Eric moved unconsciously to the edge of his seat, desperate to press Drake for an answer. He needed to know if his own lack of emotion was common or was that only reserved for professionals. He thought about the young punk, man, he corrected himself, young man he'd killed in what he thought was the defense of Drake's life. He hadn't needed to kill the guy and that realization still didn't seem to bother him. Was that numbness or something else?

But Drake's body language suggested finality. That question was not going to be answered, not tonight anyway.

Drake returned with the glasses filled. "I think that's enough with the Q and A for tonight." Drake handed Eric his glass. He sat down and picked up the remote. "Let's see what's on the tube."

The plasma television snapped on and Leno filled the sixty-inch frame larger than life.

Eric squinted at his watch. "Is it that late already? I should get home." He set the glass down and started to get up."

"Don't be silly." Drake laughed at some joke at the expense of some celebrity or politician. "I can't let you drive home. Just crash in the same room you had last night."

"Nonsense. I'm fine." Eric said but sat down anyway. He picked his glass back up and took a swig. Mojitos were no longer tasting refreshing, just dangerous. He put the glass back down.

They watched Leno finish up his monologue, show a taped bit and introduce his first guest in silence, neither man looking away from the big screen.

Finally, Eric cleared his throat as Leno announced they'd be right back. "I really appreciate you letting me stay here. I wasn't looking forward to going home tonight. Well, I don't know if I would've gone home tonight. Probably would've checked into a hotel."

Now that he'd started, he felt the words fall out of his mouth in a rush, the need to confess his reluctance ready to burst like a levy. "To tell you the truth, I don't think I can ever go back into that house. Without Emily there, that's all it is. A house. Not a home."

He picked up the now watered-down Mojito without thinking, took a sip, and almost coughed the contents of his mouth across the loveseat. It was now beyond dangerous and just pure evil. "I went there this morning." He paused, feeling the desire to spit, but swallowing. "I couldn't even get out of the car. I just sat there looking at it."

Eric suddenly felt very, very tired, as if he'd spent the whole day working in the yard on a hot day. He wanted nothing more than to find the guestroom he'd been in last night, crawl into the bed, and sleep.

Drake remained silent for another moment, but as Leno came back on, he stole a glance at Eric. "I can't even begin to imagine what you've been going through." He picked up the remote and thumbed the power button. The television screen went black. "Feel free to crash here for a couple of days. In fact," Drake stood up and stretched, looked at Eric with a smile, "I've got an idea."

Chapter 28

Two days later Eric and Drake stood at the front door of Eric's house. Drake watched as Eric held the key in a trembling hand but didn't insert it into the lock. Eric stood poised, looking beyond the front door into the house, as if seeing the interior and some invisible monster ready to leap as soon as he opened the door.

"It's okay, Man," Drake said as he took the key from Eric's hand and unlocked the door. He watched Eric closely as he turned the knob and opened the door. There was no eerie creaking like there'd be in a B-horror flick, nor was there any beast or person standing on the other side of the door, yet Eric flinched just the same.

Drake put a hand on Eric's shoulder and gently nudged him into the foyer. Eric's breathing quickened and Drake was afraid Eric might hyperventilate and pass out, but he kept moving him forward. At the foot of the stairs, Eric froze, white-knuckling the banister and staring up the stairs as if seeing the boogeyman standing there waiting for him.

"You want to wait outside while I pack your stuff?" Drake asked.

Eric nodded, not taking his eyes from the top of the stairs.

"You have any luggage?"

Again, Eric nodded, then whispered, "In the bedroom closet." He turned slowly and walked straight out the front door without looking back.

Drake watched Eric close the door behind him, thankful he'd suggested a moving company pack up the house, glad he'd rented Eric a storage space, and relieved Eric hadn't broken down. He took the stairs two at a time and found himself on the landing with four doors. Three were closed, but one was open. He peeked in. Bathroom.

Drake picked the first closed door, opened it, and walked in. Light shone brightly through the window cutting across the room, hitting a rocking chair he could have sworn had been moving when he opened the door, but now stood still, a football cradled in its seat. The walls, a bright yellow, were covered in life-size pictures of cartoon characters. On the left side of the room stood a baby's crib in white with a mobile of Dr. Seuss characters hanging quietly above it. The furniture was all matching white and covered with stuffed animals. In the corner, in the shadow, stood Emily.

Drake stepped back, slamming his head hard against the door jamb. As the stars cleared, he saw not Emily, but the Cat in the Hat, smiling in a slightly wicked way, as if the Cat had known what trick of the brain Drake had just been victimized by; knew he'd been mistaken for someone else, and found the entire episode devilishly humorous.

Drake exited the room quickly, shut the door, and took a step back into the hall. He stood there for a moment, chastising himself. He was being an idiot. Cartoon characters didn't think, didn't feel, didn't do anything. And the Cat in the Hat always had that grin on his face. There were no such things as ghosts, and nothing, absolutely nothing, other than him in the house.

Still, he felt gooseflesh crawl up his back and over his shoulder like a lizard as he reached for the knob of the next closed door. Drake watched his hand tremble and then shoot back as if he'd just grabbed the handle of a hot iron skillet.

Get a grip on yourself.

Drake clenched his fist in an effort to subdue the trembling before it could spread throughout his body. He willed himself to place his hand on the doorknob and open the door as he steeled himself against what lay on the other side. The muscles in his jaw rippled as he surveyed what must be Eric and Emily's bedroom. Just a bedroom. No ghosts. No boogeyman. No charred remains. Yet Drake felt himself hesitate to enter the room. He felt like a child, scared of the dark, standing at the top of the stairs peering down into the dark and dank basement.

This is ridiculous.

Drake stepped into the room and moved quickly to the closet door which was also closed. He grabbed the knob, flung the door open, and felt wildly around the inside wall for the light switch. He flipped it up, stepped in, scanned for the suitcase, and yanked it off the top shelf, throwing it to the ground. Fumbling with the zipper, he cursed himself for not just grabbing some garbage bags from the kitchen.

Once open, hangers and clothing were unceremoniously ripped from the rod and stuffed into the suitcase. Shoes were quickly thrown on top. Drake dragged the suitcase out of the closet, spied the hutch, and hurried to it. Dumping the contents of the sock and underwear drawer into the suitcase, Drake forced the drawer back into the hutch.

Anything I missed I'll buy him.

Drake zipped the suitcase shut, picked it up and, forcing himself not to run, walked out of the room, down the stairs and out the front door. He could feel the heebie-jeebies melting off of him as he breathed in the cold air and stared into the midday sun.

"You okay?" Eric asked as he watched Drake bolt through the door.

"Oh, yeah, sure." Drake closed his eyes, took a deep breath, and slowly closed the door behind him as if nothing more exciting had happened inside than him just packing a few things in a suitcase.

Drake locked the door. "Let's go.

As they drove back to Drake's house, Eric asked, "Are you sure you don't mind me staying at your place?"

Drake smiled. "It was my idea, wasn't it?"

"Well, yeah," Eric responded. "But—"

"The movers," Drake interrupted, "will be by your house tomorrow. You don't have to be there if you don't want to. In fact, I'd recommend you stay away. Those guys move a whole lot faster if no one's home. And," he said with a wry smile, "it's just easier to believe they handled all your personal items with the utmost concern for privacy and care."

Eric laughed uncomfortably. He didn't want to just believe they handled his personal items with privacy and care. He didn't want to think of them handling anything in the house at all. There weren't just his items in the house, and he didn't want strangers handling Emily's items, let alone personal items. He could feel a surge of panic at the vision of guys, the type of guys who whistle and catcall women as they pass by, opening Emily's lingerie drawer, pulling out her undergarments, fondling the baby blue teddy she wore for him the night they decided to get pregnant. What comments would they make? What lewd things would they say? He could feel a white-hot pang of anger that constricted his chest.

"Where'd you find this company? Are they reputable?" Eric asked, unable to keep the anger or panic out of his voice.

Drake glanced askance at Eric. "Relax," he said in a reassuring tone, "it'll be fine. They're the same guys who moved me." He slowed and stopped at a red light. "Any idea of your plans?"

Eric grunted, glad to be taken out of his jealous revelry, but also a little irritated to be taken out of his jealous revelry. "I don't know. I can't sell houses anymore." He looked out the window.

"Just take all the time you need," Drake said, accelerating as the light turned green. "No rush." He glanced in the rearview mirror, changed lanes, and stopped at another light before speaking again. "I was thinking. Since we're both unemployed at the moment, and its freaking cold, maybe this would be a good time to get outta Dodge. We could go someplace warm. How about Australia? Or maybe the Virgin Islands?"

Eric frowned. "I don't have a passport."

Drake nodded. "And it's not like you can just pop into the post office and get one like a Big Mac or Whopper."

They drove in silence for a few minutes. "Hey, I know," Drake exclaimed. "You like fishing?"

"I don't know," Eric admitted. He hadn't been fishing since he was a kid going down to one of the lakes with his grandfather, and all he could remember about those trips was how much he hated baiting his hook.

"You ever been deep sea fishing?" Drake persisted.

Eric shrugged. "No."

"Well, I hear the Keys' got great fishing this time of year." Drake turned into his neighborhood. "What say we fly down there, charter a boat, and spend the rest of the week out fishing?"

Eric didn't answer right away.

"We could use the change in scenery," Drake added.

"I'll think about it." Eric finally said, but he had to admit to himself, it was a good idea. He could use a break from all these memories.

"That's all I ask," Drake said a triumphant note in his voice as he pulled into his driveway.

Once inside, Drake disappeared up the stairs. Eric pulled out his cell phone and dialed his sister. She answered on the third ring.

"Hey, Bro," Jennifer said as if she'd been waiting not too patiently for his call.

"Hey. I just wanted you to know I've moved—" Eric paused.

"Eric, you there?"

"Before I tell you, you've got to promise not to give me a hard time."

"Well, there's a setup if I've ever heard one. Eric Messer winds up, goes into the pitch—"

"I've moved in with Drake." Eric blurted it out and then waited for his sister to respond. When she didn't, he prodded her. "Go ahead."

"What?" She replied, her eyes opened in doe-wide innocence.

"You know perfectly well, what."

"I'm not saying anything."

"Really?" Eric's eyes squinted with suspicion.

"Really." After a quick pause, she added, "I think it's sweet...in a Brokeback Mountain sort of way."

Eric rolled his eyes. "Just can't help yourself, can you?"

"Can't a sister be glad her brother's found a partner...I mean friend?"

"It's only temporary," Eric explained. "I just can't live in that house anymore." His voice cracked on the last word.

Jennifer sobered at that statement. "So you're gonna sell the house?"

"Yeah."

There was another pause before Jennifer spoke. "I really think that's a good idea." She sounded genuine.

"So, anyway," Eric cleared his throat, "I just wanted to give you the number here."

"Great." Eric could hear her fumble for a pen and paper before she said, "Give it to me."

Eric did and then felt the desire to get off the phone. He gave his love to the girls and his brother-in-law and hung up. Eric walked awkwardly around the house. He was now living here, but it still felt strange, like he was breaking and entering. The house had been on the market so long, he'd shown the house so many times, he would've sworn he knew the place inside and out blindfolded. Yet, as he walked down the hallway to the bedroom, he would occupy he could've sworn there'd been a second bedroom downstairs. He would almost bet on it. Almost.

He walked through the downstairs part of the house, checking off the rooms. Kitchen. Living room. Dining room. Den. Front door. All where they were supposed to be. But there was no sign of a second bedroom. Perhaps, he admitted to himself, he didn't remember this house as well as he thought he did.

Eric turned as he heard Drake bounding down the stairs, but all questions about the bedroom disappeared from his tongue as he heard Drake's next statement.

"Okay. We fly into Miami, pick up a rental car and head down to the Keys. Day after tomorrow, we're fishing."

"What?"

"You heard me." Drake sounded positively jubilant. "Get packing."

"But—"

"But what?" Drake interrupted. "You got some pressing appointment you're not telling me about?"

"Well, no," Eric stammered, "that's not the point. I told you I'd think about it."

"And have you thought about it?" Drake made no sign he was going to be deterred.

Eric stared at Drake, a little put off by Drake's presumption that "I'll think about it" meant "yes." Drake always seemed to be doing this, from seeing the house to basketball and hockey tickets. What he wanted was what everyone else wanted. True, Eric didn't have any pressing appointments, or any appointments for that matter, and he really liked the idea of getting out of Dodge, away from all the memories of Emily, but that wasn't the point. There was a point, Eric knew, he just couldn't seem to remember it. Nor did it seem that relevant, after all, in light of the fact that he'd leave twenty degrees with a wind chill of ten for...for...whatever it was in Florida this time of year. It had to be hotter than ten.

"I'll get packing."

Drake's face split into an "I knew it all along" smile.

Chapter 29

The chartered fishing boat bobbed on the Atlantic, or was it the Gulf, Eric wasn't sure. With the constant horizon of water and a captain who zigzagged across the seas claiming he knew a better spot, Eric had become completely discombobulated. But the sea was salty, the wind was cool, the sun hot, and the beer in the cooler between Eric and Drake ice cold.

"This is really great," Eric set his rod in the stand in front of him and leaned back in his seat. "I really needed this."

Drake grunted an agreement as he cast his line, made sure the line was clear, then set the rod in the stand in front of him. "Fishing does the mind and body good. It's very Zen." He leaned back in his seat. "I actually prefer not to catch anything. Just let my mind and spirit clear the debris of life before going back." He cracked opened the cooler and pulled out two bottles of Corona Light. "And it's a great excuse for drinking."

"Now you're talking." Eric took a bottle, popped off the cap and took a long draught. "Are you okay?"

He'd looked over at Drake, that feeling he was being watched, and saw that Drake was not looking at him or the water, but some place beyond the horizon where no one but Drake could go.

"What?" Drake seemed to come back to the boat. "Oh. I'm fine." His smile drooped a little at the corners. "The last time I was fishing was with Paul."

A silent moment passed. Eric felt Drake wanted to say more, to talk about his dead friend, but was reluctant. Eric thought back to his own desire to talk about Emily with Drake, how Drake had kept changing the subject, finally getting up and leaving the room.

Indignation bloomed on his cheeks as he looked at Drake silently waiting for Eric to take the bait, as it were, and let him talk about Paul. But Drake kept silent. Maybe, Eric thought, Drake realized he'd been rude and would be ruder still if he just started yapping away about his own loss. Or maybe he thought that talking about the death of a same sex friend was different than a spouse.

Whatever the reason, Eric felt a little guilty. After all, Drake, whether he'd intended it or not, had helped Eric through a rough time in his own life. Not to mention he'd paid for it all, including this little fishing expedition, as Drake had called it. That almost made Eric laugh out loud. *Expedition.* They'd flown first class from Chicago to Miami, rented a fully loaded Escalade, and were sitting on this private charter boat that charged seven-hundred dollars for four hours. Drake had bought eight upfront with an option for four more. He owed the guy.

"Did you guys go fishing a lot?"

Drake's smile opened a little more. "When we were young, we did. Especially as teenagers." He took a pull from his beer. "We'd go out to this little river on his granddad's property."

"Did you catch anything?" Eric asked.

"Catfish. Brim mostly." He laughed. "His granddad would always ask if he could have his trout prepared almandine."

Eric laughed too, until a thought struck him. "You haven't been fishing since Paul passed?" He'd tried to make the question as respectful as possible, but he still winced at the question once he'd heard it. It still seemed callous.

Drake, however, didn't seem to take the question that way. He looked thoughtful, pondering the question, and realizing the answer. "Yeah," he said slowly, and then a dawning of just how long it'd been since he'd been fishing seemed to take hold of him.

"Yeah, I guess I never really thought about it." He paused for a moment, finished his beer in a long pull, and dropped the bottle in a small trashcan beside him, before speaking again. "I guess we were both a little homesick and decided to go on a fishing trip. We managed to get leave together." He massaged his forehead. "We had so much fun we decided to make it an annual event, even if one of us got married. But then..."

Drake trailed off and went to that place beyond the horizon. "But then he died." His voice cracked on the last word.

Eric couldn't help but feel a little overwhelmed. This guy, whose occupation was death, had been so affected by the loss of a friend, he couldn't even think of doing something he loved like fishing. Until now. Eric felt somewhat honored and just a little cross with himself for his earlier indignity.

"So where'd you guys go on your fishing trip?"

Drake looked at him. "Your pole."

"Europe?"

"No." Drake was pointing at Eric's reel which was now screaming. "Your *pole*."

"OH." Eric had followed Drake's finger to his pole which was making a loud whizzing sound as the line quickly de-spooled. Eric grabbed the pole out of the stand and almost lost it in the water. "What do I do?" He shouted.

"Hold on," Drake yelled and grabbed the pole.

"Yeeeehhhhaaahhhh," the captain yelled from his cupola. "Looks like we got ourselves a rodeo."

Eric almost lost the pole again as he swiveled around.

"Eyes front," Drake bellowed.

Eric spun back around, swearing he saw a can of beer in each of the captain's hands. Rodeo, he wondered, was that some type of a fish? Slang for a type of fish? But Eric didn't have time to think anymore. Drake was forcing Eric's shoulders back and shouting in his ear to pull on the rod.

Forty-five minutes later, the captain was hanging over the side of the boat, netting what Eric learned was not a Rodeo, but a Kingfish.

"Now what you've got here," the captain was shouting over his shoulder, "*whff*...is...*whff*...a big...*whff*..." The muscles in the man's neck, shoulders and arms, flexed like taut rope covered in leather. He hoisted the net containing one of the biggest fish Eric had ever seen in real life and dropped it at his feet. "Whopper."

Drake slapped Eric on the shoulder. "That's a good haul for your first time deep-sea fishing."

The captain rubbed the only part of him that wasn't ripped muscle, his stomach. "First time? Well that calls for a beer." He cackled. "On the house." He climbed with surprising litheness up the ladder to his cupola.

Eric plopped down in his seat at the back of the boat. "Whew," he said as he wiped his forehead with the back of his hand.

"Oy," The captain shouted as he tossed two cans of Miller High Life down to Drake. He climbed back down the ladder carrying a can for himself. "Champagne for everyone."

Drake, who'd been staring with a dubious, if not suspicious, eye at the can, smiled at Eric. "Oh, well, if you put it that way," he said as he opened the can. "Bottoms up." He took a swig.

Eric opened his can, which promptly covered him in spray.

The captain burst out laughing. "Just like NASCAR."

"Excuse me?" Eric wiped his face.

The captain finished his beer in two swallows, belched, nodded his appreciation at the can and threw it into the ocean. "You know, after they win, they spray the car and everybody with champagne." The captain climbed back up into the cupola.

"Ah." Eric glanced askance at Drake. "Where did you find this guy?"

"Don't ask," Drake replied as he waited for the captain to disappear before pouring the beer into the ocean and depositing the can in the waste basket.

Eric stood up and did the same, saying under his breath. "I thought private charters were supposed to be a bit little less, oh, I don't know, redneck."

Drake grinned, his cheeks turning pink. "Well, when you want a private boat in less than forty-eight hours notice, you gotta lower your standards," he held up his index finger and thumb about an inch apart, "just a wee bit."

"Just a wee?" Eric asked.

Drake nodded. "Just a wee." He started laughing.

Eric started laughing as he fell back into his chair. He mopped at his face with the front of his shirt. He was feeling the sun, beer, and the fish, now. He'd had fun, but he was ready to call it a day, get a shower, some air conditioning, and a good meal. "How much longer you want to stay out?"

Drake heaved the fish into a large cooler and looked at his watch then up at the sky. Not a cloud to be seen anywhere; just a dome of sapphire blue touching the ocean in every direction. "Maybe another hour or so." He moved back to his own seat and sat down. "I'd like a chance to catch one for myself." He picked up his rod and started reeling in the line. "If you don't mind."

"Oh, not a bit." Eric said, wishing Drake was ready, but reminding himself Drake was paying for this whole 'expedition.' It was only fair he called the shots. "I'll just sit here and watch you. I'm a little tuckered out."

Drake nodded, finished reeling in his line, baited it, and cast it deep. He looked up at the sky again and back at his watch. "Come on, Baby, show me some fin."

Trouble was Drake didn't really seem all that interested in seeing some fin. Eric watched as Drake stole glances at the sky and then his watch, reeled his line in a little too quickly and cast again without making sure the line was properly baited. This went on for about fifty minutes.

By that time, Eric was beginning to feel a little rested and thought he might well cast a few more times. What could it hurt? And besides, maybe he'd get lucky and have himself another Rodeo. He started baiting his line.

Drake finished reeling in his line, looked at his watch and then up at the sky. "Okay, I think that's it." He yelled up to the cupola. "Hey Captain."

The captain stuck his head over the side of the cupola.

"Time to pack it in."

The captain looked at his watch and frowned. "You still got three and a half hours."

"I know, but we're ready."

"There's no refunds."

"A tip for helping my friend here get lucky his first time out." Drake chuckled. "That didn't come out right."

The captain nodded. "You're the boss." He disappeared back behind the wheel.

Eric had finished baiting his line but hadn't cast it yet when Drake had told the captain to pack it in, and despite reminding himself Drake was paying, he felt a little indignant Drake hadn't consulted him. He wasn't ready. Maybe he'd been an hour ago, but not now. Now he was ready to catch another kingfish or shark, or something.

Drake sat down in his chair and started stowing the rented fishing gear as the inboard engines fired.

"You sure *we're* ready to go?" Eric hoped Drake hadn't missed the sarcasm on the word 'we're.'

"Yep." Drake didn't look up.

"I just baited my line." Eric held it up to show him.

Drake moved so fast, all Eric saw was a glint of the sun off a blade as Drake cut Eric's line tossed the bait and the line into the ocean and returned the knife to wherever he'd pulled it.

Eric sat frozen from a chill not caused by the wind or the cold beer, his hands still outstretched.

Drake held out his own hand for Eric's fishing gear.

Eric flinched, expecting the blade.

Drake looked up and saw the look on Eric's face. He let his own hand drop. "Sorry, if I was a little rude back there."

Rude? That was downright Anthony Hopkins, Silence of the Lambs psycho. Eric marveled at Drake's penchant for understatement.

Drake reached up and took the rod out of Eric's slackened grip and began stowing it. "I guess the sun and lack of food got to me." He smiled as he opened the cooler and pulled out two bottles of Corona Light. "That was some haul today my friend." He offered a bottle to Eric.

Eric took the bottle but didn't drink. He could feel his heart pounding in his throat and his stomach sour. He wasn't sure what had been scarier, how Drake cut the line or his behavior after doing it. It was like a light switch where ON was maniac, OFF was sane person. Or maybe more like that movie *Die Hard*, when Hans Gruber comments how much he likes the guy's suit, even recognizes the designer, admits he has three himself, just before he kills the guy. Now that's evil.

Monsters are one thing. They hide under the bed, in the closet, in the shadows of our worst nightmares. But there's nothing more terrifying, more horrific, than the monster who looks like you, holds a job like you, maybe rides the bus in the seat beside you, says 'good morning' pleasantly to you, then guts some kid or woman just as easily as commenting on your suit, how he recognizes the designer, has three of his own.

Above the roar of the inboard engines and waves crashing against the boat and wind in their ears the captain's voice rang out.

Mommas don't let your babies grow up to be cowboys.

Worse than his voice (he was trying to sound just like Willie Nelson and failing miserably) was his complete lack of knowledge of the words to the songs he was singing. When it would finally become apparent, even to him, that he'd lost the lyric, his voice would trail off and after a silent pause would boom just as loud as ever with another tune. After Willie Nelson, he slaughtered *Folsom Prison Blues* in more of a Foghorn Leghorn impersonation. Next came *Give Me Three Steps* by Lynyrd Skynyrd with lyrics and melody not even Ronnie Van Zant would recognize, followed by Jimmy Buffett:

Hmmm Hmmm Hmmm Hmmm Margaritaville
Hmmm Hmmm Hmmm Hmmm Shaker of Salt
Some people say hmmm hmmm woman to play
But I know, hmmm hmmm hmmm it's in my vault

"It's in my vault?" Drake's eyes were bulging with mirth as he tried, unsuccessfully, to stifle a chuckle with a cough, which quickly turned into a guffaw.

Eric couldn't help himself either and burst out laughing.

By the time the boat arrived back at the dock, Eric and Drake were clutching stitches in their sides and mopping tears off their cheeks.

The captain mistook the tears for sweat and stitches for dehydration. "No extry charge," he said as he offered them each a bottled water.

Eric took the bottled water, slightly perplexed. "Uh, thanks." He looked at Drake who also thanked the captain, grabbed the fish out of the cooler, and gave Eric a 'we better get out of here before he sings again and I wet my pants' look. Eric nodded, took the fish from Drake as Drake told the captain he could have the last of the Coronas and quickly followed Eric up the dock.

Drake tapped Eric on the shoulder. "They've got a place to take pictures. We should get one of you with your fish." He pointed to a spot at the top of the dock where a huge ship's anchor stood perched beside a block and tackle for slinging up really big catches.

Eric looked at the spot. Tourist trap was more appropriate. A shack beside the block and tackle advertised pictures for ten dollars and other souvenirs with your picture for fifteen, special two for twenty-five. In front of the shack a man and his young son stood patiently waiting for their picture to be taken while the crotchety old sea bass of a photographer barked at a group of sunburnt, windswept tourists posing comically on the anchor and tackle.

Drake looked at his watch and then up at the sky yet again. Eric was about to ask him if he was maybe waiting for the sky to fall when Drake excused himself. He walked up to the man with the young son and offered his hand. The man took Drake's hand genially. Drake didn't let go as he spoke too softly for Eric to hear.

The man's eyes widened in surprise when Drake didn't release his hand; and whatever Drake said did not seem to lessen the man's bewilderment. When Drake finally released his hand, the man looked into his palm, smiled greedily, and nodded. He grabbed his son by the arm and stepped back.

Drake motioned for Eric to join him as the group of tourists broke away from the anchor and tackle, laughing, clearly pleased with what they'd done.

"Be with you in a minute." The photographer barked at Drake and Eric and motioned for the man and his son who politely gestured to Drake and Eric. "Whatever." He waved to the anchor.

Eric and Drake walked up in front of the anchor, Drake standing to Eric's right who was holding the fish.

"Why don't you both hold the Kingfish." The photographer suggested.

But Drake shook his head. "He caught it, he can hold it. I'll just stand right here."

"How about an arm around his shoulder." The old man encouraged.

Again Drake shook his head, placing his hand on Eric's shoulder.

The old photographer rolled his eyes. "Ready?"

Drake checked his watch and looked up at the sky one last time. "Now you've got a fish story and a picture to prove it. Reminds me of these old farmers who get together every Saturday for coffee and to tell stories. Well this one farmer starts telling some real whoppers and finally, his son says, 'Dad, why don't you drive and let me spread it around for a while.'" He nodded to the old man as Eric started laughing.

Chapter 30

The waitress dropped off a plate of conch fritters and two more bottles of Corona Light. She flashed her pearly whites at Eric and put a hand on his shoulder as she told them their main courses would be up in a few minutes. Upon leaving the table, she put a bit more hip into her walk. It was more than just flirting a bigger tip out of the tourists. She really did think the guy was cute, and he may have been wearing a band on the left ring finger, but he wasn't here with a wife or girlfriend. Her number would definitely be on the bill.

All of this was lost on Eric, as were the conch fritters, the beer, and the two tipsy couples at the next table who were applying liberal amounts of alcohol and laughter to soothe their flaming skin. It wasn't, however, lost on Drake.

"That woman is totally into you," he said.

Eric looked up. "What?"

"That woman," Drake was stabbing a finger after the waitress, "is totally into you."

"I'm sorry?" Eric followed the direction of Drake's finger to find the waitress two tables over, getting drink orders from a young couple, stealing glances at him, smiling, and waving furtively with her fingers at him.

Eric waved back, then felt suddenly foolish, dropping his hand quickly into his lap. It wasn't the wave, which had resembled more of a five-year-old waving to grandma from the back window of the family vehicle, nor the realization that the waitress was not only very attractive but also five to ten years younger than himself. It was the knee jerk reaction of it all. He'd looked up, a woman waved, and he'd waved back. Simple as that. No signals received and none returned. He had no interest in women. In that respect, Eric was a satellite silently adrift, a disconnected modem. His heart still belonged to Emily and their child. That's the way he wanted it. And his mind, well his mind had been absorbed in something else.

The waitress smiled even brighter at him, obviously thrilled with the acknowledgement, finally, of her advances.

"You gonna get her number?" Drake was asking as he picked up a fritter.

"No," Eric said emphatically as he picked up his beer.

Drake opened his mouth in what Eric was sure would be a protest but stopped as if a thought had just occurred to him. He popped the fritter into his mouth and chewed thoughtfully. "Emily," Drake said as he swallowed.

Eric waited, expecting Drake to start telling him, with all due respect, that Emily was dead, had been dead for seven months now, and that she'd want him to move on with his life. It was the kind of thing he'd probably have said to a friend. It was the kind of thing friends said to each other, the kind of thing that falls under the topic of easier to give the advice than to take it. He'd have said it, then gone back home to Emily knowing he'd given his buddy tough but good advice.

But Drake didn't say anything. He ate another conch fritter and sipped his beer, all the while staring at some place beyond the restaurant, beyond the ocean. Slowly, Drake came back and looking at Eric asked. "So have you given any thought to what you're going to do?"

"Well, I thought I'd try one of these conch things, drink my beer, maybe go to the men's room and take a leak."

"I meant—"

"I know what you meant." Eric interrupted. He knew exactly what Drake meant. It'd been on his mind all day; actually it'd been on his mind since Drake had asked him a couple of days previously. It had simmered on the back burner of his brain, like a sauce that takes days to prepare. Slowly, ingredients had been added, ideas of possible employs were folded in, but the sauce wasn't complete. Not until today, after they'd toured Hemingway's house in downtown Key West.

The fishing had been fun, but one day was enough for him and apparently for Drake as well, who said he was up for anything Eric was, except that again. Drake suggested they go snorkeling and found a tour that went out for the morning, returning at lunchtime.

After snorkeling, Drake took Eric to Jimmy Buffet's Margaritaville where Eric spotted a leaflet on the Hemingway House. Eric had fallen in love with Hemingway's novels during his junior year in high school, and he'd forgotten the author had lived in Key West. While they ate their Cheeseburgers in Paradise, Eric suggested they take the tour. To his surprise, Drake loved the idea.

As they toured the Spanish Colonial villa where Eric's favorite author had spun such yarns as *For Whom the Bell Tolls*, Eric's mind moved the sauce to the front burner and set the heat to high. What had Eric loved to do in his spare time growing up? Read and write short stories and poetry. What had he majored in at college? Business, but he'd minored in English, specifically Creative Writing. And as he stood staring into Hemingway's second floor writing studio, he was sure he could hear not the conversations and laughter of the other patrons, not the sounds of traffic, not even his own heartbeat. What he could hear was the slap of the typewriter arms against the paper, the ding as the barrel reached the end of the typed line, the sloosh as the barrel was pushed back. He could hear Hemingway.

"Well. I've been kind of toying with the idea of writing." The confession felt natural on his tongue, and now that he heard it out loud, right. He was more convinced than ever. But what about Drake, Eric wondered. What would he say? Or would he just laugh? Writing, after all, wasn't exactly known as the perfect board for mid-life career jumping. No money on the frontside, and maybe no or little money on the backside. He might as well be saying he wanted to become a rock star.

But Drake didn't laugh. Instead his face registered surprise then interest. "Why writing?"

"It's something I've always loved, had actually wanted to pursue at one time in my life."

"Why didn't you?" The question held nothing but Drake's complete curiosity.

Eric took a sip of his Corona Light. "Oh, well, life happens, I guess. Business seemed the safer way to go. Emily and I were already dating, planning on getting married right after college. Stories don't pay the bills 'til someone buys them, and I wasn't about to let Emily support me while I chased that wild goose."

"I bet she would have."

"Probably so," Eric admitted. "But that's not the point. My job was to take care of her. I decided I could work and write in my spare time."

"So what happened?" Drake asked.

"So I got a job selling houses. Turned out to be pretty good at it too."

"Did you keep writing?"

"No. I...I just got too busy. Look," Eric sounded as if he was trying to convince a jury his line of reasoning was the correct line. He leaned forward and looked directly into Drake's eyes. "I took care of my responsibilities. I got a good job, made good money, made sure Emily was taken care of. Writing was a hobby. Emily was my life. And when she lost her job, I convinced her to sell houses too. And she did. Who could ask for a better life? To live and love and work with your best friend?" Eric shook his head. "No, writing I could afford to lose, not Emily."

Drake nodded. "Well, it sounds like a great idea. Any idea what you'd write?"

Eric deflated. "Not exactly."

"You know, it's funny," Drake sounded a little sheepish, "but I've always thought about writing."

"Really?" Now it was Eric's turn to be curious.

Drake nodded, even more sheepishly. "Write my memoirs, maybe, after I retire. Not an autobiography. Who'd care to read that?"

"Memoirs?"

"Silly, I know." Drake hesitated a moment. "But I've often thought some of my life stories would make for some excellent fiction."

"Now that I can believe." Eric laughed and so did Drake.

The waitress brought their entrees, blackened grouper and steamed vegetables for Drake, Grouper fingers with hush puppies and fries for Eric. Emboldened by their little exchange of finger waves, she looked directly into Eric's eyes with her own "Take Me" eyes and asked, "Is there anything else you'd like from me? Anything I can do for you?"

Eric did not miss the innuendo this time, but he would not allow his knee, or any other part of him, to jerk. "I'm sorry, but I'm married."

It sounded half-hearted, but Eric set his jaw resolutely. She was young, attractive, and, as Drake said, "into him." But Eric was not yet prepared to betray his wife.

She looked quickly to Drake who only nodded affirmation. Crestfallen, she said she'd be back to check on them in a few minutes and left without another word, smile, or wave of her fingers.

Drake squeezed the lemon wedge over his fish and peppered his vegetables. "Hey, I've got a great idea. Why don't we team up? Write my memoirs together."

Eric paused, a grouper finger smothered in tartar sauce, almost to his mouth.

Memoirs? Together?

It wasn't exactly what Eric had had in mind. Okay, it was the opposite of what he'd had in mind. He couldn't decide if he felt surprised at the suggestion of the two of them taking on such a project together, or incredulous at the audacity of Drake's suggestion. He had the mental image of the two of them in Drake's den, Eric sitting on one of the loveseats, a laptop in his lap, his fingers, clamoring furiously, duteously away on the keys as Drake paced back and forth, a glass of scotch in his hand, dictating his life, his thoughts, his anecdotes to his faithful assistant.

Drake read the look on Eric's face. "I know it's probably not what you were thinking about, but it might get your juices flowing." He forked a mouthful of fish into his mouth, chewed and swallowed. "It was just an idea; at least get you writing 'til you figured out what you wanted to write."

He sounded hurt, and Eric struggled not to get eaten up with guilt. "I'm not saying it's a bad idea." He took a bite of grouper finger, using the time of chewing to think of some way to soothe Drake's feelings. "It's just that," he swallowed, "well, you don't even know if I'm a good writer or not. I mean, I just told you I used to write. You haven't read anything of mine. Your life *would* make for an excellent memoir, and I'd bet a lot of people would want to read it. But you don't know if I'm any good."

"Oh, you're good. I know it." Drake took a swig of his beer, beaming.

"Thanks for the vote of confidence, but...," Eric's voiced trailed off. How did Drake know it? Why was he so confident? How was Drake always so confident, always in the know? It was beyond confidence. Beyond cocky. Drake was...self-assured. Drake knew who he was, where he was at, what he was doing, and why he was doing it at all times. Eric couldn't help but marvel and look for a way to placate Drake. Drake was only trying to be a friend after all. That's what friends did right? They encourage you, believe in you, support you. Drake wasn't looking for a secretary or even a ghost writer, just trying to support Eric in his dream. There had to be a way to return the favor without getting stuck writing a memoir. He had a thought as he munched on a hush puppy.

"The one problem with a memoir," Eric said, holding up another hush puppy and studying it, "is that once you write it, your cover's blown. I mean it's gotta be authentic in order to be a memoir."

Drake shrugged. "I can't do this forever. Well, maybe I can, but I don't want to. I've lasted longer than most, but I'm starting to burn out. I've wanted to retire for a couple of years now, but I've always talked myself out of it. This'll give me the reason to get out and stay out."

"Yes, but a memoir may get you an invitation from the Feds or worse." Eric paused, popping the hush puppy into his mouth. "Your life *would* make for some excellent fiction."

Drake leaned forward.

"No one would know it was the truth." Eric smiled slyly.

"Only the ones that'd been there." Drake returned the smile.

Chapter 31

Drake cursed in frustration, slamming his glass down and sloshing ice water over the coffee table in the den. Drake cursed again, "I'll be right back." He stamped out of the room, mumbling something under his breath Eric couldn't catch.

Eric watched him go before turning back to his laptop. They'd been at this for three weeks, stopping and starting on one idea after another. Three weeks. And before that, they'd spent the first four days after they returned to Cary just sitting around brainstorming, as Eric called it. Drake had another name for it, which referenced a bovine's backside. Eric had asked a lot of questions which Drake had dutifully answered with great eagerness. He'd over-answered the questions in his zeal, and he found he'd taken to writing like a fish to water, like a kid to a bicycle. He couldn't wait to get started.

But as the days passed by with no progress that Drake could see, he'd grown surly. Eric began to view this man who always seemed to have it all together as more of a petulant, impatient child, prone to temper tantrums, like the one just now. And like the previous outbursts, this one had been the product of one statement. One word, actually.

Unbelievable.

Drake had stood reading over Eric's shoulder as he backspaced over an entire section of text. When Drake asked, coming around the front of the loveseat to face Eric, why he was deleting the material, Eric had answered, "Unbelievable."

Drake returned to the den with a dishtowel and a fresh glass of ice water. "It's what happened."

Eric threw up his hands in exasperation. "I've told you real life doesn't always make for real drama."

"What's that supposed to mean?" Drake wiped furiously at the puddle on the coffee table. "Ever hear the old saying, truth is stranger than fiction?"

Eric didn't miss the defensiveness in Drake's voice. He looked at Drake who stared hard into the coffee table, as if he could make it catch fire with just his gaze. Eric wondered if he wouldn't burn like an ant under a magnifying glass on a sunny day if Drake turned his gaze upon him. What had happened to this man who'd exuded so much self-confidence, so much self-assurance? Since they'd decided to write together, it was like a light switch had been turned off. Drake was no longer a man of presence, but just a follower who day by day grew more frustrated with his leader and let him know it.

That was it, wasn't it, Eric thought to himself. Drake wasn't the guy calling the shots anymore, but until recently, he hadn't seemed to have a problem with that. He was just glad he had someone to follow, to keep company as it were. And even now as he threw little tantrums and grew defensive, he still didn't seem to want to climb into the driver's seat, just put in his two cents from the back.

Drake stormed out of the room before Eric could form a reply. But that didn't matter. There'd only been one reply since the first time Drake had said it. Eric waited for Drake to return before giving it again one more time.

"I hate to beat a dead horse into fertilizer, again, but peoples' willing suspension of disbelief will go only so far. And there're some things people just don't want to believe. Yes, you lived it, but that doesn't mean anyone who wasn't there is going to buy it.

"Unless we want to write science fiction, and the problem with that is most science fiction has some political or social message like Roddenbery and Star Trek, Bradbury, Leonard Nimoy in Star Trek Four. I don't want to belittle what you and your friends went through, but as I write it down it sounds contrived."

Drake opened his mouth to protest, but Eric cut him off. "Maybe I'm wrong," Eric conceded, "it's been a long time since I've written anything," Eric was trying hard to placate what he was quickly coming to realize was nothing more than a child and you can't really reason with a child, "so maybe I need a little more experience before I can do some of these stories justice. Till then, can I stick with simple?"

Eric watched closely as the crinkle in Drake's brow smoothed. "I'm sorry. You're right." He was back to being the happy backseat passenger. "You're the writer. I'm the wannabe. I don't mean to get defensive, but I'm just so excited about us writing and I'm ready to start putting a story down." His laugh was a little more nervous than humorous. "I guess I expected us to have our first novel knocked out in a few weeks. A couple of months tops."

"That may not be very realistic." Eric smiled.

Drake nodded. "I've learned." He moved over to the bar, grabbed a bottle of Johnny Walker Blue and two heavy tumblers, and walked back to the loveseats. He set the tumblers down on the coffee table. They made a sharp crack on the glass top. He unscrewed the cap and filled each glass halfway. Setting the bottle down beside the glasses, Drake dropped onto the loveseat opposite Eric and let out a long, slow breath. He picked up a tumbler, offered it to Eric who took it, then picked up the other one. He took a sip, sat back, and rubbed his forehead.

"I think we could use some brain food. How about a western omelet?"

"At eleven o'clock at night?" Eric took a sip from his glass. The scotch was hot in his throat, but warm in his belly.

"Hey," Drake raised his own glass. "It's breakfast time somewhere." He drained the glass in one swallow, jumped up and headed for the kitchen. "Two Westerns coming up."

"Do you need a hand?" Eric didn't really want to help, didn't really want to eat. But he always felt a certain level of obligation to Drake. After all, it was Drake's house, Drake's money, and Drake's life experiences. So he'd made the offer, and was relieved when Drake had told him no, but to write.

So Eric wrote. He'd been at it for about ten minutes when the house phone rang. He looked at the caller I.D. It was his sister, Jennifer.

"I got it," he yelled to Drake and then picked up the handset. "Hey Sis." He said with a smile.

"Hey Bro." Her voice sounded exhausted. "Got a minute?"

I've got all my life, Eric thought. "What's up?"

"Sorry to be calling you so late, but I need to ask you a huge, huge favor. Are you free tomorrow afternoon and how do you feel about dance recitals?"

Eric laughed. "I'm free every day and I feel dance recitals are the spawn of Satan. Why do you ask?"

"I'd like you to spend the afternoon with Satan's spawn."

"What? You?"

This time Jennifer laughed. "No. I want you to meet me for lunch in the city and then go to your niece's dance recital."

She took a deep breath and then explained how she was tucking the girls into bed tonight, a little later than usual, but it was Friday night and the dress rehearsal for the recital had lasted longer than anyone thought possible. As she was tucking the girls in, the youngest had made the comment she couldn't wait to see Uncle Eric the next day. When she'd inquired as to why she would be seeing Uncle Eric on Saturday afternoon, the oldest child mentioned the recital with the most "Duh" intonation and inflection. Jennifer had assured both girls that Uncle Eric would of course be there, realizing she'd completely forgotten to ask him.

"I don't want to lay a guilt trip on you," Jennifer's voice sounded like that was exactly what she was trying to do, "but if you don't go, the girls will be crushed, maybe ruined for life. And then they'll appear on Oprah and let everyone know it's their Uncle Eric's fault they grew up to be prostitutes or mass murderers."

No, Eric thought with a smile on his face, no pressure at all. Eric kept silent another moment, figuring if he was going on a guilt trip, the least his sister owed him was to wait for him to wave goodbye.

"Hello?" The anxiety in Jennifer's voice sounded genuine, but he stayed silent. Finally she cursed in exasperation and started to hang up. He could hear her shouting to her husband that the line had gone dead.

Eric spoke up. "I'm here, Sis. I was just messing with you. I wouldn't miss it for the world."

"Great."

He could practically hear her body collapse in relief.

"I'm sorry," she said suddenly. "I didn't wake you up did I?"

"No, no," Eric reassured her, hesitating for a moment and then deciding to confess. "I was just writing."

"Working on a resume?"

"No. Writing, writing."

Jennifer repeated the words a couple of times in Eric's ear before the light switched on. "Wow. You haven't written since college."

"Yep." He suddenly felt like a schoolboy whose mother just discovered her son having his first crush."

"Wow," Jennifer repeated. "So what brought this on? I mean..." she stammered, "I, uh, well, I, uh, of course I know what brought that, uh, could

I have a glass of water to wash down my foot?" She took a deep "Can I have a do-over?" breath. "That's great. I used to love to read your short stories." She had completely recovered and was sounding excited again. "So what are you writing? Short? Novel? What's the story?"

Now it was Eric's turn to stammer. He might be ready to confess to his sister he was writing again. That was all well and good. After all, she had always loved reading his stories and had encouraged him to send them in to magazines. She'd even brought it up every couple of years asking when he was going to write the "Great American Novel" and put himself, Emily, and the rest of his family into a lifestyle to which they could all become accustomed. They were all counting on him. He just couldn't let her and Bill down. Oh, and Emily, too.

But just coming out and saying, "funny thing, that guy I told you about, turns out he's a former Army Ranger who's now a killer for hire and he's decided to let me move in with him and support me while I help him take some of his life story and turn it into fiction." No, that just wouldn't do. He decided on typical writer rhetoric.

"Well," he said, clearing his throat, "I've got a couple of ideas, but I haven't really decided on anything. I'm just letting it stew on the back burner of my brain. Don't want to talk about it yet, you know, might jinx it."

"Still got that superstitious streak." She laughed. "That's a good sign. Used to mean you were about to write something fantastic. You might still write that Great American Novel."

And with that, Eric's body collapsed with relief. She'd bought it. He sank back into the loveseat. "So where's this recital?"

"Oh, yeah. You got something to write with?"

Eric looked for a pen and paper till he realized his laptop was sitting in his lap, waiting for him to type something. He rolled his eyes. "I'm ready."

His sister was right in the middle of saying, "Oka-" when Eric heard ...nothing. Not even the quiet hum of the telephone line one hears after a connection is broken. He held the handset in front of his eyes and looked at it before putting it back to his ear.

"Hello? Sis?" He looked at it again, then back to his ear. Still nothing.

Setting the handset down, he called out, "Hey Drake? Forget to pay the phone bill?"

It had been nothing more than a joke, meant to elicit either no response or at least nothing more than a "what're you talking about?" called back at him from the kitchen. Certainly not the response Drake offered.

Eric heard the sound of a pan or plate set down hard, not dropped, but set down and forgotten. Before he could ask if everything was okay, Drake was in the den, his hands on Eric's shoulders, lifting him up and then away from the front windows, practically carrying him out of the den and to a bookcase, a bookcase Eric was sure hadn't been there when he'd been a realtor showing the house.

Drake touched a button recessed into the back wall of the bookcase behind a vase and a doorway opened. Now that Eric could see it, he wondered how on earth he'd missed it before.

Chapter 32

Eric felt himself shoved through the doorway into the room he'd remembered as either an extra bedroom or maybe an office, at least that's what he'd told prospective buyers when he'd shown it. As Eric looked around the fourteen by fifteen-foot room, which no longer had a window, he wasn't exactly sure what to call the room. The walls were painted a uniform, institutionalized gray. A desk, computer workstation, and chair sat in the back left corner. Next to them were two hutches. On the left wall hung an impressive array of firepower with a low, oversized credenza beneath them, on the right, what looked like breaker boxes of several sizes hung quietly humming. On the front wall were several pictures.

Drake pressed a code into a keypad and the door closed and made an airtight seal, causing Eric's ears to pop. Drake moved to the hutch beside the desk, opened the drawer and pulled out a pair of goggles. He held them up to his eyes and ran his fingers in front of his face. Remembering several war pictures he'd seen Eric figured the goggles must be equipped with night vision. Satisfied the goggles were in working order, Drake moved to one of the breaker boxes, opened the door, and flipped a switch.

The room was plunged into deep, foreboding darkness. Eric let out a gasp as he spun round looking for the doorway, unable to see his hand an inch from his own face. Claustrophobic panic gripped Eric. He wanted to scream but could not. He remembered his first experience in a cave as a kid, when the tour guide had cut all the lights, showing them what sheer, unadulterated blackness was really like. He'd hated it then and wasn't any keener on it now.

And then, it was gone. Dim red light crept down the walls giving objects back their form but obscuring their details. Shadows seemed darker, more ominous to Eric.

"Stay here until I get you." Drake's voice didn't sound harried or scared, and yet Eric swore he could hear some flavor of danger in his tone. Drake turned to the keypad, entered another code, and the airtight lock broke.

The door swung open, and Eric could see the whole house was dark. Drake entered a code and exited the room as the door closed and sealed.

Eric moved to the door and reached for the handle, his hand grasping at institutional gray. He punched the door, stinging his knuckles but only producing the softest of thuds. He thought of screaming but realized no one would hear him. This was a safe room, a panic room. Which one was it, he wondered. He sure didn't feel safe, and his level of panic was increasing at every failed attempt on the keypad.

What had just happened? What was happening? Why had Drake locked him up?

Eric spun around and fell against the door. He could feel the walls moving, closing the distance between each other. The ceiling had dropped at least a foot in the past minute. He was in a compactor, he knew it, and it was going to squash him. He closed his eyes and forced himself to breathe.

After a few minutes, his ears became accustomed to complete silence. Not really completely silent, he could hear his breathing, his heartbeat, but nothing beyond that. It was like being buried alive in a coffin.

This last thought, of course, did not comfort him. It wasn't *like* he was buried alive in a coffin. He *was* buried alive in a coffin. He had no food, no water, and, if Drake didn't come open the door, no way out. He was in an airtight space. And what about that? Air? How much had he left? Oh, he was as good as dead.

And why had Drake put him in here? To protect him? Protect him from what? It seemed more dangerous to be locked in this room. Why had Drake been spooked by a dead phone line?

Eric shivered. He was starting to see a thread running through his thoughts. Coffin. Buried alive. Dead.

Try not to think.

But then another thought quietly crept into his mind. He wasn't in a coffin. He was in a safe room. What was a safe room? A room specifically designed to keep someone...well...safe. Which implied there was fresh air, and probably provisions if he looked. And why was he in a safe room? Because Drake had wanted to protect him. From what, Eric had no idea, but killing himself with hysteria would sort of defeat the purpose, wouldn't it? He needed to keep his wits about him. He willed himself to calm down.

As his heart rate slowed, Eric ventured opening an eye and found that his vision had acclimated to the dim red light as well. He took a long, slow look around the room. There didn't seem to be as many ominous shadows. He took a step towards the center of the room and let his eyes take in objects. Under the computer station was a rectangular object. He moved towards it and knelt down. He could see *Frigidaire* dimly in the top right corner. It was a mini fridge. If he looked at it, focused on it, he could hear the soft hum of its cooling system.

So he wouldn't die. Not because of dehydration anyway. He would bet there was food stored in the workstation shelving if he looked. He didn't. Instead, he straightened up and saw the boxes mounted on the other wall, the boxes Drake had used to shut off the lights to the house. He walked over to them and opened the panel he'd seen Drake open.

Sure enough, it looked like any ordinary circuit breaker box. He saw the one marked house and moved to reset it, but paused just an inch from the breaker. Drake had turned the power off for a reason

What reason?

Eric closed the circuit box door and thought. Why would a guy like Drake cut the power to his own house just because someone mentioned the phone line had gone dead? What would Drake be afraid of?

He turned and looked around the room, his eyes falling upon the weapons covering wall. Drake was a hitman. Eric couldn't remember the movie, but he could remember a character finding the assassin dead and saying something like, "it's the first rule in assassination, kill the assassin."

Eric shook his head. That couldn't be it. He didn't know if that rule was true, but he knew that kind of stuff only happened in the movies. This was definitely not a movie. This was real life, and in real life, Drake would be coming back any minute now, opening the door, and apologizing for overreacting. Sorry for being overly dramatic, he'd say, but I just realized I *had* forgotten to pay the phone bill, how silly of me. Maybe it was time to call it a night. Laugh out loud.

Eric did laugh out loud, but it seemed strangely muted in the airtight room. The laughter caught in his throat as he slumped against the boxes. What if Drake didn't come back? What if he couldn't? What if whatever or whoever he was protecting Eric from had beaten him? What if Drake were lying unconscious somewhere in the house right now? And what about whatever or whoever was responsible for Drake's condition? What would he, she, it, do? Now the terrifying prospect of the door not opening was replaced by the more electrifying thought of what if the door was opened by a party that was not Drake?

The room seemed to brighten as the light bulbs in his brain popped on.

I need to arm myself.

Eric walked over to the wall of weapons, the scent of oil and cold, polished metal growing stronger. There was a long-barreled weapon with what looked like a nightscope and a bipod on the barrel resting on hooks. It reminded him of sniper rifles he'd seen in movies. He shrugged that one off. He had no idea how to fire it. Also on the wall was a .38, which looked awfully familiar. He kept looking, squinting at the weapons until he found what he was looking for. There, at eye level, was a Glock 9mm similar to the one Drake had taught him to shoot. Not the actual weapon. That had been disassembled and thrown into the river after he'd shot that hoodlum protecting Drake.

He picked up the weapon, feeling the familiar weight in his hands. It felt good. He checked. It had a magazine in it, but no rounds. He slipped the weapon into the waistband of his jeans and started searching for bullets. As he did, a sense of urgency washed over him. If someone opened the door right now, he could draw the weapon, but it was a bluff at best. It wasn't like a game of Cowboys and Indians or Cops and Robbers or War where you point your gun-shaped hand or stick or plastic gun if Santa had been good to you, at someone else and shouted, "Bang, bang, your dead. I shot you first."

On the bottom shelf of the squat hutch was a box of 9mm rounds and magazines. Eric snatched up two magazines and the box of bullets. Pulling the magazine out of the Glock, he loaded it as well as the two spare magazines, slammed in a magazine and chambered a round. After checking to make sure the safety was on, he stuffed the Glock back into the waistband of his jeans.

He was armed. His shoulders slumped in relief until another light bulb blazed in his brain, causing him to stand bolt upright. What good was a weapon if he was a sitting duck? Or standing for that matter. He needed to find a place to hide. Looking around the room, he quickly realized the only place that offered any protection was the desk. He swept behind it and plopped into the chair. The desk offered itself as a barrier, standing between him and whatever was out there. The chair offered itself as a sanctuary; granting comfort and solitude before whatever was to come, and Eric took it gratefully.

He rubbed the grip of the Glock. There was nothing to do now but wait. Once he heard the airlock he would drop down behind the desk, and, if it wasn't Drake, shoot the intruder in the knees. It may seem like a coward's way to make a fight, but Eric could live with that, just so long as he lived.

His eyes began to ache, but the door just stood there, steadfast. Eric finally blinked and let his eyes wander around the room, over the circuit boxes, the firearms, and then on the pictures. His eyes had fully adjusted to the red light, which now seemed almost too bright, and now he could clearly see the pictures on the wall beside the door. Eric couldn't remember any pictures in any part of Drake's house save this room. There weren't all that many, only two and they appeared to be the same picture: he and Drake on their fishing trip.

Why would he have the same picture hanging on the wall, Eric wondered, and thought he had an answer. Obviously, Drake was planning on giving Eric one as a gift. But if that were true, Eric's mind pondered, why would he hang it?

Eric felt his curiosity pricked and he got up and walked over to the two pictures in identical frames. There he was, fish in hand, laughing at the joke Drake, arm on his shoulder, had told him just before the old man snapped the picture. He grinned as he remembered the punchline. His eyes slipped over to the other picture and then bulged from their sockets. There on the same pier, the same time of day he guessed by the shadows, maybe even the same old man snapping the photo, was a young man, fish in hand, laughing at something the guy beside him, Drake, with his arm on his shoulder, must've said just before the picture was taken. He had a pretty good idea what the joke had been and an even better idea of who the laughing fisherman was.

Paul.

Bile crawled up his throat as the room started spinning. He stumbled backwards into the desk and he grasped at it for support. Eric's head was swimming. Where was Drake? What was going on? What kind of a sick joke was this? What kind of a sick mind does something like this? Just what was Drake playing at?

The walls were closing in on themselves again and the ceiling was dropping. He needed to get of here. He needed fresh air. He needed to find Drake.

He staggered to the keypad, steadied himself and then forced himself to think. He'd watched Drake enter the code. What was it? He dug deep into his memory but to no avail. He couldn't remember the sequence. He could remember hearing four beeps.

"Okay," Eric said to the keypad, "that means a four-digit pin."

Eric began entering four-digit combinations, but the door remained locked. He punched the door in frustration. Pain shot through his hand as he felt the crunch of bone on steel.

"Four digits. Think. Four digits." Eric stepped back from the keypad as he rubbed his hand savagely. He was about to give up, sit back down at the desk and wait for Drake when his eyes fell upon the pictures. He moved back to the keypad.

He pushed 7. "P."

"A." His finger pressed 2.

"U." 8.

Pressing the button marked 5, Eric mumbled, "L."

He stepped back.

The door didn't budge.

Eric stared at the keypad as his brow furrowed. He stepped up to the keypad one last time and entered another four-digit code.

This time he heard the whisper of the air lock seal breaking.

He looked at the door with a shiver. "Eric."

Chapter 33

As Eric was reaching for a doorknob that didn't exist and beating his knuckles needlessly against the safe room wall, Drake put on the night vision goggles and adjusted the fit. He ran his hand in front of his face and then looked down the hall. Everything was showing up a shade of green.

Drake put his ear to the wall and heard the softest of thuds. He chuckled to himself as he hugged the wall on his way to the kitchen. He made no sound as he saw what he was looking for. Three men dressed like ninjas and also wearing night vision goggles were standing in the kitchen. Two stood with weapons scanning back and forth as the third talked quietly into a radio. Drake moved closer, now able to discern what was being said. The voice coming from the radio was speaking Japanese.

As Drake suspected, the signal to move was the power going out. However, as the man on the radio was being told, the other team had cut the telephone line but not the power yet.

The two men scanning the kitchen snapped their heads toward the radio and watched it fall to the floor. The man who'd been holding it was holding his neck. Through the goggles they could see dark green fluid flowing through his fingers and running down his chest. It would be the last sight either man would see.

After shooting the man holding the radio in the neck to make sure he would be unable to respond, Drake quickly put a bullet in the chest of each man standing. Before either man could hit the ground, Drake was in the kitchen. He walked past the radio man who knelt on all fours, or rather three, as the other hand still clutched at his throat. He was not a threat. The other two, however, may be wearing body armor, and though thrown off their feet by the force of the bullet, still very much alive. Drake fired one round into each man's skull between the eyes and then without looking turned the silencer of the weapon towards the back of the head of the kneeling man and pulled the trigger once more.

Now Drake knelt down and surveyed the three newly made corpses. The first question was who were these men? There was no need to search the bodies. These guys weren't military or paramilitary. No self-respecting military unit or mercenary would use cutting the power as the go signal for an operation. Self-respecting units set up surveillance, waited patiently for you to go to bed, and then murdered you in your sleep. Also, the military, and especially mercenaries who had more money and therefore better equipment, wouldn't use simple handheld radios. Even so, these guys were wearing night vision, dressed in black, and carrying Uzis with suppressors. So Drake knew he wouldn't find a tag with the owner's name and phone number, but he might just find...

Drake reached down and yanked the warm, sticky blouse up on one of the dead men. Through the goggles, the man's skin glowed green, his tattoos dark green and black.

Yakuza.

Drake let go of the man's shirt and wiped his hand on the dry pant of the dead man's leg. What would the Yakuza be doing here, he wondered as his eyes fell on the radio. Despite his curiosity, he left it on the floor. Drake was fluent in Japanese, but if they called asking for a status, they would know it wasn't their man and quickly change frequencies. If they called for a status and didn't get a response, they'd change frequencies, but they wouldn't know if there was a problem or maybe just a faulty radio.

Drake heard a noise down the hall.

Eric pushed gently on the safe room door. It opened quietly. He stepped through into the hall and looked both ways. The dim red light spilling into the hallway illuminated only about three feet in each direction and then was swallowed by the darkness. A chill scurried over him like a cockroach, but anywhere in the darkened house had to be better than the confines of the safe room.

He had no idea where Drake might be, but the house wasn't that big, and eventually he had to run into him. Right?

Eric moved slowly, not wanting to stub his toe or smack his head. Both, however, seemed to be his fate. He let out a yelp as he smacked his toe against some piece of furniture.

This is ridiculous.

"Drake?" He called out in a hoarse whisper. "Where are you?"

A voice spoke from behind him in what he could only assume was some Asian language. Chinese, maybe? Japanese? He wasn't really sure. He was too distracted by the feel of cold steel on his neck. Eric raised his hands slowly, the Glock hanging off his finger by the trigger guard. It was quickly snatched from his hand. He took from the nudging he was to turn around. He did so. Slowly.

The voice came from a man who, by what little natural night vision Eric had acquired since leaving the red light, wore dark clothing and goggles similar to the ones Drake had pulled from the safe room hutch. In his hand was a weapon Eric didn't recognize beyond the realization it could and probably would kill him.

The man spoke again, in Japanese Eric guessed, as he raised his weapon and pointed it at Eric, then grunted, a look of surprise on his face. If he wasn't ready to wet himself, Eric would have thought the look on the man's face comical. As the man fell, Eric heard a very familiar voice.

"I told you to stay in the safe room until I came back." Drake's voice was soft, even, and icy. He reached down, picked up the Glock, pulled off the deceased's night vision goggles and handed them to Eric. "Put these on."

Eric accepted the Glock and the goggles, slipped them on his head, and then almost yanked them off again after looking at Drake. It wasn't that the other man looked evil in the green gaze of night vision, but more that he looked totally devoid of anything human.

"Stay right here." Drake pushed Eric up against the wall. "Don't move." With that, Drake moved quietly off.

Eric followed him through the goggles, hazarding several more hoarse calls with no response.

Drake disappeared, leaving Eric alone. Eric looked around the hallway, amazed. He'd seen night vision goggles in movies, of course, some of which even showing the camera's eye view through the goggles, the green, graininess, but he'd never actually worn a pair. It wasn't like it was the middle of the day, but he could make out everything, including the machine gun still clutched in the dead man's hand before him.

He stuffed the Glock into the waistband of his jeans, reached down and yanked the machine gun out of the cadaver's hand and held it up before himself. It was like a cold, cumbersome metal box with a trigger and a small hole in the front. And it was heavy, especially with the suppresser, which was longer than the weapon itself. But he felt stronger because of this weapon in his hand, safer, more secure. If only...

Eric looked both ways down the hall. To his right was the direction Drake had moved. Left led back to the safe room. Machine gun in his hand or not, right about now the safe room sounded...well, safe. What harm would there be, Eric wondered as his grip tightened unconsciously around the suppresser, in heading back to the safe room.

Making sure his finger was poised on the trigger, Eric set off down the hall back to the safe room. The red light, which looked brighter and whiter through the goggles, was this time a welcomed and relieving sight. He checked over his shoulder every few steps to make sure the dead man was staying dead and that no one else was following him.

As he stepped into the room, he felt his stomach jump up, kiss his brain stem, and then drop down past its normal position before bouncing like a Wilson basketball off his pubic bone and back to its normal space within his body.

There in the room were two other men, dressed the same way as the man he'd encountered in the hall, right down to their Asian speech. The men were rifling through the desk and hutch drawers.

Eric let out an audible gasp and raised the machine gun as the men turned and faced him. They were dressed in black like ninjas, but they'd removed their goggles. The one by the hutch was tall, had a short thatch of hair and a whisper of a mustache. The other was squat, young, with a long mane of black hair, clean shaven and round glasses. He looked like an overweight John Lennon.

Both had the same machine gun as Eric, but theirs were slung over their shoulders like metallic purses. Eric shouted for them to stop as they reached for their weapons. They obeyed, smiling as if they'd just shared some inside joke between them.

"Keep your hands where I can see them," Eric commanded as he pointed the machine gun at one and then the other. The men, smirking, slowly lifted their arms in mock surrender.

Eric felt unnerved at the two men's reaction. He felt another shiver starting in the small of his back, the same shiver he'd felt back in the parking garage when he'd first learned the truth of who Drake, or Paul as he'd known him then, was. It was a kill or be killed emotion. Eric suppressed the shiver as he pulled the trigger which moved approximately a quarter inch and then stopped. He pointed at the other intruder and pulled the trigger, but it did the same thing.

Eric turned the machine gun over in his hands, trying to assess what might be wrong with it when a blade of fire stabbed at the back of his skull. He went blind as the white light of a welder's arc seared his vision. He thought he heard the crack of a major leaguer's wooden bat sending a ball over the centerfield wall as his knees turned to gelatin, no longer able to support his weight. The floor swept up to catch him as gently as a jackhammer. He could taste the warm, metallic flavor of blood as he lost consciousness.

Chapter 34

So this is death.

Eric felt himself floating in what he could only imagine was the abyss. He thought about all the stories told by people who'd had near-death experiences and as far as he could tell, they'd been a huge crock. There was no bright light, no voices of welcome, only darkness and some phantom pain in the back of his mind. It must have been the blow that killed me, he thought, I guess it follows you into the afterlife. Hope it goes away.

But it didn't. Instead the throb advanced on him faster than he moved through the abyss which now that he noticed did seem a little less dark. Yes, it was getting brighter. He wasn't moving towards a light but was surrounded by light. And as the light grew brighter and the pain grew sharper, he realized he *could* hear the voices. Only they weren't welcoming him, in fact, he couldn't understand them at all, but they didn't sound happy.

And now he began to feel his body. He couldn't move his arms or his legs, but he could tell he was prone, lying on something that scratched his face. And he could taste blood, warm and fresh.

Wait a second.

He shouldn't be able to taste blood if he were dead, should he? You don't bleed in the afterlife. You've got no body so there's no reason for blood. And, come to think of it, did the afterlife really smell like glue and carpet and wood and...people?

The voices were much clearer now. It wasn't a heavenly or a hellish language, but one of humans. Asian? Japanese maybe?

Eric's eyes fluttered open. He could see something dark in front of him. He concentrated on focusing his eyes. He was facing the desk, not more than six inches away. The pain in the back of his skull was now excruciating and even moving his head slightly to see the carpet nauseated him. Moving just his eyes he glanced at his arms. Black duct tape kept his wrists tightly bound and to his surprise and dawning horror, duct tape had also been used to bind his elbows together as well as his palms so that he looked lost in prayer.

Eric could not see all of his legs but he could now feel tape binding his ankles and knees. These guys weren't the two young punks in the parking garage. These guys, whoever they were, were professionals.

He tried calling out to Drake to warn him, but he couldn't open his mouth. He couldn't even move his jaw. Duct tape wasn't just covering his mouth in a nice little swatch like it did in the movies. Instead, these guys had wrapped the duct tape around his entire head.

The talking stopped immediately. Eric hadn't been able to warn Drake, but he'd made enough of a murmur, he'd obviously been heard.

One of the voices spoke. He couldn't understand it, but he knew it'd been a command. At the sound of the voice, Eric could hear footsteps moving towards him and then hands were on him, grasping him roughly, turning him over with no thought to Eric's comfort. Eric wanted to fight it, get away, but he was as helpless as a newborn.

Waves of nausea swept over Eric and bile filled his mouth as the tall man he'd seen before lifted him completely off the ground as if he'd been nothing more than a trash bag and dropped him into a chair facing the desk.

At the desk sat a man Eric hadn't seen before. He too was Asian, bald, thin, the skin taut across his face. He sat rubbing the nub of where his right pinky used to be. Behind him, John Lennon stood arms crossed, but ready to move.

The man behind the desk gave another command to the tall man. Once again, he advanced on Eric, this time pulling a Tanto out of thin air.

Eric began squealing like a pig realizing he's just been led to slaughter and shrank into the back of his chair.

The tall man pinned Eric into the chair with one arm and with the other brought the blade down on Eric.

Eric squealed again as he felt the cold steel brush his cheek, but a moment later realized he was not dying.

Instead, the tall man grasped the now cut tape on Eric's right cheek and yanked hard.

Eric felt the skin on his face and scalp burn; sure the tape had taken several layers of flesh with it. He yelped unconsciously and tried to rub his face but instead he looked more as if he was bowing his head to pray.

This last thought must have also been on the man behind the desk's mind for he chuckled to himself before speaking. "I must apologize for my rather rude behavior at our first meeting," the man's English was flawless with only the slightest tinge of his Asian heritage bleeding through, "but I was afraid you might figure out how to remove the safety before my associates could get to you."

"You...you're the one who hit me?" Eric's voice sounded weak in his own ears, and he wondered if he could've possibly asked a more obvious question.

The man behind the desk, however, didn't seem to think the question was obvious at all. "Yes. I hit you a little harder than I'd wanted to. I was afraid I'd killed you at first."

The tone of the man's voice didn't sound like he'd been afraid at all. On the contrary, Eric heard a matter-of-factness in the man's tone that made him shiver. Just how many men had he *not* been afraid he'd killed?

"I'm glad I did not. However," the man looked directly into Eric's eyes, "we do have a problem, Mr. Messer."

"Are you going to kill me?" Eric blurted out.

"The problem," the man replied evenly, "is that Drake Wetherford is still alive while several of my colleagues are now dead. I would like you to speak to your friend on the intercom system, convince him to turn himself over to us, and then you may go."

"You're just going to let me go?" Eric hoped his voice didn't sound as incredulous as he felt, but that didn't sound right. Eric only had the movies and television as a reference and the guy in his position always died. Why should real life be any different?

The man behind the desk didn't hesitate. "You have my word."

Eric watched the man for a silent moment and found that he believed him. He wouldn't be harmed if did what the man said. But what if he pleaded their case to Drake and he didn't turn himself in? Would the man behind the desk change his mind? Would he give the command for the tall guy to slit his throat, and would the pudgy Asian John Lennon laugh at his Columbian necktie? Can you call it a Columbian necktie if it's given to you by a Japanese thug?

Eric wiped his face with the back of his prayerful hands. He looked at the man behind the desk. He was waiting patiently for a reply. Eric wanted to shake his head to clear his thoughts (where did thoughts like that last one come from?), but he was afraid the man behind the desk might take that for his answer.

Did that fear mean he was going to do what the man asked? And what was the man asking, exactly? He wanted Eric to trade Drake's life for his own. And he was considering it, wasn't he? If he were really honest with himself, he'd admit, shameful as it might be, that he was. But what if the situation was reversed and it was Drake sitting here? What would Drake do?

Eric looked at the man behind the desk. "No."

The man behind the desk glanced over his shoulder at John Lennon.

The tall guy wrapped an arm around Eric's neck and yanked back, lifting Eric up off the seat.

Eric was now only afforded a view of the ceiling as he felt the icy steel of the tall man's tanto against his skin. The tall man wielded his knife in one fluid motion, again, not cutting Eric, but slicing the front of his shirt open, exposing his chest and midriff.

Eric could feel his windpipe compress but not collapse, as he choked on the tall man's breath in his face, could feel the man's sweat mixing with his own.

John Lennon came around the desk and pulled out his own blade. It was sharper, much sharper than the tall man's blade and had but one purpose, to which he now employed it. Without hesitation, he placed the blade on the left side of Eric's abdomen and made his incision across Eric's stomach. The blade cut down through the thin layer of fatty tissue, nicking the abdomen muscles.

It felt like a torch lighter had been struck and the flame dragged slowly across his stomach. As air and sweat invaded the wound, the open flame was replaced with hot iron pressed into the laceration.

Eric screamed like a child throwing a temper tantrum. His body writhed, but the tall man's iron clamp wouldn't let him move, wouldn't let him cover up his stomach. His arms burned with lactic acid, as they pumped and pumped to defend himself, to strike out at John Lennon. Tears dampened his cheeks as blood dampened the top of his jeans.

John Lennon waited for the screaming to stop, the crying to die down before placing his blade on Eric's stomach, a half-inch below the first incision.

At the frigid touch of the blade, now stained red, Eric screamed. "No, no, no. No. Please. Don't."

John Lennon left the blade idling on Eric's stomach and looked back.

Eric looked at the man behind the desk and found him meeting his gaze, an expectant expression on his face. Eric gave the man his answer.

The man behind the desk looked at John Lennon. The blade cut through Eric's abdomen for the second time.

Now Eric's body was screaming as if a boiling water, salt, and vinegar solution were being poured over his wounds. Eric writhed in agony and still the tall man's grip left Eric anchored to the chair. His whole stomach felt as if it were raw meat cooking over an open flame. Tears were streaming uncontrolled down his face and sweat poured from his body.

But as the blade came to rest a third time on his belly, something happened to Eric. Like steel tempered in the forge, Eric's resolve, his defiance hardened, strengthened in the fire of his belly. There was no way on this good earth he would ever do what they wanted him to do now. They'd have to kill first before he'd give them the satisfaction. He had no idea how many times they would cut him, and he really didn't care. There was no shame in crying or screaming, but this was really no different in his mind than bullying and Eric hated bullying. Eric was not known for having a high threshold for pain tolerance, and tonight was not going to be any different, but he wasn't going to call Drake and talk to him, even if that meant biting off his own tongue and swallowing it.

For his part, the man behind the desk looked hard into Eric's eyes and saw what he had not expected from this American. The fear was gone. He'd lost his advantage with Mr. Messer with the use of torture. It was time for a different tack.

"Mr. Messer, I am impressed by your loyalty, truly." He leaned forward. "But I am afraid it may be misguided."

The tall man released Eric after a nod from the man behind the desk. Eric doubled up in the chair, collapsing on himself which caused a spasm of pain. Eric felt no shame in whimpering.

John Lennon moved back behind the desk and assumed his previous position of arms crossed, staring hard at Eric. Just where the knife had gotten to, Eric had no idea. At the moment, he was just grateful he wasn't feeling the cold steel resting on his stomach.

"You will hurt for a while, Mr. Messer," the man behind the desk was saying, "but do not worry there will be no lasting damage. A scar maybe, but nothing else." He leaned back. "And now, Mr. Messer, I should like to tell you a few things about your friend, Paul Stephens, or as I have recently discovered, Drake Wetherford.

"Where to start. Were you aware Mr. Wetherford was a paid assassin?"

Eric nodded.

"He told you of Japan and Ricky Patrelli?"

Eric nodded again.

"Did he tell you that a month later he murdered Ricky Patrelli at the request of his uncle, Mr. Frank Patrelli? A request he'd made of us, which Mr. Wetherford interrupted."

Eric stared blankly.

The man behind the desk smiled. "I did not think so. Did he share with you his failed attempt to kill Ernesto Fabozzi?"

Eric had no idea whom Ernesto Fabozzi was, but the name did sound familiar. "No, I didn't think he would. You *are* familiar with Mr. Fabozzi though are you not?" When Eric didn't respond, the man behind the desk frowned in disappointment. "I would have thought you would remember the name of the man who owned the house where your wife and child died."

Eric felt the blood in his veins run cold. He forgot the pain in his stomach.

The man behind the desk continued. "Mr. Wetherford had originally intended that little roast for Ernesto Fabozzi. Your wife, pardon the cliché, was at the wrong place at the wrong time.

"Mr. Wetherford finally did track down Ernesto Fabozzi in Mexico over Christmas, but by then the damage was already done. C.N.N., Fox News, the major networks carried the story of the pregnant realtor killed by happenstance in a gas explosion. They even mentioned Mr. Fabozzi by name, his links to the Patrelli crime family, and that he could not be located. Of course, Mr. Fabozzi will never be located. But by then I had been contacted by Frank Patrelli."

The man behind the table paused, letting all he'd said sink into Eric and when it looked to him that it had indeed sunk deep into Eric's soul, he stood up, moved around to the front of the desk, and leaned against it.

"Mr. Messer, we do not usually work this way. I can assure you this is a once in a lifetime opportunity. You speak to your friend, convince him to come to the door, and I let you walk away never to see or hear from me again." He leaned forward, smiling. "Just don't ever come to Japan."

He looked pleasantly, expectantly at Eric as if the man were a game show host waiting patiently for a contestant to make up his mind if he would like to stay with what he's got or go for it. But Eric sat there stone-faced.

Iciness swept across the man's face, and standing up, he slapped Eric. Bright light blinded Eric and once again, he tasted blood. He watched as the man moved to a console set into the wall by the door. How'd I miss that, Eric wondered.

"Mr. Wetherford," the man said calmly, "I know you are still in the house. You're security system is quite impressive. Obviously Japanese. I will give you ten seconds," he nodded to the tall man who produced his tanto and placed it to Eric's throat, "to produce yourself at this door or Mr. Messer dies."

Not a heartbeat in Eric's chest had passed before the soft hiss of the airlock disengaging could be heard. The safe room door swung open.

Chapter 35

Drake stepped into the room, hands behind his head.

The man standing at the console let Drake walk past him before punching Drake in the kidney.

Drake grunted as he dropped to his knees but kept his arms behind his head.

The man nodded and John Lennon sprung over the desk, this time producing a roll of duct tape as the tall man pulled Eric from the chair and pushed him to the floor, which caused Eric to scream. His stomach felt as if it'd just been torn open wide.

John Lennon hoisted Drake onto his feet, moving Drake's right hand into a wrist lock. It was unnecessary, however, Drake did nothing to resist but allowed himself to be manhandled into the chair, each wrist bound to an armrest of the chair and ankles bound together with the duct tape with no regard to his comfort. He said nothing, only grunted as the tall guy cuffed him in his ear as he stood up and backed away.

"Mr. Messer, you are free to go."

Eric was dragged up by his bound arms by the tall man. He pulled his tanto out yet again and with one swipe sliced the tape binding Eric's arms, wrists, and palms. Eric immediately hunched over, taking the strain off his stomach, massaged his wrists, and looked at Drake.

Drake's head hung low on his chest. His eyes downcast. He didn't look up at Eric nor ask him if he was all right.

"Mr. Messer, I grow weary of you."

Eric looked at the man whose hand gestured toward the open door, and Eric decided he didn't need any more prompting, but his head was swimming from what the man had told him about Fabozzi, about his wife. His world had been ripped from him and torn to pieces in June. With Drake's help, he'd started putting the pieces back together only to have those pieces torn from him again. He felt nauseated just thinking about it, and he found himself staggering towards the door.

As he reached the doorway, he stopped and turned back. Drake hadn't moved. Eric had no idea what he could do, but he knew it couldn't end like this, not if he could help it. It just wasn't right for him to walk away and leave Drake to these thugs. He had to do something. But first, he had to get out of this room. He turned and stepped out of the safe room.

The man turned away from the door as Eric stepped into the hall. He walked over to the desk and sat down behind it. He leaned back, set his elbows on the armrests, and interlaced his fingers, watching Drake. After several moments, he finally spoke.

"Mr. Wetherford, I am pleased to finally meet you. I would like to say I wish we could have met under better circumstances, but that would be a lie. I could not imagine a better situation."

Drake didn't look up or in any way acknowledge the man behind the desk. The tall man grabbed a handful of Drake's hair and pulled his head up.

"I am sorry. I have not introduced myself yet. Where are my manners? My name is Tadeo Suzuki. We have never met but you crossed paths with my brother in a nightclub almost twenty years ago."

With that Drake knew exactly what this was about. Revenge. Drake had walked up to the door knowing the Yakuza were here to settle a vendetta, to exact payment on him for what'd happened all those years ago. Like the American and Russian mafias, the Japanese memory for crimes against the family ran long and knew no statute of limitations for reciprocity. But this was not going to be just business, this was going to be personal, very personal. Drake had killed this guy's brother, probably his little brother, and the guy had had the last twenty years to think of ways to make whoever was responsible suffer. Oh he'd make good on the promise to make him pay and pay with interest.

Drake had no desire to postpone the inevitable, that he was going to die, with torture. He had to get this guy off his game. Make him mad, really mad. He nodded to Tadeo's hand.

"Was that because of me?" He snickered. "You know, I've always loved the Japanese, but I have to admit some of your traditions are stupid. And that one's got to be about the dumbest."

Tadeo's eyes narrowed to slits.

Drake continued.

"No, I take that back. Keeping your honor in your pinky has got to be even dumber. Although," Drake's eyes dropped from Tadeo's hand down to where he imagined his crotch was, "I guess you go with your biggest appendage."

The tall guy's hand, still holding Drake's hair, tightened into a fist. John Lennon's right hand flinched. Tadeo's pupils shone like black onyx on fire. Drake, his scalp on fire, his kidney still aching, pulled one last punch.

"I haven't thought of that day in years. Which one of those punks was your brother? The guy whose neck I sliced open or the guy I put a bullet through his brain. I bet it was the guy on his knees begging me for his life just before I set him on fire."

Drake could practically hear Tadeo's teeth grind as his jaw clenched and the muscles in his neck popped. Tadeo inhaled deeply, his body ramrod straight, his hands, white in the knuckles, balled into fists. And then his body relaxed, collapsing into the chair, his neck muscles loosened, and he exhaled in a knowing laugh. "A clever adversary to the last. Just as I had been told."

Drake felt his hope for a quick death sink faster than the Titanic. This was going to be a very long night.

"You will die, but first things first." He nodded to John Lennon. "An eye for an eye, as the Old Testament says, or in this case, a finger for a finger."

John Lennon sliced the duct tape holding Drake's right hand to the armrest.

Panic seized Drake as John Lennon seized his hand and dragged it to the desk. He heard his voice utter unintelligible words. It wasn't the pain of having a finger cut off, or even the loss of a finger causing him agony, but the sudden realization he was no longer in control of the situation, of his life. Maybe he'd never been in control, ever. But he'd always won. Never been left holding the short end of the stick. Until now. He looked wild-eyed around the room for someone, something to stop them, when his eyes fell upon Tadeo sitting across from him, his face twisted in a smirk.

Drake twisted his wrist and yanked it free from John Lennon's hand. Before Lennon could respond, Drake slapped his hand down onto the desk as he stared unblinking into Tadeo's eyes.

Tadeo nodded. The tall guy stepped up and tied a tourniquet around Drake's pinky and then placed his hand over Drake's wrist. John Lennon placed the point of the knife into the desktop between the ring and pinky fingers.

Drake's focus moved from Tadeo's eyes to the blade poised, gleaming evil, between his fingers. It was liquid, beginning to flow slowly, now picking up speed as it poured downward. The hand grasping his wrist tightened in anticipation so that he could now feel the tall guy's pulse in his skin. And then, the tall guy's grasp loosened as the blade and his hand suddenly rusted. No, his brain told him, not rust. Blood. But not his. His finger was still intact. The tourniquet dry.

He looked towards the tall guy who folded like an accordion, his skull protruding rudely through his scalp, sliding down the desk like fingernails over a chalkboard.

John Lennon turned towards the doorway, exposing his stomach to Drake, the wicked purpose of his blade forgotten.

Drake reached up, and grabbed John Lennon's hand in a wrist lock, turning the blade inward towards Lennon's stomach. The blade, not caring what it cut so long as it cut, performed an assisted *hara-kiri*, entering and slicing Lennon's stomach open. Lennon's eyes popped in surprise as he looked down and saw his entrails slipping out of him like grotesque sausages slipping out of their casings.

Drake took the knife from the dying man's hand and sliced the duct tape trapping his left hand and his ankles. Looking up, he saw Tadeo rising from the desk, a 9mm pistol in his hand, aiming at the door. Drake threw the knife at Tadeo, the blade finding the flesh of Tadeo's neck and burying itself to the hilt. Tadeo dropped the weapon as he reached for the blade, and not thinking, pulled it from his neck. Blood gushed from the wound like water from a broken water main. Tadeo was dead before he fell across the desk.

"Thanks," Drake picked up Tadeo's 9mm.

"I was aiming for you."

Drake spun around to see Eric slouched over grasping his stomach, the 9mm still in his hand. He nodded understanding and slowly placed Tadeo's pistol back on the desk. "You know."

Eric pointed the gun at Tadeo. "He told me."

"What did he say?" Drake sat down.

"Does it matter?" Eric gritted his teeth as he aimed the 9mm at Drake. "You killed my wife, my child." His knuckles whitened on the grip as he remembered. "You said that everyone you'd killed deserved it, that they were all bad people, no loss to society." The last words carried spit that landed on the desk. Eric stood there trembling. He wanted to pull the trigger, to put a bullet in Drake's head just like he'd taught him, but he didn't. He just stood there. This was his chance. Drake was unarmed, unprotected. He could put an end to it right now. But he didn't. This man was the reason he no longer had a home or a wife. A family. And yet he stood, rooted to the floor.

"For what it's worth, I'm sorry." Drake offered, not making any move to stop Eric.

"It doesn't change the fact you killed them." Eric could pull the trigger, and put a stop to this. Just pull the trigger and walk away.

"I feel horrible." Drake sounded as if he was telling Eric how bad the sushi he'd eaten for lunch was making him feel.

Eric took a step forward, pistol trembling but steady enough not to miss its intended target from this range.

Drake raised his hands in supplication. "You don't know how hard I've worked to make amends for that day. I tracked Fabozzi down and finished the job." Drake waved his hands around the room. "I bought this house to help you get back on your feet financially."

"The house, and the hockey tickets, Bulls games, trip to Vegas? They were just some emotional bribes to ease your conscience." The 9mm trembled violently as rage and adrenaline coursed through Eric's body. Now. He should just shoot him now.

"It wasn't like that at all." Drake was calm, not at all alarmed by Eric's emotional response. "There was a reason why I took you to those games, invited you to lunch, to Vegas." Drake smiled coyly. "Do you remember where you were, what you were doing when I called you and invited you to the hockey game?"

Eric knew exactly where he was. How would he ever forget? It would be easier to collect a tsunami in a paper cup. The question alone produced a metallic flavor in his mouth, his bones could feel the cold of that day; his fingertip could feel the rough gradation on the trigger. He knew all right, but what did Drake know? A chill raced up his spine as Drake got up, walked behind the desk, sat down (in much the same way as Tadeo had), reached down, and then laid Eric's .38 snubnose revolver on the desktop.

"Where'd you get that?" It was one of those knee-jerk questions people ask. He knew the answer of course. Drake had broken into his SUV and taken it.

Drake realized the superfluity of the question as well. "I couldn't take the chance you'd get to drinking again."

The silence that passed between the two men would've given Jack Frost the shivers as horror dawned on Eric as sure as the realization of Drake's words. "You...how long've you been following me?"

Drake leaned back in the chair with all the air of a businessman dictating a letter to his administrative assistant. "Except for Christmas Eve and day, you haven't been out of my sight in months. I was gone those days on business—"

"Fabozzi," Eric interrupted. "Finishing the job."

Drake continued as if nothing had happened, "but otherwise I've been watching over you, protecting you, trying to redeem myself."

Eric shifted his weight, making sure he hadn't locked his knees, the 9mm growing heavy in his now sweating palm as the word, "redeem," staggered around his brain, unsettling him. This must be how a priest feels at confession, he thought, when the confessing party asks what they can do to gain God's forgiveness, how many "Hail Marys," how many "Our Fathers." What penance will wipe away the sin? It was something for which a priest might take pity, might mean when he says, "Your sins are forgiven." But Eric wasn't feeling pity or particularly forgiving.

Drake rubbed his forehead, looking very tired. "I just wanted the nightmare to stop."

"What nightmare." Eric was reeling, the room felt like it was suddenly raked thirty degrees.

"That doesn't matter now."

"So this, all of this, has been about you." The 9mm felt a little lighter as a shot of anger hit his brain, the urge to twitch his trigger finger growing steadily again, to just end it before Drake could say anything else. But still, he didn't.

"At first," Drake admitted, still rubbing his forehead. He stopped, ran his hand through his hair, and looked up at Eric. "But then I really clicked with you. I started seeing you as a friend. And I haven't had a friend in a long time. Not since Paul."

"Paul, huh?" Eric wasn't feeling fear or even horror, but a sickening realization of what was happening. He turned to the wall, tore the pictures of the fishing trips off it, grunting from the fresh sear of pain across his stomach, and staggered back to the desk. "You think of me as a friend," he laid the two pictures down on the desk, "or Paul?"

And now Eric saw what he didn't see, couldn't see before under the red light. Under the dim red light and its shadows, he could see two different men posed with Drake. But now, under the naked glare of white light, Eric could see just how uncannily similar he and Paul resembled each other. Not twins, like it would undoubtedly be in a film, but brothers. They could pass for brothers. He, Eric, could pass for Paul.

Drake picked up the picture of him and Paul as Eric yelled. "Do you realize how twisted this is? Do you realize how sick in the head you must be? Did you really think you could live your friendship with Paul vicariously through me?" He watched Drake stare through the photo in his hand with dawning horror. "No, not live vicariously." His body erupted in gooseflesh. "Replace Paul with me."

But Drake no longer seemed to be there with Eric. He was somewhere a million miles and a lifetime ago, when he and Paul were in the Keys on a fishing trip. Eric looked at Drake and felt not fear or anger or hate or even loathing, just a deep-seeded disgust and he exploded. Forgetting the pain in his abdomen, he wrenched the photo out of Drake's grasp and slammed it down hard on the desk, shattering it.

"I'm. *Not*. PAUL."

Eric looked towards the chair, but Drake was not sitting in it anymore. He'd already crossed the desk, taken the 9mm from Eric's hand, and slammed Eric up against the wall, jabbing him in the chest with the barrel.

Eric screamed. It felt like talons had clawed his stomach open even more.

Drake's eyes blazed with fire that could have only come from the lake where Lucifer rules and his chest heaved with hard, heavy breaths.

Perhaps six months, a year ago, Eric would have wet himself with terror, begged for his life with tears streaming down his cheeks, but he was no more in that place than Drake had been in the room just a moment ago. He remembered how scared he'd been when he bought that .38 and he'd wanted to die. Now? Nothing. No, that wasn't the right word.

He looked from the barrel to those demonic eyes and felt…vacant. "Go ahead," Eric said, "You've already taken my wife and my child, my reasons for living. I'd rather be dead than a scab, just a replacement friend."

Drake pushed the gun harder against Eric's breastbone, but he didn't fire.

"What're you waiting for? It's what you do, isn't it? Hand out death, like candy to kids on Halloween? That's your one, true friend, isn't it? Death. Seems to follow you wherever you go, doesn't it? Even the ones you care deepest about."

Drake looked up, no longer in the safe room in his house in Cary Illinois, but back in a country to remain nameless on a mission to remain classified, setting up a perimeter. He'd heard the whistle of incoming mortar fire during live-fire training, but it had never sounded so loud, so clear, so deadly. He heard someone scream, "incoming" and then the pandemonium of war in all its chaos and havoc fell upon them like a pack of rabid dogs. His ears were ringing from a cacophony of claymore mines, grenades, and bullets. Smoke and gunpowder burnt his eyes and lungs, and now he understood that in the heat of battle, no man fights for God, King, or country, but for his brothers-in-arms.

He screamed into the storm for Paul, sweeping right and left. And then he saw a figure, ghostly in the smoke, rise up in front of him, holding something, ready to hurl it at him, he was sure, and now something his Ranger instructor had drilled into him came to the front of his mind. "Do unto others before they get a chance to do it to you."

Drake raised his M16 took aim and fired.

The flare exploded in Paul's hand and now his screams rang loudest in Drake's ears, the stench of his burning flesh burnt his eyes and lungs.

Eric listened to Drake's confession of Paul's death with an overwhelming sadness. Not about Paul's death. Yes, it was tragic, even more so at the hand of his best friend, but that wasn't it. Nor was it over the pain one must feel at being responsible for the death of a friend or loved one.

Since he'd first met Drake, he'd been completely enamored, infatuated with the man. If it could be taken without the homosexual overtones, he'd had a crush on him. Drake had appeared to be what every man wanted to be: completely self-assured, self-reliant, completely at peace with the man he was.

But that's all it was. Appearance. Drake was nothing more than a house of straw with a brick facade. He was incapable of being his own person because he wasn't a real person. He made attempts, but he's completely devoid of humanity, no more real than the Barbie's in his niece's platoon. So instead he lived off Paul, then the memory of Paul, and lastly the reincarnation of Paul. In that respect, he was like a parasite, leeching life force off some more complex, complete creature.

Drake wiped his eyes. "I'm sorry, truly sorry." The 9mm Drake had been keeping a limp grasp on, now fell to the floor.

Yes, Eric thought, I believe you think you are. "I'm not your priest, Drake. I won't grant you absolution." He looked Drake in the eye. "There's no redemption here."

And with that, Eric suddenly felt weary. He missed his wife, the child he would never bounce on his knee, throw a football with, and he felt a strong desire to hug his nieces. There was nothing here for him. Hugging his stomach, he turned to leave the room but stopped as something else on the credenza below the gun collection caught his eye. It was the pipe belonging to Paul's grandfather, Randall Stephens.

"You never did call them, did you?"

"What?"

"Paul's parents, you never called them, did you? They said to call them once you'd figured your own life out. But you never called."

Eric looked over his shoulder and saw the dawning realization on Drake's face. He'd never called Paul's parents. He'd never figured his own life out. Eric nodded and left.

Drake watched Eric leave. He'd hoped Eric would stay, put an arm around his shoulder, and tell him he'd teach him how to be a man. But when Eric turned, he knew that would never happen. He walked over to the desk and picked up the picture of him and Paul, brushing away the remaining shards of glass. Eric was gone just as surely as Paul was.

And now the irony of an old cliché drifted across his brain, "No good deed goes unpunished." All of this, not just tonight with the Yakuza, but the past twenty years, killing Ricky Patrelli and Ernesto Fabozzi, and Emily Messer had happened because he'd tried to help someone twenty years ago in a bar. He'd tried to help Eric, make up for what he'd done, do right by him, and now he was gone too. Drake mopped his face with his sleeve and sat down heavily in the chair.

Eric's hand was on the knob of the front door when he heard the report of a .38 snubnose revolver. He didn't hesitate but opened the door and closed it behind him.

THE END